The
Luxembourg
Run

THE
LUXEMBOURG
RUN

Stanley Ellin

Random House · New York

Library of Congress Cataloging in Publication Data
Ellin, Stanley.
The Luxembourg run.
I. Title.
PZ3.E4558Lu [PS3555.L56]   813'.5'4   77-4751
ISBN 0-394-49646-9

Manufactured in the United States of America
2 4 6 8 9 7 5 3
First Edition

for Jeannie, with love

CONTENTS

THE
INVISIBLE
PRINCE

Part I

Once upon a time, I was ten years old.

In a photograph taken of me on my tenth birthday—that, by simple calculation, had to be in the year 1955, in the time of Eisenhower—I, David Hanna Shaw, am standing alone on the summit of the Acropolis against the whiteness of the ruined Parthenon and the dazzling blue of Grecian sky, garbed in a flawless replica of the evzone military regalia. A small musical-comedy hero with those pompons on my slippers, short pleated skirt, ornamental jacket draped with cartridge belt, tasseled cap and all.

When you know that it was my mother who was inspired to thus fantastically garb me, putting me through endless fittings in order that I might be presented to a select gathering of Foreign Service families and their Greek opposite numbers at a birthday party for me that afternoon, and that she then forgot to send out invitations to the party, you know pretty much what there is to know about my mother. Divinely featherheaded. And, before she started to put on her middle-aged weight, divinely beautiful.

My expression in the photograph is interesting. All done up in costume for a party that wasn't being held, I am facing the camera with a smile. Not forced either. Evidence that after only one decade of existence I had attained a marvelous emotional balance. For eight years of that time I had been hauled around European capitals by a scatterbrained mother, a pompous father, and a succession of governesses, and what with that and the peculiar boarding schools I was occasionally dropped into, I had absorbed the lesson that yielding to the current is the way to go.

Of course, I had luck on my side. Where other Foreign Service kids from the States were usually planted in one specific alien place and raised there in an Americanized hothouse, I had a father whose office was always on the move. His title was Commissioner of the United States Economic Agency in Europe, a title much more formidable than any powers of the agency, but which provided deluxe living quarters, staff, limousine, chauffeur, and a popgun salute on arrival. It cost my father somewhat more to maintain his position than it cost the government, but it was the position he wanted, the title and perquisites of which made up his idea of glory.

At ten years old I already had a vast amount of such information tucked away in my brain because I had the gift of tongues. I was fluent in French and Dutch, competent in Spanish, Italian, and German, and had a fair smattering of what might be called kitchen Greek. Also, I had pretty much a free run of any quarters we occupied, and it was the domestics, taking small notice of this silent, apparently uncomprehending little American boy, who not only filled in my command of their native tongues, but supplied fascinating opinions of those they served.

It stung sometimes to overhear the backstairs analysis of my mother's idiocies and my father's overbearing stupidity and endless cheapness with money, but I was wise enough to understand that if I raised a voice in protest I would be cut off from the backstairs gossip. Only once I came near blowing the whole thing. That was in our Brussels apartment where I found that to his servitors my father was known as Monsieur le Bécoteur. Title of honor, perhaps? But no, there was something about the way it was said that suggested otherwise. At last, itching with curiosity, I approached my then

Ma'mzelle, a middle-aged Walloon lady, and faced her with the question. Her immediate reaction was an involuntary hoot of laughter. Then she put on the familiar frowning dignity. *"C'est dégoûtant.* Disgusting. Where did you hear it?"

"I don't remember. But what does it mean?"

"Ah, you really are something, you know that? Well, I will tell you, so that you do not say it in front of decent people. It means a man who touches women where he should not. Now you see how disgusting it is? So you will kindly put it out of your mind."

Far from putting it out of my mind I seized on it as the clue to those late-night conversations between my mother and my father when, in my bedroom that adjoined theirs, I could catch heated words and phrases. "Incorrigible womanizer," went the treble, and "Oh, yes, I saw you with her! I saw what was going on!" while the bass rumbled and grumbled angry denials.

Womanizer. *Un bécoteur, hein?* So now I knew.

By all the statistics ever extracted from case histories I should have been as neurotic a kid as was ever destined to wind up on the couch, but somehow I wasn't. True, now and then I did suffer fits of melancholy. I would sit alone, a lump rising in my throat, tears welling in my eyes, savoring a delicious self-pity. But it never lasted long. Even through the woeful moment I was fortified by the awareness that I knew things no one else around me knew; I was the Invisible Prince.

I was, in fact, mostly content with myself and my lot. I suppose it never struck me in my childhood that I wasn't supposed to be.

$\mathbf{T}$he man who took that photograph of me as midget Greek warrior was named Ray Costello, and he was a sort of gift from my grandmother and grandfather Hanna in Florida, shipped across the Atlantic to serve as my bodyguard in Athens. Whatever news of Greece during that period reached the *Miami Herald,* it must have portended for those folks on South Bay Shore Drive at least the kidnapping of their grandson. The one and only grandchild. The J.G. Hanna son, who would have been my uncle had he lived, was killed in World War II at Anzio. The Hanna daughter, my beautiful, scatterbrained, egomaniac mother, had produced me, then gone out of production, and, I suppose, had made it clear to her family that she had no intention of ever returning to it.

So one day Costello showed up at the mansion in Athens, a chunky, hard-faced man who wore a gun in the shoulder holster under his jacket and who never spoke unless directly addressed. And, even then, with the absolute minimum of words. Altogether a heroic image, but not really much of a companion.

Of course I was not completely marooned in Europe. Once or twice a year I would spend time basking in the adoration of grandma and grandpa Hanna in South Florida, and if there was any outside agency which could be credited with the perhaps unnatural equilibrium that sustained me through most of my very young life, it had to be those folks in that house on South Bay Shore Drive who obviously thought I was the greatest thing to ever come down the pike. My grandmother was the more demonstrative addict. Everything I said dazzled her.

"Tell me what you and grandpa did today, darling."

I would tell her.

"Now tell it to me in French."

I would tell it to her in French.

"Perfectly beautiful," my grandmother would say. Then motioning over Mrs. Galvan, the Cuban housekeeper, and aiming me at her: "Now tell it to Emiliana in Spanish, darling."

My grandfather, not quite so overt in his enthusiasms, was, however, the more potent influence on me. A slight little man, always cool and neat, he was the one for the boat outdoors and the checkers and chess indoors. The boat, moored at Dinner Key, was named the *Carrie H.* in honor of my grandmother, and it was an imposing forty-footer, rigged for deep-sea fishing, and capable, as my grandfather solemnly assured me, of going right across to Europe if one chose to take her there. There was also a captain and a one-man crew, the captain generally looking very uncaptainlike to my critical eye, the crew always in patchwork clothes and smelling strongly of fish and beer. Each morning at dawn we would set out with full bait buckets for the trolling lines, and return at noon in time for lunch, sometimes with a catch on display considerably larger than I was.

For a while I had the impression that my grandfather made his living as a fisherman, and it came as something of a disillusionment to be informed by my grandmother that no, he was a lawyer, and a very good one. There was never any question in my mind that whatever he was he would be good at it. Always soft of voice, he never had to raise that voice to command attention. At most, there was a small, unfunny smile he took on that was like a danger sign. Once there was a scene behind the closed doors of the living room where he and some men were closeted on business, the men's voices alarmingly angry, his voice hardly to be heard, and when they all emerged at the end, the men slamming out of the house red-faced with bad temper, my grandfather wearing that little smile, my grandmother said complacently to me, "Grandpa can drive a hard bargain, dear, and some folks just seem to resent it."

Whatever that meant, I could see he was more than a match for three very angry men, all of them much larger than he was.

Sometimes I practised that little smile in the mirror, but I could never make it very impressive.

The evening of my partyless tenth birthday in Athens, the simmering relationship between my father and mother finally came to full boil.

That midnight I was wakened by my mother, and drugged with sleep was helped to dress and led downstairs to the car, where Costello was waiting for us. Then we were driven to a hotel off Syntagma Square where we spent the rest of the night. Next afternoon we were on our way to Paris by train, and the following day set up in the Hôtel Meurice on the rue de Rivoli.

It was not until then that my mother took me into her confidence. She was in no mood to mince words. Father had made Mother very, very unhappy, so they were separating now and would divorce later. Mother had done her best to make a loving home for all of us, but it was simply no use.

She squeezed my hand. "You do understand, darling, don't you?"

"Yes," I said. Then I said hopefully, "Will we live here in the hotel?"

"I will, darling, but you'll be living at school. A delightful school. Le Lycée Anglais d'Auteuil, not a half-hour from here. You start next week."

C'est la vie.

Well, it was a lycée, a "middle school," and it was certainly planted right there in Auteuil on the outskirts of town, but how that *Anglais* came to be part of its title is something else again, because of its several dozen youthful boarders—we ranged in age from the innocent eights to the sophisticated sixteens—I was the only one to whom English was the native tongue.

In his brochure describing his institution, Monsieur Stampfli, founder and headmaster, summed it up neatly. *Here is a school which allows the growing child himself to determine his course of study so that in the end he emerges as a gloriously creative force in society.* In practice, this meant that one attended classes which entertained one and disregarded those which didn't, a process that made for a sketchy education at best. But the atmosphere was amiable, the cuisine sufficient, and the library well stocked, so I had no complaints in that direction.

The one item in the curriculum that required at least a show of attendance was outdoor athletics, and a large, unevenly marked-off football field with wobbly goal posts and torn net was provided to that end. Here it was that I discovered I had an undreamed-of talent. I was agile and tough, I was brainlessly unafraid of getting a boot in the shins or an elbow in the eye, and with very little effort I could make that battered old soccer ball do tricks.

This became one of my distinctions among my peers. The other was awarded me much against my will when the news of my parents' divorce hit the press. Stuck away here, a few thousand miles from America where the divorce proceedings were being held, I could not, of course, get a first-hand view of the mess, but I didn't have to. My schoolmates—especially the seniors, avid scandalmongers—were right on the ball.

For a couple of weeks they had all the grist they needed for their mill. It was a mess all right, considering my father's hitherto secret career as elderly Don Juan; it was featured in the Paris papers, earned a gaudy half-page in the London *News of the World* illustrated with photographs not only of my father and mother, but also of a lissome British beauty in a barely discernible swim suit. And finally, courtesy of Jean-Pierre de Liasse, our senior of seniors, I was shown the two-page spread in the magazine *Paris-Match* where my parents now appeared in the pictorial company of several Continental beauties out of my father's past. *Paris-Match* also played up the aged husband-youthful wife theme, thus making me aware for the first time that my father was almost the age of my grandfather Hanna, and somehow this seemed the most shocking revelation of all.

A mess all right. *"Un vrai micmac,"* as Jean-Pierre de Liasse cheerfully put it in kitchen French.

He and a handful of the other seniors, smokers and winebibbers all, took to using my study as a sort of clubhouse during this bad time. I lived with that, not only because I lacked the nerve to order them out, but because I sensed that they were, under the hard-boiled talk, trying to be kind to me. Trying, in their way, to fortify me against the wallops the older generation keeps landing on the younger in their wild swinging at each other.

Jean-Pierre, at least as hard-boiled as a twenty-minute egg and the school's reigning nobleman—he was, in fact, Monsieur le Comte de Liasse ever since his father had hit an oil slick at Le Mans while under full acceleration—Jean-Pierre it was who put it in a nutshell. *"Il jete sa gourme, votre père.* Your old man's getting off his rocks while he can, that's all. No harm done. That's how it is with all us men."

"It doesn't hurt to be a little discreet about it though," remarked another senior, and Jean-Pierre shrugged. "One gets careless at times. Then you get a stink in the papers, especially if they can call papa a distinguished diplomat and mama an international beauty. But our David is a tough one, right? He looks the situation over, he says that's life, that's how it is with the old folks, no sweat for me. *J'm'en-fichisme.* It's the only way."

Right. *J'm'en-fichisme,* that was the name of the game. Total indifference. No sweat for me, baby, whatever goes on out there. It's the cool one who's the real hero.

Not bad at all, having those seniors mark me as a cool one.

Now and then, mail arrived. Affectionate little notes in violet ink from my mother on the Hôtel Meurice stationery, each violet *i* capped not by a dot, but by a perfect tiny circle. Stern messages from my father on State Department stationery in which I was admonished to practise thrift—hard to do otherwise, considering my meager allowance—and to heed my instructors. Long, chatty letters from my grandmother, with a few teasing words appended by my grandfather.

Finally one day there arrived, not one of those notes from the Meurice, but my mother herself, driving up in her own shining new little car and with a stranger in tow. A smallish, gray-haired man, deeply tanned, and speaking in an almost too precise Berlitz English. This, my mother said so brightly that it raised my hackles with premonition, was a very dear friend, Mr. Periniades. Milos Periniades. A Greek gentleman who lived in Rome and had business here in Paris. And when in departing my mother said to me sotto voce, "You do like him, don't you, darling? I can see you do," the sense of premonition was overwhelming.

I didn't like him. I didn't like him any better on their next visit either. So when the marriage took place in Rome, although I was invited to attend, I made a point of reporting to the infirmary with an imaginary disease a day before the event and spent the occasion malingering.

Then, from a copy of busybody *Paris-Match,* I learned of my father's remarriage and, incidentally, that his career as diplomat had been abruptly terminated by the colorful way he had conducted the nondiplomatic side of his life.

This news was soon after followed by my father himself who paid me a rare visit at school, his bride, Olivia, splendidly befurred and deliciously perfumed, on his arm. Since the lady wasn't wearing a bikini it took me a while to realize that here was the nubile British beauty from the *News of the World,* and once I did realize it I found myself terribly embarrassed by the whole situation, speechless to the point of appearing hostile to the fair creature.

Caught hell for it too when Olivia went off to the ladies' room and I was pinned down alone by my father. What emerged was his conviction that my mother had set about poisoning my mind against him, and he didn't intend to stand for that kind of nonsense. No use trying to tell him that in her last note my mother had specifically charged me to always be properly respectful of her former spouse. *Always, darling. After all, as your n. father he deserves that much from you.*

And certainly no use telling him that when, in bewilderment, I had asked her over the phone what an n. father was, she had informed me that of course it meant my natural father, the one who had helped bring about my entrance into the world.

Back to *J'm'en-fichisme* with a vengeance. Say "Yes, sir" and "No, sir" to my n. father, try to make conversation with his new wife, gratefully wave good-by when they departed. And then turn to the sardonic and sympathetic Monsieur le Comte de Liasse for some urgently needed spine-stiffening.

Above all, recognize that if I had any goal in life after this, it was to stay as far away as possible from any parents who might lay claim to me, n. or otherwise.

No luck in that department.

At the early summer break between terms when I had expected to be basking on the deck of the *Carrie H.* in the Gulf Stream I was firmly ordered by my mother to report to her in Rome, and for all the foot-dragging I did that was where I wound up. Once more or less settled down as houseguest to Mr. and Mrs. Periniades in their apartment in the Parioli district, I could only wonder why they wanted me here. My host was polite and no more, and my hostess, after a spell of nervous, overeager chatter about my life at school, quickly reverted to her old sweetly forgetful self.

What saved it from being a wholly dismal two weeks were the neighbors in the adjoining apartment, Signore and Signora Cavalcanti, transplanted Florentines and now evidently dear friends of the Periniades, who had two offspring near my age, Umberto about a year older and Bianca about a year younger than I. Now my days were full of soccer practice in the park with Umberto and Bianca, swimming parties at Ostia, movies in the Piazza Barberini, and always, as a late-afternoon climax to events, a visit to a place in Piazza Navona called Tre Scalini where we stuffed ourselves with ice cream and assorted pastries.

Along the way I made my first conquest. I wasn't aware of it at the beginning, but then I took notice that Bianca, who usually walked between us holding Umberto's hand, after a while was holding my hand as well, and then only my hand and not her brother's at all.

I took notice, and I liked it. It was not only that Bianca, blonde, gray-eyed, and with a neat little tip-tilted Florentine nose was nice-looking, it was also the sense I suddenly had of a powerful proprietorship over someone.

Not long after I returned to school I got a letter from her solemnly explaining that she had been granted permission to write me as long as mama and papa could read her letters and, if I chose to answer, any I wrote in response. After which the entire message was that she was well, Umberto was well, and she hoped I was well.

From the distance and with the passage of time, she began to look more and more slender and pretty to me, so I finally did write to her, my letter, with a wary eye on the board of censors, largely consisting of a list of books I was now reading.

That Christmas was the first in a long time that I didn't spend with my grandparents. Instead, as soon as my mother suggested that perhaps I might want to share the week with her and my alternate father in Rome, I jumped at the chance. What she absentmindedly forgot to mention until I arrived on the scene was that the entire Cavalcanti family had hied itself off to the mountains for the holiday.

I emerged from that permafrost week with a squint. Fourteen movies in seven days—some of them viewed twice over at a sitting —can do that to you.

By my sixteenth year, several memorable items could be credited to my account.

Item. I had become the senior of seniors at the lycée, as Jean-Pierre de Liasse had been in his time. Jean-Pierre might have been Monsieur le Comte, but I was more than that: High Priest of *J'm'en-fichisme,* all-around man of mystery, and revered dispenser of wisdom. I was also the football hero of the place, idol of every goggle-eyed beholder as I rammed home those apparently unmakeable goals.

Item. I had taken a woman to bed. This was Suzie Cinq-heures who did the cleaning up of the tobacco and stamp shop near the school and at five o'clock—*cinq heures*—each afternoon was ready for business on a cot in the back room there. And despite a touch of nerves and my lover's depressingly flabby breasts and dirty feet, I felt I carried it off very well indeed.

Item. I had discovered Paris, fantastic Paris. I covered it block by block on foot, seeing, hearing, and smelling with avidity, but ultimately came to roost most of the time in outdoor cafés in the University quarter, nursing a citron and soda, trying to be mistaken for a University man myself. Paradise on earth, that's what I knew it must be to be one of those University men.

The next time my n. father showed up, now accompanied by wife number three—Darlene was her unbelievable name—I broached the subject. I had been given intimations that what he envisioned for me was the good old Ivy League college he had attended, then a stretch at Georgetown in Washington for training in international diplomacy, and then a climb up the State Department ladder. But these dismal prospects still seemed in the balance, and I felt that if I made a proper case for my choice, logic might prevail.

I should have known better.

That left one court of appeal to turn to, my n. mother, and as soon as my visitors were gone I wrote her a long letter setting forth the case and asking that she plead it before my father. Her answer came a week later addressed to me from Bagnio, Italia.

Darling boy,

Arrived here yesterday—a dreadfully smelly place with all this sulphur in the air—to take the famous Bagnio waters. Please do not worry about my health which is v. good but did put on 4 kilos over the past few months and must try drastic measures.

Re: your education, dear Milos and I are v. short of funds at present, so all costs for college must fall on your n. father. He has now made it plain that for his "investment" you are to live with him at his home in Old Westfield, Long Island, N.Y. and this summer will be tutored for college admission to his old college. Your dear grandpa approves this. He said to tell you there is some inheritance for you when the time comes, but would most like you to inherit his v. good law practice. Says he will try to live long enough to hand it over to you personally. Do write, once you are established at Old Westfield. Milos joins me in sending fondest regards.

Your mother

D uring my freshman year at college my grandmother suddenly and unexpectedly died of a heart attack. My initial reaction was incredulity that this bright spirit, my most uncritical admirer, should be so illogically snuffed out, and after that a sort of dull toothache of the spirit set in for a long time. One of those situations, I could see, when *J'm'en-fichisme* didn't seem to work.

My mother arrived from Italy, red-eyed and much subdued, just in time for the services, which were a three-ring circus for the immense crowds packing the church and the street before it, and which included a bevy of newspaper photographers. After that came several uncomfortable days where I was expected to remain around the house for introductions to weighty visitors who all voiced the same mournful phrases in the same hushed tones. Then my mother and the visitors went their way, and I was alone with my grandfather.

There was a tension between us now which, I think, bothered him as much as it bothered me. On board the *Carrie H.*—no crew along this time, just the two of us out in the Gulf Stream taking furtive stock of each other—he abruptly said, "You feel I let you down about going to college in Paris, don't you? You hoped I would stand up to your father about it."

"Yes."

"Glad you've got the guts to speak your mind, Davey, but this was one of the few times I agreed with your father about anything. You're going to practice law right here in this country. And you can possess all the graces God offers, but they're not worth a damn if you come off as an outlander to the people you have to deal with."

"Fine," I said. "But what if I don't want to become a lawyer? What if I want to become something else?"

"Such as?"

I couldn't answer that, although my grandfather gave me all the time I needed to come up with an answer. Finally he said, "No ideas on the subject? Well, considering how nature abhors a vacuum, Davey, you just slant your course toward a law degree. And a place with me when the time comes. You're not having any big troubles with your father, are you, living there with him?"

"No."

"And that latest wife of his? What's her name this time?"

"Wendy. No, we get along."

"And school's not too unbearable?"

"No."

"So there it is," said my grandfather.

So there it was.

A
n acronym.

Dear Old Dad Weds Persistently.

Dorothy. Olivia. Darlene. Wendy. Phyllis.

The handiest device really, after my n. father's fifth trip to the altar, for keeping the sequence straight without a scorecard.

The marriage to Phyllis, an actress with all of two TV commercials to her credit, took place during my second year at Old Ivy. What it indicated to me after I met Phyllis was that my father, his whitening hair suddenly an unconvincing blond, was determined to sooner or later present me with a stepmother who was younger than I was. Darlene had been ten years my senior, Wendy five. Phyllis, it turned out, was only two years older than I and quite willing to overlook all seniority.

I wondered sometimes, in the face of her embarrassingly affectionate reaction to me right there in my father's presence, whether she was simply unable to approach any male except by way of flirtatiousness, or whether she was deliberately playing off son against father just to keep the kettle boiling. Either way, it made for a highly volatile situation, and more and more I took to spending holidays and other free times at the college, a safe distance from it.

Not that the situation at Old Ivy was any less volatile. The over-ripe smell of Southeast Asia was wafting over the student body, and there was a choosing up of sides I wanted no part of. And there was the Negro problem starting to simmer on campus. Or the Colored problem, as some called it. Or the Black question, which a few were starting to call it. Sort of a semantic one-upmanship, the latest word for it evidently drawing the hottest heads and greatest glory.

Back to *J'm'en-fichisme.*

Back to the Self, the one stable element in this scrambled universe.

The only activities that did come to claim my interest, aside from the perpetual search for the ready and willing female, were the Old Ivy Historical Film Society—the title had been selected by its founder, my roommate, a beady-eyed hustler who knew what to call a private club dedicated to old movies, pot, and beer—and my house team in the Intramural Soccer League where I was prime mover in getting the team its winning cup.

Sporadically, I'd devote myself to a journal I was keeping, a good means, I had discovered, of working off frustrations generally brought about by my latest contact with my father whose greatest pleasure in life, it seemed, was in making me beg for the scanty allowance he was supposed to provide me regularly. More and more, he became the subject of the journal, and I recognized after a while that what I had here was a devastating biographical study of Shaw, Sr., which after his death could do the job on him that obviously was not going to be done in his lifetime. I even went to work adding to my own reminiscences and insights by digging through newspaper and magazine files in the library to round out the picture. I could gauge the amount of therapy I required this way by the steadily increasing height of that stack of typed pages tucked away in the bottom drawer of the desk in the study I shared with my roommate. There were enough of those pages after a while to make a very large volume.

Once, I sat back to read through the accumulation, and it added up to a picture both sad and funny. Shaw, Sr., came off as a pompous, tight-fisted, thick-skinned gent, insufficient to any task he set himself in or out of marriage, desperately hanging on to his long-gone youth by wedding the overly youthful again and again, a father distressed by the existence of a growing son who didn't fit any standard mold, and yet, so that the family name might be kept burnished, driven to keep the son close and try to steer his course for him.

It was, I judged immodestly, a well-written, well-documented psychobiography, and the only thing to spoil my pleasure in it as author was that I also happened to be the son in question.

Through all this, my roommate was a born Connecticut Yankee by name of Oscar Wylie. The beautiful world of buying and selling was his province. Used textbooks, secondhand golf balls, football tickets, tax-free cigarettes, a poor grade of pot at outrageous prices, all the way up to—or down to—advance copies of test questions.

It was Oscar, of course, who sold me my first car—his own beat-up, bathtub-sized MG—by allowing me, in lieu of the two-hundred dollar asking price which I couldn't possibly meet, to sign on as indentured servant, doing his literature and foreign language papers for him. And by reminding me, whenever I felt that I had bought my freedom from bondage, that he was sole judge of that.

To do him justice, he was not on the hustle just to pile up wealth. No, Oscar had an obsession into which most of his money went. He was a movie nut, someone who took it very seriously, a worshiper of every strip of film that had ever come out of any movie camera from the time Tom Edison had perfected the motion picture camera.

Some day, Oscar said, he was going to make movies in Hollywood. Great movies. To this end, the furious hustle, the profits from it devoured by equipment and more equipment and film and the cost of its processing. To this end, when he wasn't on the hustle or in class he was out shooting scenes with that battery of apparatus or working over his films in the quarters provided him in the Performing Arts Center. To this end, he had founded the Historical Film Society, and there arranged showings of film classics, again at a profit to himself.

Considering the endless variety of goods that Oscar, as hustler, offered his clientele, it was hard to imagine that he could yet come up with something new and different to market, but eventually he did.

Me.

That was on a hazy October day when I was out on the soccer practice field with a few house-team members booting the ball around for fun. Then I noticed that Oscar was on the sidelines watching the action in the company of a couple of others. The only thing he ever seemed to admire about me was that I had earned a column in the college paper during last year's soccer tournament— he had even come to watch part of the playoff game—but it was a surprise to find him, as it were, conducting a tourist party to these premises and obviously pointing me out as the main attraction here.

When he motioned me to join him I strolled over out of curiosity and recognized one of the tourists as Shields, a second-string quarterback on the varsity team. The other man I didn't know. An ex-jock from the look of him, bald, middle-aged, tossing a football from one hand to the other as he took me in. This, said Oscar, was Coach Muldoon of the football team. Kicking coach. Oscar had explained my uncanny abilities as kicker to him and Coach Muldoon was here to get a look at me in action.

So, simply for the pleasure of wiping that cynical smile off Coach Muldoon's beefy face, I kicked a few goals for him, Shields holding the ball. Twenty yards out, thirty yards, and forty yards, varying the angle on request, neatly splitting the bar for an imaginary three points each time.

When the performance was over Shields said to me, "Money in the bank, baby," and Coach Muldoon's smile was no longer cynical. He gave me a nod. "Head Coach Neiderhoffer'll be in the Field House five o'clock. You be there then. We'll have a little talk with him."

They took themselves off, and Oscar, up to now under twitching self-restraint, burst out with it. The team desperately needed a kicker, he said. The hell with soccer; this is what counted, real football. And here I was, sent from heaven and eligible. And the payoff? A set of top-price tickets to scalp every home game. Alumni waiting to stuff money in your pocket. And best of all, there were all those pro teams now on the hunt for any kicker who knew how to use that weird sidewinder soccer style I did. The pros! The bonus money alone! So what I must now do is let Oscar take over for me as business manager on commission. First, he'd talk with Neiderhoffer, squeeze some juicy perquisites out of him. After that—

Grotesque as it was, this picture of my joining the sweaty, crop-headed, master-and-slave world of jocks, he was desperately serious about it. Why not? A nonpareil hustler, here he was working out the fanciest hustle of all, the managership of a profitable jock. Start with Dave Shaw, show what you can do for him, build up a whole string of profitable like numbers. After that, man, you can bankroll any movie you dream of making. He didn't have to spell it out for me. I knew Oscar's way of thinking.

"Sorry," I told him, "but the answer is no."

"Listen to me, Dave. You can't even begin to guess the kind of money that's waiting for us."

"No again," I said.

"You owe me two hundred bucks," Oscar said. "I want to see my money right now. The whole two hundred."

"After all those papers I did for you?"

"Two hundred cash," said Oscar, "or I get my car back. But if you go along with this football deal—"

I saw myself at the training table making conversation with such as Shields and Coach Muldoon about the Big Game, and I had to laugh. The laugh was a mistake. Oscar said grimly, "You think it's funny turning down a deal like this for both of us? And after I got Muldoon himself to come over here to take a look at you? Wait and see."

So I not only lost my unpaid-for car but, since Oscar was dictator of the Film Society, my unpaid-for membership there as well. I even lost Oscar himself for a little while when he abruptly packed and departed our quarters. I think what drove him to it was that I took my punishment so lightly. After all, how much joy can one get from inflicting deserved punishment when the victim yawns through the proceedings?

But he was back within the week. There wasn't another dorm room available until the end of the term, and I gathered that the boarding house he had tried out was too far from the action to be a proper base of operations. Now he settled down to a small, self-defeating vicious cycle, where the more he sullenly loathed me, the more I was indifferent to it, and the more I was indifferent to it, the more he loathed me.

But silently, all communication cut off between us.

There seemed no point in confiding to him that of all things I might cherish in a roommate it was just that kind of total silence.

During Thanksgiving week, a

letter from my mother.

When I opened it a photograph slid out. My mother and a young woman smiling at the camera on the terrace of the Periniades apartment in Rome. My mother, alas, had put on much more than the original four kilos she had once gone to Bagnio to lose; she seemed, in fact, to be taking on pouter-pigeon dimensions. The young woman beside her was beautiful. Dark hair, exotic eyes, a delicately featured face.

Well, well.

Roma, 20th Nov.

Darling boy,

This is all v. confidential, so do not discuss it with your n. father.

In your last note you mentioned that you are not happy about the careers planned for you by your n. father or by grandpa. Dear Milos is v. sympathetic. Also he has v. extensive interests on the Continent but cannot find a young man in the family to represent him there. Believes only in family does one find true loyalty. And only family member he could persuade to leave Greece and join him here is v. young niece, Sophia Changouris, a dear child. But while she assists in his office she speaks only Greek and Italian, so cannot handle many important matters.

Milos feels that you—member of family, v. intelligent and fluent in languages—should consider joining his business after graduation and eventually becoming a partner. To this end he will send round-trip fare to Rome and generous expense money, so you can share Xmas week with us and discuss all details with him.

Sophia is also v. anxious to meet you. She is shy about op. sex, and Milos hopes you can bring her out of her shell. He asks I send this photo so you will know you are not being lured here to become victim of a dragon.

Please wire your answer immediately.

Remember all this is v. confidential as yet.

Your loving mother

I looked at the photo again. The thought of entering business with dear Milos was one degree more abhorrent than the thought of becoming the diplomat my father intended me to be or the Dade County lawyer my grandfather wanted me to be, but devoting a week to helping bring Sophia out of her shell? And with all expenses paid?

That was a different story altogether.

At Fiumicino Airport, there they were. Milos looked me over doubtfully, and my mother openly expressed distaste for what she was seeing. "Really, darling, with that hair and those clothes you look like one of those disgraceful hippie ragamuffins in the Piazza di Spagna."

Sophia made up for this ungraciousness. Wrapped in a luxurious high-necked fur coat, her face flowerlike against the collar, she smiled shyly at me as we shook hands. "Did you have a good voyage on the airplane?" she asked me in careful English.

"Yes, thank you." She was surreptitiously trying to work her hand free of mine, but I refused to let go. "A very good voyage. But I speak Italian. *Parlo l'italiano molto bene.* And Greek."

"Ah, no. Always the English, please. I much desire to learn the English. You will help me in that, yes?"

"Of course," I said.

Of course.

What I discovered as day followed frustrating day through that

Yuletide was that Sophia Changouris had come on a marvelous device for forestalling seduction. Linguistics. Start to woo her in Italian and she'd immediately press a silencing finger to your lips. Try it in English, and it became a language lesson.

What made it worse were the wasted opportunities along the way. The family apartment was often empty and available, and, even more trying, Sophia's own little apartment on via F. Lippi was not merely available, it had been made into something so harem-like that it was an agony just to stand there, car keys in hand, waiting to remove her from it. But standing there, car keys in hand, was as far as I ever got in that apartment.

We covered a lot of territory around Rome that week, hosted by the offspring of my mother's innumerable friends at house parties, clubs, and cafés, and though there was always wine and sometime pot for the asking, it seemed that demure Sophia drank very little wine and smoked no pot.

Meanwhile, Milos was working his wiles on me. Now and again he would lead me into a conversation about my future and the reasons for putting it in his charge. He dealt in commodities, it seemed, contracting for future delivery of goods he didn't even own today, the cash flow was enormous, the profits considerable. And to keep all this in the family—

I fended him off each time, and in the process of fending him off one morning I touched a nerve. He was deep in a description of a coup he planned, and, casting about for any topic which could turn him off, I was led to think of the Cavalcanti family. I knew they still lived next door because their nameplate was over the bell, but they never appeared on the Periniades's doorstep, and no mention of them was ever made. Why was that, I inquired.

There was a sudden chill in the dining room. Then as my mother started a flurried explanation Milos cut in. "I invited Cavalcanti to invest in some grain futures a few months ago. Really a gift to him on my part. Last month when I handed him his profit he felt it was not sufficient and told me so to my face. That, of course, was the end of it between us."

"After all these years," my mother said wistfully. "I still think that if you simply went next door—"

"No," Milos said, "we will have nothing to do with those people. Ever."

"Yes, dear," said my mother, although her furtive expression suggested to me that she was, against orders, still having something to do with those people.

"Also," Milos said to me, "it's just as well you stay away from that Umberto. Really a scandal. Already in trouble with the police."

"What kind of trouble?"

"Oh, a political madman that one."

"And Bianca?"

Milos waved the question aside. "Please. No more of the Cavalcantis, if you do not mind."

I did not mind. Despite some fond memories of plump little Bianca clutching my hand with sticky fingers as we strolled Piazza Navona after ice cream at Tre Scalini, she was, of course, out of my remote childhood. It was Sophia Changouris who was the proper concern for me in my overheated young manhood.

On New Year's Eve, I found that at last I was making progress in my concern. The generations came together at a party given by Milos and my mother, the music was eardrum-shattering and blood-quickening, and the champagne, ouzo, and retsina flowed like water. Wine, steadily applied in small amounts to my hesitant Sophia, worked its magic on her.

Timing it near midnight, I pulled a coat at random from the rack in the master bedroom and hauled my prey out to the terrace, draping the coat over her shoulders against the chill. When I slid my arms under the coat and locked them around her waist she said, "Please," in gentle protest. It was almost no protest at all.

I said, *"Ma lei ha freddo, gioia mia."*

"No, I am not cold." She giggled. "But your hands, they are cold."

Maybe. But they were warming up fast.

The door of the terrace clattered. Uncle Milos's tone was peremptory. "Young people, it is almost the midnight. Join us, please."

Sophia went through the door, but I remained where I was. "Later," I told Milos. "I need the air. Too much to drink maybe," and he said, "Yes, the air may cool one's blood," and closed the door behind him after he stepped through it, each of us understanding the other.

Then, to make it worse, I saw I was not alone with my bleak thoughts. The door of the apartment beyond the dividing wall of the

Cavalcanti's terrace was partly open, a head thrusting through it, an arm beckoning. "Sss. David."

"Bianca?"

"Certo, buffone. Vieni qui."

After how many years I am addressed by this once admiring child as a clown? And come over there for what? *"Perché, ragazza?"*

"Don't ask questions. Just come over here."

I vaulted the terrace wall and followed the *ragazza* into the Cavalcanti living room. Empty. "Where is everybody?" I asked.

"Cortina. For the skiing." She suddenly went into a convulsive fit of sneezing, then said unnecessarily, "I've got a cold. No use my going with them in this shape."

She was in pajamas and robe, a big girl now, on the borderline of plump. But not bad-looking at all, though the neat Florentine nose was pink and the large gray eyes watery.

We stood there looking at each other. "Well," I finally said by way of conversation, "it's been a long time."

"That's not my fault."

"Ah, come on, *bambola*—"

"And don't *bambola* me. I'm not really a kid any more."

Through the wall, the remote sound of celebration in the Periniades apartment suddenly rose in volume. I looked at my watch. "Twelve o'clock. Happy New Year."

"Happy New Year," said Bianca and went into another sneezing fit. She finally controlled it. "What's going on with you and that girl?"

"Sophia?"

"Of course, Sophia. Who else have you been carrying on with all week?"

"Oh? And how would you know that?"

"Everybody knows it. Umberto knows it. And his friends. They've been seeing you around town with her everywhere. For that matter, anyone can stand right on that terrace out there and see what's going on through your door. Like all the work you've been putting in, trying to get her clothes off in the living room."

"Is that how you caught your cold? Watching the action from your terrace?"

"I don't think you know about her at all." Bianca shook her head wonderingly. "You really don't know she's Milos's mistress, do you?"

Again we just stood and looked at each other. Then Bianca's face crumpled as if she were doing a Stan Laurel imitation. "I should never have told you! I don't know why I told you. I am absolutely crazy. And look at the mess I am. And letting you see me like this. I must be crazy."

"You need something to drink," I said. "I think we both do."

In the kitchen the espresso machine was steaming. There were movie-fan magazines scattered over the kitchen table. Bianca hastily cleared them away and set down two cups of coffee. Into each she poured a small dollop of cognac.

"Now," I said, "what about Sophia?"

"Yes. Well, there's this Greek tourist agency on the Corso. Athenikos."

"And?"

"Sophia was receptionist there. Their showpiece."

"And?"

"And Milos picked her up right out of the agency. Because your mother is such an innocent really—"

"Or chooses to be."

"Well, whichever way it was, he got bolder and bolder about it. Took Sophia into the apartment as a relative, gave her a nonsense job in his office, finally set her up in her own rooms. We knew about it all along. Milos needed a lot of cash fast and got Papa to go along on the deal with him, so Papa had a desk there while it was happening. After the deal was settled and Papa got his money back, we just cut off from Milos. What we couldn't understand was why he practically invited you to go to bed with his woman."

"I wasn't invited to," I said. "And I didn't."

"You didn't?" Bianca said. "You know, I believe you. Am I being stupid about that?"

"No. But are you sure my mother doesn't have any idea what's going on? Absolutely sure?"

"Absolutely. So you'll have to be the one to tell her. You're really the only one who has a right to."

"Tell her? Not a chance."

Bianca, her cup poised halfway to her mouth, gaped at me. "Are you going to deny she has the right to know her husband is betraying her with that slut?"

"You're giving it the grand opera treatment, baby. I'd say Mama has every right to be happy. She seems perfectly happy this way."

"But that's shameful. Don't you have any pride? Any sense of decency? My God, I'm only sorry I didn't know what you were turning into. It would have saved me a lot of foolish daydreaming about you."

I had a feeling that even if I were less muzzy-headed it wouldn't be easy keeping up with her. "*Coccolina,* the last time you and I went around holding hands, you couldn't have been more than twelve years old. Now what kind of daydreams can a twelve-year-old kid work up on an ice cream and pastry high?"

"What kind? *Romàntico. Romàntico.* Pinwheels in the head. That's what kind."

"Now let's not—"

"Don't you dare sit there and look amused about it! You don't know anything about girls, big or little. I was crazy about you."

"More coffee," I said.

"Get it yourself."

I got it myself and poured a very large slug of cognac into it. Bianca said, "You wind up drunk, and then how do I get you back next door?"

"I won't wind up drunk. Besides, why worry about next door when right here seems to be all ours for the night?"

She fixed those large watery eyes on me. "You mean, because you can't get into bed with Milos's girl friend you'll settle for bed with me?"

"Forget about Milos's girl friend. Look, now that I know what's going on I'm taking the plane back to New York tomorrow, but meanwhile the night is ours. *Io ti bramo, carissima. Che ne diresti?*"

"The way I look right now? And with this cold? That sounds absolutely perverted."

"It happens to be perfectly natural. And possibly curative."

"No. Now listen very carefully. I haven't gone to bed with any man yet. I will certainly not do it under these conditions."

"But—"

"No. It would be wrong, that's all, because you wouldn't be caring, and I would. You know how those daydreams always ended?

You'd walk in here, and I'd be so slender and glamorous—certainly I wouldn't be spraying germs all over the place—and you would say, 'Here I am, Bianca. Now I know you are the only one for me,' and I would see you meant it. Then when you said, *'Che ne diresti?'* I'd say, 'Of course. That's the way it was always meant to be with us.' An idiotic dream, you understand. Part of the growing-up sickness. But I'm almost eighteen now. It's time I was over it."

"It is," I said. "And since I'm not that eager to rush back next door after the great enlightenment, do you suppose you could just sit and talk to me a while as if I were an old friend and not a product of your fevered imagination?"

"No. Now please go. Please."

"Why?"

"Because I'm in no mood for a friendly talk. I don't feel like your friend."

I went the way I had come, over the terrace wall. I had the impression when I rejoined the party that no one there had missed me for a moment.

There were still three days left of the holiday vacation when I walked into the dormitory, and the place was almost empty. In the lounge, the TV set was tuned in to the Capitol where Lyndon B. Johnson was being re-enthroned, but there was no one in the lounge to cheer the coronation. My own quarters also looked more than usually barren. It took me a few seconds to realize that this was because Oscar, in my absence, must have finally relocated himself and had cleared out every vestige of his unpleasant person.

Easy come, easy go. The immediate objective was to crawl into bed and sleep off jet lag and the remnants of my Roman hangover. And possibly to cool off an overheated conscience. My passport wallet was unusually plump, stuffed with almost four hundred dollars, the remainder of the astonishingly generous expense money Milos had thrust on me soon after my arrival at his home. When I departed it, after the coolest of farewells, it had taken considerable rationalizing to keep me from thrusting it back at him. After all, if my mother had any suspicions of Sophia's place in her husband's life, I had done a yeoman job of allaying them with my wooing.

That, I suspected, had to be one reason Milos had wanted my presence on the scene, no matter the expense. Now, however, conscience was jabbing me again, but not enough to keep me from falling sound asleep as I weighed the idea of shipping him back his money first thing tomorrow.

I was wakened by a hand prodding my shoulder and a voice asking me something about a break. A break? I tried to open my eyes but couldn't. "What?" I said.

"You can see what a break it'll be for me, Shaw. It's a hot story. UPI's been on the phone with me about it. If I can get an exclusive—"

"UPI?"

"The press service. I'm a stringer for them."

I managed to open my eyes and focus them on this intruder. Don Schaeffer, a staff man on the college paper. The one who had done the admiring column about my soccer prowess. "What the hell are you talking about?" I asked.

"What do you think? That spread in the *Weekly Graphic.*"

The *Graphic.* One of those national tabloids that feature sensational headlines, soft-core porno photos to illustrate fake news stories, and a large section devoted to lonely-hearts ads, bring your own vibrator and whip. "I still don't know what you're talking about," I told Schaeffer.

"Ah, stop fooling around, Shaw." He pulled a rolled-up newspaper, tabloid size, from his overcoat pocket and held it up to display the front page. "It came out this morning."

I looked. And what I beheld was a large photograph of my n. father, many years younger, tête-à-tête with Dwight D. Eisenhower.

And I didn't so much read that glaring headline as seem to hear it bellowed into my unbelieving ears.

SEXUAL FEARS MADE STATESMAN INTO BLUEBEARD, SON REVEALS

Of course, none of this was really happening. I had fallen asleep fully clothed and landed in the middle of a nightmare.

I took the paper from Schaeffer. Real. And looking at the small print below the photograph which advertised *Story and Other Pix on Pages 4 & 5,* I knew that worse was to come.

"Well," Schaeffer said, "what about the interview?"

He retreated a couple of steps as I stood up. "Out," I said, speeding him on his way with a hand against his chest.

I closed and locked the door. I laid the paper out on the study table and opened it to pages four and five which, side by side, presented a vivid display of my father's personal history.

Dorothy. Olivia. Darlene. Wendy. Phyllis.

I was directly quoted only once in the text. In the opening paragraph I set forth the premise that my aging dad was seeking his Fountain of Youth in perpetual remarriage. The rest of the text had been, like that quotation, lifted from the journal in my desk drawer, but whittled down and sharpened to the worst effect. The total presentation did what it was intended to do. No one reading it could doubt that I had spilled all this to an evil-minded interviewer.

A good hater, Oscar Wylie. And shrewd. Because he had not only murderously scored against me but must have been paid by this rag for the pleasure of doing so. Thirty pieces of silver, no doubt.

If there was a record for covering the distance between the dormitory and the Performing Arts Center, I broke it in that headlong run. I found Oscar in his workroom, the small room he had wheeled out of the Dramatic Arts Department, full of Movieolas, dismantled cameras and projectors, and the rest of the stuff necessary for bringing out his genius. He was at a table with a couple of assistants doing some close work on a piece of machinery. One look at me in the doorway and he knew what I was there for.

When I moved he dodged around the table, but too late. I caught him flush in the mouth with a punch so hard that it sent him reeling into the cluttered shelving on the wall. The assistants grabbed me and I shoved them off with no effort. But now when I moved toward Oscar he was holding something shiny in his fist, waving it menacingly as he sputtered warnings at me through a spray of blood from his mouth.

It could have been a length of pipe, an iron bar, a machine gun for that matter. It was all the same to me, all of no account, because I joyously knew I was capable of charging a battery of cannon if that was the way to him.

That was my mistake.

I was in the college infirmary, I knew as soon as I opened my eyes, and those figures hovering over me were the doctor in charge there and the nurse who doled out cough syrup and pills with a miserly hand. For the rest, I understood that I was stretched out on a receiving table still fully clothed, and that my face had a weight resting on it. I ran a finger over the weight and discovered gauze and tape covering my nose from cheekbone to cheekbone.

The doctor shoved my finger away. "Know who you are and where you are?" he said.

I told him, and he said, "Perfect score," as he checked my eyes with a pocket light. He seemed satisfied with the results. "In layman's language," he said to me, "a badly busted nose and a pair of lovely black eyes. Your father's already been notified about this, and we're waiting for him to call back and tell us what he wants done with the body—kept here or sent home. Meanwhile, you can look through your wallet on the table there and sign a receipt for it. It'll be kept locked up until your discharge."

He left, and a little while later the nurse left, and I was there alone. I looked into the wallet and found the four hundred dollars and my passport as I had last seen them.

The receiving room was on the ground floor. Outside its window a block away was the cabstand where one could get a cab to the bus terminal, a bus to New York, a plane to Paris.

The plane to Paris.

THE
KING OF
VONDEL PARK

Part II

In the last week of June, in the year 1971, I became King of Vondel Park.

De Koning Vondelpark.

The event was manufactured by journalist Berti van Stade in her column, The Woman's Eye, which regularly appeared in that estimable daily, *Het Oog Amsterdam.*

A tall young man, 26 years of age, lean and muscular. An unkempt shock of hair, a drooping mustache, a massive beard, a broken and battered nose. Tattooed on a powerful forearm a tulip crossed by a dagger. The clothing? Sandals, a pair of jeans hacked off at the thigh, no more. Dark glasses conceal the eyes. Altogether a piratical figure, yet, as soon becomes evident, a most attractive and compelling one.

Who is he? His name is Jan van Zee, and he is indisputably king of that troublesome territory in our midst, Vondel Park.

That was just for openers. From there on, in equally lush prose, followed the account of how Berti, one of the many who had been outraged that the city of Amsterdam should allow its lovely Vondel Park to become a hippie haven, was advised by Inspector Hendrick Spranger, in charge of the park police, to meet with a strange young man named van Zee and see why the experiment might work out. Van Zee, it seemed, was paterfamilias of Amsterdam's hippie horde, its adviser, travel agent, interpreter, intermediary with the authorities, and propagandist against hard drugs. Most surprising of all, he had won not only the respect of the youth movement itself, but also that of the police in several cities for his moderation and good sense.

And so Berti had arranged for an interview with this wonder-worker right there in Vondel Park and had been terribly, terribly impressed. And that was how Jan van Zee—once David Hanna Shaw—came to be *de Koning Vondelpark.*

The evening of the column's publication, Hendrick Spranger showed up at the Salamander Café in Rembrandtplein on one of his accidentally-on-purpose visits, plowed through the mob like a walrus hunting its mate, and dropped into the seat next to mine. "Jesus," he said, "you could choke to death from the stink of pot in here."

He was a big, gray-haired, amiable hulk, the only cop I knew whose presence would not stir up a shock wave in these surroundings, because he never made an issue of small sins and tried to be fair about large ones. "The young ones today," he would say, shaking his head in honest bewilderment. *"Ach, de jongelui."*

Now I said to him, "I don't like publicity, Hendrick. What made you turn that newspaper lady loose on me?"

"Pressure from the top, boy. She's got a lot of clout, that bitch. Also I knew that if she fell into your hands, she'd be charmed to death, which is exactly what happened."

"Thanks," I said.

"Not at all, Your Majesty," said Hendrick.

And how had David Hanna
Shaw become Jan van Zee and entered into this curious kingdom?

The hard way.

I had landed at Orly Airport in Paris masked by surgical gauze
and tape, all my worldly possessions on my back, and very few
dollars left of my hoard. As soon as I managed to clear the barrier,
no easy job considering my bandaged and indistinguishable features,
I destroyed my passport with a sense of burning all my bridges
behind me. More important, with the hounds certainly following
close behind—at least one outraged n. father and a whole roster of
outraged mothers—it was better to carry no papers than the wrong
papers. Now what I desperately needed to close the books on David
Shaw and open them on an alter ego was a French passport. A
forged passport, of course, such as I was sure could be obtained for
a price, although where to obtain it and how to get up the price were
beyond immediate reckoning.

Meanwhile, the name of the game was survival. Harder yet, survival without a *carte d'identité.* That closed every door to me where proper identification was required, and Paris, I soon learned, was one such door after another.

Paris in the springtime is one thing. Paris in January, especially for someone in my pauperized condition, is another. In the grim time that followed, it was a moot point whether I suffered more from cold or from hunger. In a way they alleviated each other, the cold sometimes so marrow-piercing that it made me forget my hunger, the hunger sometimes so acute that it left no room for any other sensation. Bearded, unkempt, exuding the fragrance of the unwashed, I became a beggar, a scavenger, a petty shoplifter in food stores, a sleeper in doorways.

What saved me was *La Société des Cousins.*

It did not exist in any records, it was not known in polite society, and I heard about it miraculously from a café sweeper-up who took pity on me. In Montmartre, he said, on the Boulevard de Clichy and its adjoining streets were cheap restaurants that sometimes needed an extra hand in the kitchen for a day or two. And, most important, where the inability to show a work permit would be overlooked. If an inspector did walk in, the temporary help would promptly become the proprietor's Cousin So-and-so in from the provinces to help out in an emergency.

As I learned, moving from kitchen to kitchen in the guise of Cousin Jean Lespere from Decazeville, the alleys around the Boulevard de Clichy swarmed with cousins any busy night of the week. Most were derelicts, perpetually foggy with wine, moving slow motion through their jobs. I came to be the golden exception, a cousin really to be desired, as, steadily eating my way back into form, I handled my chores full speed and with a will.

It was not work for the fastidious. One went shoulder-deep into slimy pots to scour them properly. Disassembled broiling units to scrape every bit of crusted fat from them. Got down on the knees with a bucket of soapy water and brush to scrub dirt-caked floors back into shape. Performed magic on reeking lavatory bowls. Stayed sober, pacific, and outwardly smiling, no matter how ungrateful my employers, until I finally won recognition as the best of all possible cousins. *La fleur des pois.* The pick of the crop.

Inevitably, such a pearl among cousins was destined for upward mobility.

When I reported for duty at one of my usual locations one night the proprietor told me not to strip for action, but to hie myself around the corner to rue Houdon and make myself known to the operator of La Maison Chouchoute there. To Chouchoute herself. She might have a steady job for me, papers or no papers.

As I instantly understood on entering the premises, Chouchoute's was hardly one of your fancy places, but was, in the local parlance, *une maison d'abattage.* A cut-rate whorehouse made for quickies. And, judging from the attendance in the waiting room, highly prosperous.

I was ushered into Madame's private quarters on the top floor where she was getting dressed for the evening, and, in the process, unselfconsciously showing a great deal of her stout self. She looked me over with the eye of a moray eel. "I've heard about you. Hardworking, mannerly, tends to keep his mouth shut, they said. Doesn't seem to be a boozer. True?"

"Yes, Madame."

"Then what's the catch? *Le noir? Le blanc? Chnouf?*"

Hash? Cocaine? Heroin? "No, Madame." I rolled up my sleeves to demonstrate the absence of needlemarks. "Only a joint now and then, when one can be had."

"We'll soon find out." While she talked she was wrestling herself into a bulky corset. She turned her broad back to me. "Here, lace it up tight. Put those muscles into it." She held her belly in while I laced as tight as I could, sure that as soon as she took her first deep breath the whole contraption would explode in my face. Against all laws of science, it didn't. "Good," said Madame. "All right, you can try out as handyman here, starting with the kitchen. The chef is useless when he's more than half drunk, so see he's never more than half drunk. And clean up that filthy kitchen of his once and for all and see that it stays clean. Same for the rest of the place, top to bottom. And tend the furnace. Is that enough to keep you out of mischief?"

"Yes, Madame."

"Not quite. Because sometimes a customer here gets the idea he's a real tiger. When that happens your job is to restrain him without damaging him seriously. Think you can do it?"

"Yes, Madame."

"I hope so. An honest day's work for an honest day's pay, that's

---
45
---

what I expect of you. And let me inform you, citizen, I'm no one to be trifled with."

That was probably the most gratuitous piece of information I had ever been offered in my life.

Earn while you learn.

Not only did the job guarantee survival, but the more I came to know Chouchoute, the more I was convinced that if anyone could help me lay hands on a forged passport, Madame was it.

So to win her stony heart I gave my duties all the devotion Cousin Jean Lespere from Decazeville was capable of. The duties of scullion, of course, I had already mastered. My other duties—house cleaner, furnace tender, assistant chef, corset lacer, sergeant-at-arms, and psychotherapist for a houseful of manic-depressive, case-hardened females—well, they did offer challenges now and then.

For example, one learned not to poke too enthusiastically into an ancient French coal-burning furnace because then the grates immediately collapsed. And not to keep urging sobriety on a moody Algerian chef because eventually he would enter his demurrer with a carving knife in hand. And, in providing a sympathetic ear for the inmates of a place like Chouchoute's, not to believe a word any of them spoke, however plausible it sounded. *Le noir, le blanc, chnouf*

—all the ladies here were either smoking it, sniffing it, or shooting it. Plausible but spaced out, one and all.

For their part, despite early suspicions that Madame had hired me to be house stool-pigeon, they finally came around to treating me as a member of the team. Someone you could confide your many troubles to, knowing he'd cluck his tongue at the right places. Janot was the nickname they came to tag me with. Used as an insult, that word can invite a black eye. In my case, it was used affectionately. On the Boulevard de Clichy, Dopey in *Snow White* would be called Janot.

Even Madame took to using that nickname and to confiding her troubles to me, always winding up the narrative with the phrase, *"C'est du bidon, bébé."* Meaning, in rough translation, that it's all a snow job, baby. The world is a great big snow job, and we poor innocents—Madame in the forefront—are always getting snowed under.

Then traces of springtime appeared in the 18th arrondissement. Flowerpots appeared on the windowsills along rue Houdon. And on the Boulevard de Clichy, potential customers stopped to study the pictorial displays before the strip joints instead of scurrying past them, heads sunk in their collars.

It was time to test Madame's good will.

I picked that hour for the test when she was usually, if not in a sweet mood, at least in a neutral one. Noon. Her breakfast hour. She was in bed at her coffee and croissant and newspaper. She looked at me and put the paper aside. "Something's in the wind," she said.

"Yes. I need a lead to someone who can provide me with a passport. A false passport that can pass as the real thing."

There was no suggestion of surprise in that blobby face, not a quiver of those jowls. "So it's just as I thought. You're on the lam, aren't you?"

"Not as a criminal, Madame."

"As some species of revolutionary then? Some agent seeking to crawl out of the underground and make trouble for decent people?"

"No, Madame. Strictly a *J'm'en-fichiste.*"

"A sensible policy, if you mean it. But why come to me with your problem?"

"A fair question, Madame. You see, I've taken notice that among our neighborhood clientele there are certain declassé gentlemen—

pickpockets, fences, con men—with whom you are on excellent terms. I believe that one of them, at your suggestion, might steer me in the right direction."

Madame shrugged. "Small-time types, Janot. False passports are big-time. That means big money is involved."

"Given time, Madame, I can pay off any money required. A lot of companies around town are offering good wages to personnel who are fluent in foreign languages. I'm well qualified for such work. And a few months on the payroll means I can meet whatever price is set. First, of course, I must have the passport to get the job."

Madame's eyebrows went up. "The passport on credit? Small chance."

"Why, Madame? Whoever sells it to me has the best possible collateral. If I miss any payments for it, all he has to do is make an anonymous call to the Sûreté about me."

Madame sat studying me. *"Formidable,"* she said at last. "Everything planned to perfection, isn't it? Well, I'm a fool. Always too softhearted for my own good. I'll see what I can do for you."

"Thank you, Madame."

"No thanks yet. Just get back on the job and keep that mouth tight shut about this."

If I thought she would act out of sentiment, I would have known better than to expect results. I had learned at La Maison Chouchoute that, contrary to all mythology, Madame and every one of her girls without exception had hearts like cash registers. But that was in my favor now. The passport would cost plenty, and of that plenty Madame was undoubtedly expecting a fat payoff.

The accuracy of this was proved when I was called to her room a few days later. "The price of that item you asked about is ten thousand francs, including my commission," she said. "But there are a couple of small strings attached to the deal."

"How small, Madame?"

"Well, a French passport is out of the question right now. So what you'll be getting is the genuine article issued by the Dutch government itself to someone about your age who had no police record and is now very much dead. That shouldn't bother you any. I've heard you speak Dutch like a native to those Eindhoven truckers that drop in here."

I thought it over. "Are you sure there's no police record?"

"None. A little correctional time done as a juvenile, but to the police that kind of thing is a joke."

"How did he happen to die, Madame?"

"God moves in strange ways, Janot. He died in a boating accident in the Channel, and there was no use reporting it to the family because there was no family. He was a war orphan and a street child in Rotterdam. Nor was the death reported to the authorities, because," Madame shrugged broadly, "who knows which authorities have jurisdiction over all that cold water."

Who indeed?

"All right," I said, "when and how do I make the arrangements?"

"When is immediately. How is someone else's business. You'll meet with him today and find you're in for a pleasant surprise. You'll work off your ten thousand francs all right, but in just one little job. A pleasant trip accompanying a young lady who must bring some merchandise from Marseille to Paris. After that, the passport is yours, free and clear."

"And the merchandise?" I said. *"Chnouf?"*

"Where would you get such an idea?"

"Marseille means either fish stew or heroin," I pointed out. "And I can't see someone giving me credit for ten thousand francs for transporting a pot of fish stew across the country."

"Hardly," said Madame. She seemed rather pleased by my surmise. She leaned forward and rapped me gently between the eyes with her coffee spoon. "Brains. They rattle a little sometime, but they're all there. Yes, you'll do very well for yourself, I think."

I would be met at three o'clock at the far corner of the Place de la Chapelle, Madame said, and all I had to do was be there on time and make myself visible. At three o'clock I was there. A sedate black Renault station wagon was also there, very dusty and a little battered around the edges, and on its side was a large white cross underneath which was inscribed *Les Amis du Bon Évangéliste.*

The particular Friend of the Good Evangelist who apparently chauffeured it was on the sidewalk handing leaflets to unwilling passers-by, and a sharply pointed evangelical nose she had, perfectly in keeping with that mousy hair drawn into a tight bun and those sallow features and the schoolmarm dress inches longer than any other in view. She approached me and thrust a leaflet at me. When I started to crumple it in my fist she said between her teeth, "Read it, Monsieur Janot from rue Houdon. The address on it is not far from here. Wait until I leave."

I waited until the wagon scooted off, then followed its direction.

The address was on a dreary block, all ruinous buildings, most housing hole-in-the-wall bistros, but one curtained store front revealed the neatly lettered sign on the door, *Les Amis du Bon Évangéliste*. The Renault was parked across the street from it.

I stepped into the place. A one-time bistro all right, its past now largely stripped from it. The bar remained, but on it was an array of missionary tracts. And on the wall behind the bar were posted various messages. *No Alcohol Permitted!* And *No Smoking Permitted!* And that ultimate secret of salvation: *Our Coffee Contains No Caffeine!*

Beautiful. All beautiful down to those freshly whitewashed walls, the glossy linoleum flooring, the half-dozen rows of slat-backed chairs facing a lectern at the far end of the room, behind which was an upright piano and a large crucifix. But the most beautifully convincing touch of all was the occupant of one of those chairs, the sharp-nosed young lady of the leaflets who sat there, head bowed in deep meditation. I scraped a foot on the floor and she turned to regard me. Then with a sharp little motion of the head she indicated the back door of the room. As I pushed open the door and entered the room beyond, she was right on my heels.

I was in a kitchen now put to other use, because aside from the usual kitchen equipment there were a filing cabinet, a typewriter on a stand, and a few open cartons of books. And a kitchen table, behind which stood a man giving me a toothy smile. About thirty-five, with a beefy red face glowing with good nature, and done up in a tweed suit and white turtleneck sweater, he had to be anybody's idea of a born scoutmaster.

"Prettig kennis te maken," he said jovially, and, taken aback at encountering Dutch where I had expected French, I hesitated before politely responding, *"Aangenaam met U kennis te maken."*

"Ah, goed." He nodded approval. *"Zeer goed."*

"Pas de ça!" the young lady said sharply. "Speak French."

The scoutmaster gave me a big wink. "That is Marie-Paule Neyna," he informed me, then shifted to fluent French. "From Namur. One of your Belgians who think those Dutch-speaking countrymen of hers north of Brussels should either learn to speak French or keep silent."

"Buffoon," said Marie-Paule.

"And of course," her tormentor remarked to me, "no sense of

humor at all. By the way, my name is Kees Baar. A Netherlander, need I say?"

"Jean Lespere," I said.

"Dear Chouchoute's Janot. You know, the old biddy thinks very highly of you. Considering that she views the world through a vinegar bottle, that's as glittering a recommendation as you can get. She gave you an idea of what the deal is, didn't she?"

"More or less. A Dutch passport in return for helping transport some merchandise from Marseille to Paris."

"Right." He dug into a pocket and came up with a passport which he tossed on the table. "Here's the trophy you're shooting for."

I carefully examined the passport. Issued to a Jan van Zee in January of this year, it was the real thing all right. Only one hitch. The photograph in it bore not the least resemblance to me.

I pointed this out to Kees, and he said, "No problem. This evening we hold services here which you're to attend so you can get the feel of the thing. That gives you more than enough time to visit a certain photographer on the Boul' Magenta and then leave everything to me. Before you've even completed your assignment, the passport will be in perfect order. Incidentally"—he motioned at my paper sack of belongings—"is that your entire complement of luggage?"

"Yes."

"Then after you have your pictures taken, stop in at a secondhand shop along the boulevard there and pick up a cheap suitcase for yourself. Something suitably drab and Calvinistic. And a wedding ring. Brass will do nicely."

"A wedding ring?"

"You and Marie-Paule will be partners on this missionary tour, and we don't want any eyebrows raised along the way." He shrugged. "Naturally, no operation like this can be completely air-tight, but we do try to plug any conceivable pinhole. Of course, the biggest asset is an ability to improvise on the spot convincingly. In those terms, I think you're going to make a worthy member of the team."

I didn't like the direction in which he seemed to be aiming. "A member of the team for one job," I pointed out. "This job. None other."

Attendance at services that evening was meager. Besides staff there were only five present, all of them looking like charter members of *La Société des Cousins*. The program opened with the grim-visaged Marie-Paule issuing books to us—from the bulk of it, *Le Recueil Complet d'Hymnes* must have been the fattest hymnal ever published—and this was followed by a doleful singsong, Marie-Paule thumping away at the piano, the rest of us caterwauling hymns, and was closed by a hellfire-and-brimstone sermon by Kees who, indeed, made a highly convincing Reverend Davidson. Then Marie-Paule awakened a couple of sleepers, collected the hymnals, and, after stacking them away with great care, presided over a buffet of bread and *café sans caféine*.

At eight-thirty it was all over, and the redeemed departed for their night's rest in their chosen doorways or under their favorite bridges. The staff, or unredeemed, gathered in the kitchen to clean up, and while we were at these chores Kees said to me, "Starting tomorrow evening, services in Marseille. Three days of that, then back to Paris, and there you are. You have only two things to remember. First, you're to follow all Marie-Paule's instructions to the letter. Second, you'll also be her strong-arm boy. Her protector. Chouchoute said you're good in that department. That you know how to use your muscle without getting murderous."

"Glad to get the recommendation," I said, "but protector against what?"

"Not the police, if that's what's on your mind. However, there's a species of waterfront animal who may show up at our place in Marseille looking for trouble, and that must be discouraged. But no weapon is permitted. Nothing that might have the police move in."

"One's best weapon is a pure heart and a loving spirit," I pointed out.

"Exactly. That's what gives us hope for the future of mankind, isn't it? And now, since you're going to be up before dawn, Mijnheer, I'd suggest you bed down early. The room upstairs overlooking the street is all yours."

I bedded down on an army cot somewhat harder on the hip than even the floor would be, so in the end I settled for the floor. I was awakened in darkness by Kees poking my shoulder and saying, "Time to be up, Sleeping Beauty. It's four-thirty. Get a move on or you'll catch an earful from the lady."

The lady herself, a wedding band now conspicuous on her finger, was hard at work in the kitchen when I walked in and was in no sweeter mood than she had been last night. Under her instructions I loaded into the station wagon cartons of books and leaflets, a wicker hamper of food, and finally her suitcase and mine. As a reward, I was allowed all the coffee and bread I could put away in one minute flat, and then on the stroke of five we were in the car and heading south.

She drove expertly, always staying just within speed limits, and traveling thus, we arrived at Marseille in midafternoon. It came as no surprise to find that, just as the Paris tabernacle was planted in a rough neighborhood among cheap bistros and auto supply shops, the Marseille tabernacle, a couple of blocks from the docks, was planted in a rough neighborhood of cheap bistros and boat supply shops. And, as I saw after I rolled up the corrugated metal sheet that sealed it in and Marie-Paule had unlocked its door, the place itself was a facsimile of the Paris salvation center. Same general size and layout, and, one flight up, even the same sort of bedroom waiting for me, no furniture in it but a cot.

So to work, unloading the car, and then, shoulder to shoulder with Marie-Paule, tending to an accumulation of Marseille grime with rags and mops.

In the midst of this I was handed yet another duty, to get to a bakery for a few loaves of bread. Watching Marie-Paule working away with the mop as I departed, I could only wonder where she got the energy. It was some satisfaction, therefore, when I returned and laid the warm breads on the bar, to see that my partner must have gone human for a moment and decided to take a breather. She was not on the scene but her mop was, resting against the bar. Nothing wrong with that, but, curiously, the kitchen door which we had left open through our labors was now almost closed, only a thin band of light showing through it. And on that newly mopped floor, were those the prints of men's shoes other than mine? Two distinct sets of them?

I moved toward the kitchen, but stopped short of it. "Marie-Paule," I called, "I've got the bread here. Where do I put it?"

A silence followed, a few heartbeats of it, and then in a warmly inviting lilt came Marie-Paule's voice. "Right in here, *mon cheri.*"

Mon cheri? From that lady?

I came at the door like a battering ram and hit it full force with my shoulder, trusting that anybody waiting in the kitchen to waylay me would be behind it, and luck was with me. The door crashed into someone, sent him staggering back, but I didn't have time to finish him off on the spot. Marie-Paule was seated in a chair in the middle of the kitchen which was a scene of wild disorder, and standing over her, one hand twisted in her hair, the other gripping a long-bladed knife, was a big, hard-looking specimen, astonishment on his face. As training for combat, soccer has its advantages. Before he could turn the knife in my direction I drove my heel into his shin, and when he doubled over in agony I kicked him in the jaw with impact enough to drive it right through his skull, and down he went. I wheeled around, expecting the other man to be on my back by now, but that one had had his bellyful—faceful, actually, and I knew how that felt—and before I could grab him he was through the outside door and gone.

I closed and locked the door and quickly returned to the kitchen.

Marie-Paule, still seated and very white of face, was regarding the man stretched out on the floor. Most of the acid seemed drained from her as she looked up at me. "My God, you are efficient, aren't you?"

"You helped considerably. That *mon cheri* was very clever."

She gave me a pallid smile. "And you are too, for guessing what it meant. When he motioned me to call you in here I didn't want to, but that knife at my throat—"

"A very convincing argument, a knife at the throat. But who is he?"

"I don't know." She got unsteadily to her feet and didn't seem to mind that I put an arm around her waist to support her. "Small fry probably. They live on what they can steal from proper dealers. See what he has on him."

I did, and found I wasn't the only one in these parts traveling without papers. There were a few franc notes in one of his pockets, and that was it.

"Now what?" I asked Marie-Paule. The man stirred and made a sound in his throat. The unnatural angle of his jaw indicated it might be broken, but he looked tough enough to survive a broken jaw and a few missing teeth. "He'll soon be coming back from dreamland," I pointed out, "and I can't just cart him out outside and dump him there."

"I'll run upstairs and phone Kees about it. Meanwhile, tie that animal up and get him down to the cellar. Use the rope from the book cartons."

She didn't wait to see me tie my victim's hands behind him, then bring him around to consciousness by slapping a wet rag back and forth across his face so that he could do his own walking. When he dragged his feet I urged him on with his own knife—eight inches of razor-edged fisherman's knife—and he sullenly led the way to the chilly cavern below decks which must have once been a wine cellar. The racks were still there along with a few wooden crates and a scattering of dust-covered empty bottles. I tied him to one of the iron posts supporting the ceiling and left him to his reflections.

It took Marie-Paule long enough at her phone call for me to do some straightening of the kitchen before she returned. Not only had its shelves been ransacked but our cartons of books and leaflets had been emptied on the floor, a couple of the cartons stove in by hard kicks. I managed to fit the printed matter into the unbroken ones, then squatting there, one of those hefty copies of *Le Recueil d'Hymnes* in my hand, I wondered why anything this cumbersome should be used as our text when it would more practical to use a lightweight hymnal. And after the Paris singsong there had been that business of Marie-Paule's almost fanatically careful repacking of each copy before she undertook to dole out refreshments.

I flipped through the pages of the book, found it no more or less than what it was supposed to be, and, moving fast now, emptied the carton on the floor and repeated the process with the rest of the hymnals. Of the two dozen, four had sections of pages cut away to make neat little nests in the middle of the book, and each of the four was identifiable by a rough spot dead center on the spine. By moderate estimate, the nests provided transport space for at least half a kilo of heroin.

Tiens. So during the Marseille services, four of the redeemed known to my partner would be handed these special volumes and would plant the goods in them. Marie-Paule herself would collect the books and carefully pack them away. In Paris, select members of the congregation would then remove the packets from the hymnals and that was all there was to it.

I made no move to conceal what I was doing when Marie-Paule reappeared before me. She frowned and then decided to take it with good grace. "So you've solved our little puzzle," she said.

"I trust I haven't offended."

"I'm in no position to be offended. After all, I owe it to you that I'm not lying here right now with my throat slit. Yes, that's the truth. I told Kees about it, and he's very grateful too. Almost as much as I am." She looked almost dewy-eyed about it.

I tucked away the last of the hymnals. "More important," I said, "what about our friend downstairs?"

"Yes, that. Kees doesn't believe he was on his own. So you're to see he's tied up tight and stored away where he is. Tomorrow after we leave, some men will come here and work him over. They'll try to find out who put him up to this, then dispose of him."

"Clumsy," I said. "This is supposed to be a mission. Suddenly there's a crew of toughs coming in and out, doing something mysterious. It can endanger our whole cover."

Marie-Paule shrugged. "These are the chances one takes."

"But what if I can find out who this type is working for? And then send him back to his boss to warn him that he's now a marked man?"

Marie-Paule shook her head. *"C'est un dur cela.* That's a hard case downstairs. If you think you can make someone like that sing with a kick in the belly, you don't know what you're dealing with."

"Perhaps not. But I'd like a few minutes to find out. Meanwhile, you can get the shop ready for the evening trade."

I didn't give her a chance to debate this—or to consider that somehow I was taking charge—but picked up a length of rope and the knife and made my way down to the cellar. The man watched expressionlessly as I planted a whiskey crate underneath a pipe running along the ceiling. I stood on the crate to lash an end of the rope around the pipe and made a noose of the remainder. Before releasing the condemned from his post I bound his ankles and made sure his hands were tightly tied behind him.

If anything, he seemed contemptuous of the proceedings. The contempt faded as I maneuvered him to the crate and manhandled him on to it. When I draped the noose around his neck he finally seemed to grasp that there was something seriously wrong with his situation. He had trouble speaking with that twisted jaw but he managed to get the words out. "What the hell is this?"

I said cheerfully, "That's how it goes, *copain.* You win some, you lose some."

"You're crazy! Just because of a little break-in you'd kill somebody?"

"If he's doing a job for Big Milos Periniades, yes. Sorry, chum, but those are the orders." Giving myself a foot up on the crate, I snugged the noose around his neck. "My boss has a bug in the brain about Big Milos. And anybody on his payroll."

"I'm not on his payroll! Big Milos? I never even heard of him. I swear on my beloved mother's life I never even heard the name."

"Sure, sure," I said soothingly. I stepped down from the crate and braced a foot against it, poised for the shove that would leave the body dangling.

"Wait, for God's sake!" Beads of sweat stood out on his stubbly face. "Listen to me! It was Renaudat who put me up to it. I swear it. Only Renaudat."

I scratched my head thoughtfully. "Renaudat," I said.

"I swear it. You know how he operates. Out for easy pickings as long as somebody else does the dirty work. He told us it would be some kind of sickly woman and a miserable little Dutchman who'd faint if you showed him a knife. He never said a pro like you would be on the job."

"So now you know." I prolonged the agony a little longer, then slipped the noose from around his neck and slashed away the rope binding his ankles. He stepped shakily down from the crate. "Look," he said, "any time I can do you a favor—"

"Right now. Get back to Renaudat fast and let him know he's in big trouble. Tell him he has one hour to get out of town, because after that it's open season on him in Marseille. You'd better convince him of it, too, or the same goes for you."

"Yes, sure. Believe me, I'll take care of it."

I paraded him upstairs and past Marie-Paule who stood there open-mouthed at the sight, then at the front door I cut loose his wrists and shoved him out into the street. He lurched away, picking up speed as he went.

Marie-Paule was still open-mouthed when I returned to her. "You let him go?" she said.

"Renaudat," I said. "Know of anyone by that name?"

"Yes."

"Well, he's the one who arranged for our friends to hit this place."

"And that animal told you about it?" She pressed her fingertips to her forehead. "But of course he did. How else would you have known about Renaudat?"

"Right. And now that I do I advised his boy to get him out of town fast or disaster sets in. And he will. I guarantee it."

"You guarantee it." She slowly shook her head back and forth. "You know, I think I'm ready to believe anything you tell me after this. Incredible. I've never met anyone quite like you."

"I must say the same about you," I told her truthfully.

Sudden color showed in those cheeks. "Yes. Well, we do seem to complement each other, don't we? But now I must call Paris again and explain how things turned out. Incredible. What did you do to him? He didn't look badly hurt."

"I converted him. That's our business, isn't it?"

Services that evening varied little from the services in Paris, except that now, as my partner doled out hymnals, I gave a dramatic reading from Revelations, and afterward, while she led the hymn-singing, I was the one who collected the hymnals and carefully stored them away. Very carefully. The street value of the cargo some of them now carried made them worth at least as much as a Gutenberg Bible.

That night, out of painful experience, I rejected my rump-sprung cot and prepared for another bedtime on the floor by gathering together anything that might cushion my slumbers. I was at this when Marie-Paule appeared in the doorway. She was wearing a flannel robe that would have done credit to any missionary, but in contrast to the image this offered, her hair was down. Surprisingly heavy and lustrous, it fell almost to the middle of her back, and the effect considerably softened the harshness of her features.

"Well?" she said.

"Well?" I said.

She abruptly opened the robe to demonstrate she was wearing nothing under it. A bony body, but feminine. Distinctly feminine. "Do you find this of interest to you, Monsieur van Zee?"

"Of great interest, mademoiselle. But consider. No imbibing of alcohol, no smoking, no caffeine. I'm not sure where the list ends."

She laughed. "It ends right there, *cheri*. And there's certainly room in that old bed inside, if you don't mind a tight fit."

I didn't mind at all.

Nor did I mind that during our three days in Marseille Marie-Paule spent much of her time single-mindedly building up her role of Madame van Zee, devoted wife. She fussed over me, prepared meals to my taste, and even seemed to take pleasure in washing my clothes. And in bed went far beyond mere devotion.

Our last morning in town I was wakened by a finger gently playing back and forth along my arm. I opened an eye and saw Marie-Paule standing there in that dismal robe holding a tray with a cup of chocolate and brioche on it.

"Breakfast in bed?" I said, helping myself to it. "Now this is what I call high living, *mon ange.*"

"You deserve it, *chéri.* And don't gulp it down like that. I've just been on the phone with Kees, and he said there was no need to rush back to Paris. To take our time, as long as we were there before evening."

"And my passport will be waiting for me?"

"Yes. But there's a detail Kees advises you to attend to." She rubbed the finger along my arm again. "Van Zee had a tattoo right here. A red tulip with a dagger crossing its stem. After breakfast, you should go to one of those places on the waterfront where they do that kind of work and get yourself decorated with the same design. Even those who never met him knew of him as the man with that marking on his arm."

"I'll see to it. Anything else to know about Mijnheer van Zee?"

"Nothing pleasant. A treacherous little toad, that one. And once he learned who our connections were, he set out, in effect, to go into business for himself. No honor at all. For that matter, no courage. Can you see the difference it makes to me, having you as a partner?"

She sounded positively maudlin about it, bless her corrupt little heart.

I was not the only one to whom the maudlin was apparent. Back at home base in Paris, Kees led me into his kitchen-office and closed the door behind him. "I understand you handled all problems most capably," he said. "Also," he gave me a roguish look, "that you've quite turned Marie-Paule's head. I hardly recognized her when you two walked in here. That glowing appearance, those ready blushes. Love does make a difference, doesn't it?"

There was something too cat and mouse about this. I said flatly, *"Mag ik mijn paspoort even zien?"* Dutch seeming more emphatic than French when it came down to serious business.

"The passport? Of course. And as bonus, van Zee's driver's license, now with your photo attached. And some money. In round numbers, two thousand francs."

"Fine." I held out my hand expectantly. "Every little bit helps."

He smiled very broadly. "A nice payoff for three easy days, isn't it? And there's a lot more of the same to come. A little trip to Marseille now and then—"

"No. I'm out of missionary work for good."

Kees looked startled, then slowly the smile reappeared. "I'll be damned," he said at last. "You know, on the phone this morning Marie-Paule told me what you were like, but of course I took it with a large grain of salt. She actually sounded like a schoolgirl in the throes of her first romance. I should also have taken into account that, throes or not, this is a very hardheaded female."

"Very. And now the passport, please."

"Look, I can't see a talent like yours going down the drain. Missionaries of your caliber don't come along every day."

"The passport, please."

Kees held up a hand in protest. "First you are going to do yourself one favor. There's a certain philanthropist I want you to meet. Someone who takes a great interest in our mission."

"Is he also the one who decides whether or not I get my passport?"

"No, he has nothing to do with any such small matters. Don't even mention it to him. Just hear him out. Give him an hour of your time this evening, and that's all."

"On one condition. The passport now. And anything else you want to throw in with it."

Grudgingly, Kees pulled a bulky envelope from his pocket and laid the contents out on the table. Passport. Driver's license. A sheaf of banknotes. "Good enough," I said. "When will your philanthropist be here?"

"He won't be. I'll pick you up at nine wherever you say."

"The Café Cambronne. Rue Racine near the Boul' Miche."

"Nine sharp," Kees said. "But one thing. Don't mention any of this to Marie-Paule. It's not her department."

The name was Rouart-Rochelle.
Yves Rouart-Rochelle. The address was just off Avenue Foch in the
Parc Monceau district. A mightily imposing building behind spiked,
ten-foot-high iron palings, its door was opened by a uniformed maid
who led Kees and me up a broad staircase to a sitting room. There
were three couples in the room having coffee, and this was a surprise,
considering the nature of the business Mr. Big wanted to discuss
with me.

At the doorway I said sotto voce to Kees, "Are they all in on
this?" and he whispered in alarm, "No, no, for God's sake. None of
them. Not even Madame. Only Yves." So it appeared that if a
philanthropist wanted to stake a company of missionaries to their
good works, he might also want them to be visible to his friends on
occasion. Nothing to be ashamed of in good works, is there?

A pale, pudgy, sleepy-eyed man with sleek black hair and narrow
mustache—he resembled a sea-lion freshly emerged from the water
—came forward to greet us. "Jan van Zee," Kees said. "Yves

Rouart-Rochelle," and so for the first time ever I was presented to the world at large by my now proper name. I shook hands with my host, and his was a damp, flaccid little hand indeed. And then there was an en masse introduction to the company, drawing from it polite murmurs of, "Ah, yes. *Les Amis du Bon Évangéliste.*" "Yes, I've heard of it. Splendid work."

But the last one in that semicircle broke the pattern. She stood up and said, "Kees Baar, it's been much too long," and said to me, "I am Madame Rouart-Rochelle, but do call me Vahna, and this is a pleasure," all in one breathless trill which sounded as if she really were bubbling over with the pleasure of it. Madame. As exquisite an Indo-Chinese *objet d'art* as any collector could imagine in his wildest dreams.

Lucky me. The conversational semicircle was now extended to include Kees and myself, but where Kees, at one end of it, drew the master of the house, I, at the other, drew Madame. Vahna. A Siamese name. "And," she confided, "that is only a little bit of it. If I told you my whole name, you would be quite bored with it before I finished."

My delighted response to this delighted her in turn. She drew her chair a little apart from the others and closer to me, and next thing we were tête-à-tête on the subject of Holland—she had never been there—and of Bangkok itself—a very dull place, really, and of Paris. Ah, Paris. The little shops, the large stores, the boutiques, the couturiers—all the best things in the world were here in Paris. Those exotically slanted eyes glowed at the thought of it.

When the rest of the company took itself off Madame gave every indication of remaining, but her husband gave her notice to go and so she did, trilling a warm appeal to me to return very soon. Yves waited only until the door closed behind her before saying to me in chilly tones, "One surmises you made a strong impression on Madame. She usually finds these little gatherings extremely dull."

Kees hastily cut in on this. "We've waited long enough to take up our business, Yves. Let's get to it."

"Our business," Yves said. He studied me with eyes as unblinking as a serpent's. "Yes. Kees tells me you have a talent as missionary. A great capability for that sort of vocation."

"Didn't he also tell you I've given up that vocation?"

"He did. But he feels it's because you have no clear idea of the rewards offered by it. So let us consider what may be a fantastically rewarding ministry for you. Have you ever been in America?"

"No."

"But you speak English fluently, I'm sure. All you Hollanders have that facility."

He wasn't joking, I saw. He really was taking me at face value as Jan van Zee.

"Yes," I said, "I speak the language."

"Excellent. Now there is a people that is prodigal with its money, the Americans. So consider the possibilities if we were to extend our mission to such coastal cities as New York and Miami."

"A French mission in America?" I said. "Would that make sense to the Americans?"

"The word evangelist makes a perfect cover," Kees said. "The authorities there will be even more inclined to deal with it cautiously than they are here. We've already appraised that aspect of it. For that matter, the police there seem wide open for business."

"And," said Yves, "we'll guarantee to deal in honest goods. Nothing adulterated. Now what would you say, Monsieur van Zee, to becoming our man in America?"

What to say? Certainly not that I still planned on instant retirement from his racket. Try that, and next thing I might find myself at the bottom of the Seine.

The only thing left to do was temporize. "Well," I said, "it's not a decision I want to make on the spur of the moment."

The lids over those serpent's eyes were raised almost imperceptibly, a sign, I took it, of profound surprise. "I don't understand," said Yves. "Anyone else would jump at this offer."

"Perhaps," Kees put in smoothly, "our Jan is concerned with whatever unpredictables may come up in a foreign mission. But given another day or two—"

"One day," Yves said flatly, "and that's all."

"Excellent," said Kees. "Then we'll meet here again tomorrow evening."

In the car he gave me a sly poke in the ribs. "Don't think I can't guess why you'd like to prolong negotiations, my friend. Another chance to hold hands with Madame, right? But beware, Casanova." He gestured at the building behind the high iron palings. "That whole monstrous place is a dollhouse, and she's the Siamese doll it was bought for. And nobody plays with dolly but her husband. Remember that if you value your skin. Now where do you want me to drop you. Marie-Paule's apartment?"

"No, I can stay at the tabernacle tonight. Tomorrow I'll find a place for myself."

At the tabernacle he left the motor running while he unlocked the door for me. "I'll see you in the morning, *copain*. Meanwhile, guard against dangerous dreams."

In the office-kitchen I made myself a dinner of soup and bread, then took out my new passport and examined the signature. There was paper and pencil in a cabinet, and time to spare. On one sheet of paper after another I practised the signature until it came easily. Then I worked out the kind of script that would fit it, a jagged, almost vertical handwriting, until I finally had samples that looked to me as if the original Jan van Zee might have produced them. Satisfied at last, I stretched out on the floor, my jacket serving as pillow, for a series of fitful naps until the first light of dawn showed through the window.

Then suitcase in hand, I strolled to the nearby Gare du Nord. There, after buying a ticket to Amsterdam, I invested in a picture postcard. I took my time mulling over a proper message and settled for *Education continuing*. I signed it *David*, addressed it to my grandfather, and dropped it into the box just as the warning sounded to board my train.

I could only hope he would understand that it was a small repayment for past kindness and not a bad joke.

Amsterdam. Then, when the mood seized me, I moved north and west through Scandinavia and England, and as the days shortened I turned south and east through the Continent to the Mediterranean. I was not alone. Back and forth a whole tide of the counter-culture flowed, northwest and southeast according to the seasons.

Total freedom. Total commitment only to the moment. Even the ritual of sending a postcard to my grandfather once or twice a year was undertaken only in response to impulse, and, impulse or not, I made sure to mail it from whatever town I was leaving that day. It was the last lingering vestige of David Shaw letting it be known that any reports of his death were greatly exaggerated, a concern that Jan van Zee shrugged his shoulders at next day.

As for survival now, having a *carte d'identité* allowed me the sweaty privilege, whenever money ran out, of loading and unloading trucks, doing harvesting during crop seasons, and in the most dire emergencies turning to kitchen duty again, although, thank God, no longer as a lowly member of *La Société des Cousins.*

To the counter-culture, among whom I led my nonworking life, this occasional spasm of proletarianism was utterly baffling, but it didn't keep the more helpless or troubled from turning to J. van Zee when occasion demanded. Need a medical adviser, a travel guide, a psychiatrist, an interpreter, an expert on local customs, an advocate who could talk you out of the hands of the fuzz? See van Zee.

I knew I had a reputation among my kind. What I didn't know for a long time was that the reputation had spilled over into various police headquarters along my meandering path. I discovered it one summer day in Amsterdam, my home base if I had any such thing as a home base.

It was the Provos, the youth activists, who first hit on Vondel Park as a gathering place, but they were essentially street people, and the park soon lost its appeal for them. So after a while it became a haven for the flock, allowing for some halfhearted raids by the fuzz—*de smeriss*—when neighborhood pressure became intense. Halfhearted or not, as far as the flock was concerned *de smeriss* was *de smeriss* the world over and always a bad scene. It was an attitude I shared with them until that summer day when along came a distinctly different breed of fuzz.

I was playing chess with a girl, Anneke Brun, who had become very important to me, when I was aware of an outlander trundling a bike across the rolling meadow in my direction. A bulky, middle-aged man with a walrus mustache and, despite the summer heat, wearing jacket and tie.

He parked the bike near us and showed me a police I.D. card. "Hendrick Spranger," he said. "And you're Jan van Zee, right?"

"Right."

He said, "For my sins they've put me in charge around here. I thought the smart thing was to get together with you about it."

"Why me?"

"Because at headquarters while I was going through all the park reports they dumped on me I noticed that your name kept popping up in them. Favorably, too. So I checked you out with some police bureaus outside the country, and you seem to be in their good graces as well. A concern for the kids but a level head. Somebody we can talk to."

"That's my Jan," said Anneke, whose Jan indeed I was.

Spranger bobbed his head at her. "I'm glad to hear you say that, Juffrouw—?"

"Anneke. Just Anneke." She was a big sunshiny girl who could charm the birds out of the trees, and Spranger, I could see, was as susceptible as any other bird. He said, "Anneke. Yes. Well, I don't know how to make either of you believe it, but I'm not the enemy. In fact, I got stuck with this detail because I have a name for being easygoing about the youth movement."

"Is it possible," said Anneke wickedly, "that you're in the wrong line of work?"

"I might be. But now suppose you and your young man arranged for me to speak before this crowd in a friendly way. Tell them very honestly what's expected of them and what the government offers in return. From them, decent behavior in public. From us, medical services, welfare money in an emergency, counseling—"

"Who'd listen?" I said.

"I would," said Anneke.

So I put my imprimatur on the proceedings and saw to it that a fair number of the flock attended them. That they did any good was doubtful, but, as Anneke pointed out, they did take some of the onus off Hendrick as plain unadulterated pig. It didn't make anyone very happy to have him show up, but since he kept his eyes tight shut to the soft drug scene he could at least show up without the alarm being set off. And show up he did, not only on duty in the park, but even off duty at our cafés to talk out his troubles with Anneke and me.

Most of what he had on his mind concerned youth—*de jongelui* —and what it was up to nowadays. *Ach, de jongelui!* Why this way of life, especially for those who came from prosperous and devoted families? This was largely directed at Anneke, whose prosperous and devoted parents, preparing to emigrate to South Africa for business reasons, found that their precious teen-age daughter would not abandon the crazy Dutchman, van Zee, and go along with them. Pleas, tears, and anger, and in the end the parents went off without her. But why, demanded Hendrick. A bright and pretty girl who could live like a princess in Johannesburg—why would she settle for this ragged and wasteful life? What about the future?

"But there is no future," Anneke said, only half-teasing. "There is only today."

"Only today," Hendrick echoed hopelessly. "Live for today and count on staying young forever." He pressed his hand on the chessboard before me, fingers spread wide. "Sixty-four squares," he said. "No more than eight in any direction. But where are all you young people?" He tapped the edge of the café table. "Out here. Outside the board on Square Nine. A fine game that is."

"*Ach, de jongelui,*" said Anneke with great solemnity.

That was the Hendrick Spranger who led columnist Berti van Stade to me and, through her column, won me the title of *de Koning Vondelpark.*

And, in all innocence, drew the attention to me of someone out of my past whom even the tolerant Hendrick would never have approved of.

I t was the combination of An-
neke and the inflation that undid me. Our plan had been to leave
Amsterdam by midsummer, go to Brussels where Anneke's dearest
girl friend had sent out a call for the flock to rally for some urgent
good works, and from there cross the Channel to do England as far
west as Cornwall.

Ordinarily, a few weeks labor on the docks would have provided
enough capital to see us through the whole tour and back. But that
year strange things were happening in what the newspapers referred
to as The Economy. Instead of doling out a few coins for the necessi-
ties, you found yourself peeling off paper money for them. A loaf of
bread brought cake prices. The cheap pad where half a dozen of us
could settle in became a luxury item on the landlord's books. And
I now had two mouths to feed and two bodies to shelter.

So the few weeks on the docks stretched on and on while I
hoarded what I could of each pay envelope, trying to accumulate
enough to provide a fair stretch of freedom. And what this did was

tie me down in the same place for a much longer time than I had been tied down since I made the transformation to my Dutch self. At least long enough to allow the slowest-moving reader of Berti van Stade's column to search me out right there in Amsterdam.

That was in early October, and by now Anneke and I had removed from autumnally cool Vondel Park to a commune run by some flower children on a canal boat moored in the Heerengracht.

This weekend evening I came home beat-up by overtime on the docks, and Anneke, self-elected baby-tender for the commune, greeted me with an infant in each arm and with news that there'd been a visitor looking for me. An old friend of mine who had seen Berti van Stade's flattering column some time ago and had finally decided to look me up.

"An old friend?" I said. Considering the broad definition of the word friend among *de jongelui,* this covered a lot of territory. "What's his name?"

"He just said he was an old friend. And that once when he was doing missionary work you helped him out."

"A solidly built Dutchman? With a red face? Smiles easily?"

"That's the one. He said he'd be back later this evening for a good talk."

"But we won't be here for any good talk. We're leaving for Brussels right now."

"Right now?" Anneke was used to my making precipitate decisions, but none quite this precipitate. "But you said it would take at least another week—"

"Right now," I said. "Park those kids somewhere and get your stuff together. Anything not packed in ten minutes gets left behind."

"That man," said Anneke. "A bad karma?"

"Very bad," I said.

$\mathbf{B}$russels was not my kind of town. Aside from its perpetually gray, wet climate, it seemed to be a place that had never put itself together. To my eye at least, the leaden-weighted medieval stone buildings, the baroque gilded structures that enclosed Grand' Place, and those naked-looking steel and glass high rises shooting up everywhere rubbed against each other abrasively.

And this was a town where the bulldozers had been unleashed with a vengeance. That was what had led to the good works Anneke's girl friend Trude was involved in. Marolles, the shabby old southwest corner of the city, was now scheduled for the bulldozers, and that district—*gemütlich* and low-priced—was where the counter-culture had gravitated. So the counter-culture was rallying its forces, and Trude and her Alain who had a pad on the rue de Renard in the heart of Marolles were leading members of the general staff.

We arrived by train at midnight, settled into the pad, and next morning were pressed into service with the troops. Their banners were already hung high across the street from building to building —LA RUE DE RENARD VIVRA and LA RUE APPARTIENT A SES HABITANTS—although this information that the street would live and that it belonged to its inhabitants did not seem to me likely to stampede the bulldozers when they showed up. The service itself consisted of a cosmetic job. A host of blue-jeaned, mostly barefoot volunteers was out with buckets of paint, toiling away on every weatherbeaten building-front along the block.

As a sort of uncertified master painter I was assigned the task of supervising the section of the block at its rue Blaes end and of instructing the painters there how to get more paint on the buildings than on themselves. I was on duty at noon when a familiar voice behind me said, *"Ah, de Koning Vondelpark."*

I turned to face him. He had put on a few additional pounds around the belly since I last saw him seven years before, but otherwise it was the same red-faced, smiling Kees Baar. I said, "I suppose the canal boat brethren in Amsterdam told you where to find me?"

"Approximately."

"Well, you're wasting your time, Kees. I gave up missionary work long ago."

"Oh, as far as dealing in the hard stuff, so have I." He put on a mock reproachful look. "Still, you shouldn't have run out on me yesterday. After all, I had to answer to Yves for your leaving us in the lurch last time around."

"Too bad. And how is Yves?"

"Out of the hard stuff too. That American venture of his—" Kees stepped back as some volunteers lined up buckets of paint almost at our feet. "Look, let's take a little walk. There's a street fair over on rue Haute. I have a weakness for street fairs."

"For private talks?"

"Believe me," said Kees, "when it comes to real privacy I'll take a crowd of strangers over an empty room any time."

There was a street fair on rue Haute, block after block of it, and it didn't take long to see why Kees liked street fairs. Sausages, black and white, beer by the pint to wash them down, slabs of rich cake, he passed nothing by.

"That American venture," he confided with his mouth full, "went badly. A disaster. We finally moved into New York and then found ourselves up against the brotherhood that claimed a monopoly on the trade. All right, nothing so tragic about having to give up on America, but *zut!*"—he snapped his fingers—"like that, the Marseille connection was gone too. That brotherhood has a long arm all right. They put Yves out of business in one day."

"So now," I said, "he's cleaning up the kitchen at Chouchoute's."

Kees laughed. "Hardly. Still the money doesn't come in the way it once did. And Vahna—you remember Vahna, I'm sure—"

"Yes."

"Well, she's really impossible in her extravagance. Been piling up gambling debts at an unbelievable rate. And Yves, poor fish, is so insane about her that he just foots the bill without a whimper."

"She could do that to a man," I said.

"Oh, she's a looker all right—still as beautiful as ever—but she couldn't do it to me. Also, her papa was some species of tinpot aristocrat in Thailand, and now she's got this itch to get in with the *aristos* here. The real blue bloods. And Yves is supposed to buy her way in. He'll wind up bankrupt before that happens."

"So," I said, "to keep himself solvent he'd like me to do a little job for him."

"No," Kees said, "as it happens, I'm in business with someone else now. A Britisher. Really a gentleman. And his line of work—"

"I can imagine."

"It's respectable," Kees said, unperturbed. "Almost completely respectable. But it needs a certain type of personnel to handle it properly. And someone like you without any police record—in fact, someone who actually stands in well with the police around the Continent—"

"Where'd you pick that up?"

"Where?" Kees raised his eyebrows. "To start with, that newspaper piece in *Het Oog*. To finish with, I had a talk with the cop mentioned in that piece. Spranger. A great admirer of yours. I produced flawless credentials and made it plain that I was ready to offer you a proper career if you measured up to your notices. And, as he then said, he'd be glad to help remove you from your present useless life and see you started up the ladder of success."

"I happen to like it down here, Kees."

"Please don't talk like a damn fool." He jerked his head in the direction of the rue de Renard. "You're not really like that gang of retarded children. None of them could have handled that mess in

---
77

Marseille the way you did. And Spranger spilled it all about your way of life. Does van Zee live by begging or borrowing? No, when this paragon needs money he goes out and sweats for it. *Vous travaillez comme un nègre.* And the longer you live, the harder you'll have to sweat."

He was addressing to me the same thoughts that sometimes rose to my mind while I was at my dock work. I gave him the same answer I had given myself. "Plenty of time to worry about it," I said shortly, and moved off down the street to indicate that the subject was closed.

He hastened after me. "Don't be stupid, *jochie.* All you'd have to do is take a few trips a year. A couple of days on the road in your own little car—yes, you'll be supplied with a car—and that's it."

"I see. And what do I transport in my own little car?"

"Paper."

"Paper," I said. "Of course. Printed by the government. And with pretty pictures and large numbers on each piece."

He gave me a sidelong glance. "That brain didn't get rusty while you've been off playing with the kids, did it? Yes, it's currency we're moving around. And your cut for helping move it will be five thousand gulden a trip. Five thousand a trip, mind you, meaning not less than twenty thousand a year."

I wanted to close my eyes to them, but visions of sugarplums danced in my head. Then they became visions of handcuffs. "A load of currency is nothing to be caught crossing the border with," I pointed out. "It can leave me with a lot of explaining to do. Also, it's not merchandise you can tuck away in hymn books."

He snorted. "Give me credit for a little intelligence, will you? We ran *Les Amis* for three years without a whisper of trouble, and it wasn't the cops who finally closed us up either. This new set-up is even prettier. I'll let you test it for yourself. I'll plant a load of scrap paper in the car, you can have all the time you want to hunt for it, and I'll guarantee you won't come up with one little piece."

"Kees, you can probably find a dozen men—"

"But what the devil good are they? They look like what they are. They smell like what they are. Naturally, they all have records. If somebody with a badge runs a check on any of them, this whole thing comes apart, but somebody like you innocently touring along —and with the blessings of the Amsterdam police, no less—"

We were at the Place de la Chapelle now, where the fair petered out. The last food stall in sight was offering *beignets au pommes,* sizzling hot apple fritters coated with sugar. Kees ordered one for each of us, and when I refused mine he slowly and voluptuously ate both of them. Impressive to see the way he did it, not a drop of juice oozing down his chin. A perfectionist, Mynheer Baar, in whatever he did.

I said, "Is Marie-Paule in on this?"

"No. She is working for my Britisher, but in a different department. Movies."

"Movies?"

"Porno. Kino 96 Produkt in Copenhagen. She manages the place, tries to get it to show a profit despite all the competition. Funny to think of her in that line of work, isn't it? Can you see her at it?"

As a matter of fact, I could. I could also see across the square a trio of leather-aproned workmen rooting up loose cobblestones, lugging them to the curb, stacking them there. Kees followed my eyes. "Seeing yourself in the mirror, *jochie?*" He pulled out a handkerchief and carefully dusted powdered sugar from his fingers, ruminating aloud. "Twenty thousand gulden. Three hundred thousand Belgian francs that is, for a few easy weeks of travel during the year. I wonder what those roadworking donkeys there would think of that."

As if he didn't know, and I didn't know, what those roadworking donkeys would think of it.

The name of his Britisher—and Kees would come out with it only after our handshake agreement —was Simon Leewarden. He was in Bruges now, but it was too late to arrange a meeting with him there this weekend. However, we would meet a week from today in Bruges. "Do you know the town?" Kees asked.

"Yes."

"Well, there's that bookshop on Sinte-Katelijnestraat, the big one. Be there at twelve noon. You'll find me waiting."

"For an Englishman," I said, "your friend seems devoted to Bruges, doesn't he?"

"Devoted to his daughter. The apple of his eye, believe me. She attends the girl's school there run by the Sisters near the Beguinage."

Back at the pad I broke the news to Anneke in a roundabout way. "How would you like to become the mother of a pretty little Volkswagen, *lieveling?*"

"Fine, as long as you're the father." She gave me a sharp look. "Are you serious? A car? Is that what you've invested all your hard-earned money in?"

"No, it comes with a job I'm taking. I travel for this company a few weeks a year, and not only do we get the car but enough money to carry us the rest of the year. A good deal."

"Is it? Wait a second. Does it have anything to do with that man who looked you up in Amsterdam? The one with the bad karma?"

"As a matter of fact, yes."

"Then, as a matter of fact, I seem to have missed a big scene in the movie. In Amsterdam, you wanted no part of him. Now, suddenly, it's a job with him that pays remarkably well. Traveling? What kind of traveling? What kind of business is he in?"

"There are some businesses, *mijn lieveling,* which are not in any directory. And that's as far as it goes."

She could see I meant it. "All right," she said obediently. But, as I had good reason to know, my pliant, clownish, long-legged Anneke with those innocent blue eyes and those childish freckles was not always as pliant as she looked. She said nothing more about the matter until late that night in bed, and then it came out without warning. "When you're traveling on business do I go along?"

"Anneke, it'll amount to only a few days now and then—"

"No. We've been together more than a year now, and we've never been apart one night. Daytimes I know it can't always be helped but nights are different. You're not to be away from me then."

"Unfortunately, we can't always do what we want in this cruel world."

"Liever een mep dan een lengen, jochie." It was the hard-boiled "Don't hand me that crap, pal" response that sometimes stopped poor Hendrick Spranger in his tracks. "I know how females are about you even without a car. Don't let these little-girl freckles fool you, *meneertje,* because I happen to be very grown-up jealous when it comes to my man."

That I believed.

"All right," I said, "I have to go to Bruges next week about the job. Come along if you want to."

"I'm glad you're so reasonable," said Anneke.

"But you'll be on your own there while I'm dealing with these people. You'll have absolutely nothing to do with them, now or ever."

"Of course," said Anneke. "I'm at least as reasonable as you."

It was her first time in Bruges. Pack on back, we walked from the railroad station along the broad and empty Begijnenvest in fitful sunlight, and when we reached the Minnewater road she stopped short and said, "Oh, look."

The lake was glassy smooth, the only ripples on it made by swans which could not have been more regal. The foliage on the surrounding trees was now October-thin, but there was still enough of it to set everything against a gauzy, pale green backdrop. The beautifully proportioned old buildings and the wall of the Beguinage down the road were out of a remote past when much of this Flemish world must have been as empty and quiet as it was now.

"Oh, God," said Anneke, "it's so lovely it hurts."

Toward the center of town, however, there was a steady thickening of traffic. From Sinte-Katelijnestraat I pointed at the Bell Tower rising high above the main square not far away. "That's Gros Markt Square. My meeting is down the block here, but if you go over to the square you'll find enough to keep you entertained for awhile."

"How long will you be?"

"Let's allow a few hours. There's an eating place, Oscar's, on Sint-Amandstraat just off the square, and we'll get together there at five. Next door to it there's a movie house, the Mini-Bioscoop, that shows classical stuff. You can kill some time that way."

"You said we might stay overnight. Couldn't I just get a room for us?"

"Not yet. If that car is waiting for me, I'm not sure where we'll wind up tonight."

The rain, which had obligingly remained cloud-borne all morning, suddenly dripped down as we kissed good-by. "Wherever it is, it had better be someplace in the south," Anneke warned me. "Somewhere in the sunshine."

At exactly noon I entered the bookstore on Sinte-Katelijnestraat and found Kees waiting. "I hope you haven't eaten," he said. "No? Good. Leewarden told me to bring you around to his house for lunch as soon as you showed up. And Monika—the housekeeper—cooks like an angel." Under a gentle drizzle, he led me down Oude Gentvig. "He rents the place here year round so he can be with his kid weekends. But she'll be away from the house for the afternoon, so we'll have all the privacy we need."

"No wife?"

"Oh, she ran off with another man a few years ago. But after the divorce she kept going to court about her rights to the daughter until Leewarden planted the kid in school here just to keep her out of range. He's very embittered about it all. And not reticent about it either, once he gets a bottle of wine down."

It was an accurate forecast. Leewarden—a forty-year-old, bald, popeyed version of Bertie Wooster—ate very little of the excellent lunch served by the motherly Belgian housekeeper, but applied himself diligently to the wine. As the second bottle was being opened, the conversation, politely meaningless up to now, took a turn in my direction. What, Leewarden asked me heatedly, was my way of life all about? All right, present company excepted, of course, but look at the company I kept. Dirty, foul-mouthed, sexually loose, drugging itself silly, deafening everyone with its idea of music—what the bloody hell was going on nowadays?

Kees shot me a warning glance. "Nothing much," I said, a picture of the impending Volkswagen vivid in my mind. "It's harmless."

"The devil it is," said Leewarden. "My wife was infected by that kind of harmlessness just long enough to wreck my life and her daughter's. And what about Sarah herself? My daughter. Thirteen last month and just ripe for infection if she's let loose among it. It's a great inconvenience, let me tell you, to have her educated in an out-of-the-way hole like this, but, by God, it's one way of keeping her from being corrupted."

I was hard put not to ask my highly moral host how business was with Kinema 96 Produkt, Copenhagen, his porno film factory, and Kees, as if reading my mind, hastily raised his glass in a toast. "To Bruges," he said, straight-faced, "the last refuge of decency."

"But," said I to Leewarden, putting aside the larger malice for a smaller one, "some day Sarah will have to go back to England. Will she be ready for England when the time comes?"

"It'll be a long time coming," said Leewarden, reaching for the wine bottle again.

"Doesn't she even visit there now?"

Leewarden glowered. "So my ex-wife can get her shiny claws into her and show her the beauties of life backstage?" He squinted at me over the rim of the glass. "You might have heard of the lady. Emmaline Bell? Second best parts in the West End? Some film bits?"

"Sorry."

"Nothing to be sorry about. An over-the-hill ingénue with the morals of a mink. What's more—"

It was a long and detailed "what's more" and it went on until Monika cleared away the remnants of lunch and, under Kees's instructions, departed to the kitchen to wait any further orders there. "Business," said Kees sweetly. "Let's proceed with it, Simon."

"Business," said Leewarden. "Right. Our arrangements."

"About those arrangements," I said to him, "I'm the one doing the dirty work. Transporting the currency, that is. Now I'd like to know what it's all about. Otherwise—"

"Oh, there's nothing terribly dishonest about it. And let's face it, van Zee, if we don't do it, somebody else will be bloody well skimming the cream off the pail."

"Do what, exactly?"

"Well, let's put it in plain language. International airlines are largely dependent on travel agencies to bring them their trade. Naturally, there must be a quid pro quo."

"Rebates," Kees said. He gave me his best smile. "Not legal, of course, but highly essential in the tourist trade."

I said, "And Simon here is the agent of agents. The one who collects the rebate money and sees that it lands in the right hands."

Leewarden nodded. "For a commission. An extremely generous commission."

"And consider," said Kees, "that the airlines involved—sixteen of them at present—are among the most respectable corporations doing business here and in America. We're not moving among the underworld. We're dealing with people who at the slightest smell of scandal will throw all their weight into protecting us."

What could be more considerate? Not only was I being handed a car and a fair income for my occasional services, but if anything went wrong there would be a battalion of corporation lawyers leaping to my defense. Anything to make sure I remained content and close-mouthed.

"So there it is," Leewarden said. "As for the details of your job, I'm not really that familiar with them, but Kees can fill you in there."

"Including," said Kees, "the question of how you came into possession of the car, should anyone ever ask it."

"And how did I?" I asked.

"You're now going to buy it. I have the papers here for you. My signature on them indicates I've received payment in full." He seemed very pleased with himself. "Believe me, *jochie,* you'll never get a better bargain."

Papers tucked away in my pocket, I went out with him and Leewarden, all of us warmed by a bottle each of excellent Burgundy, to look over my new acquisition. In the garage behind the house was a Bentley saloon and a fire-engine-red, gleaming new Volkswagen— the classic Bug—dwarfed to insignificance by the Bentley but still far more beautiful than it in my eyes. The VW, I observed, had Dutch license plates.

Kees patted it affectionately. "There are a half dozen newspapers tucked away in here. Now I challenge you to find them."

I went over the car from one end to the other, inside and out. The VW, of all cars, is not one to hide anything bulky, and it didn't take long to decide that anything hidden here had to be in an unreachable area beneath the chassis. There must be a flat metal container welded under it.

When I announced my decision Leewarden shook his head. "Wrong," he said. "Although that's just the conclusion any inspector would have to come to, the bloody bugger."

"All right," I said, "where is it?"

"Watch," said Kees. He used a small screwdriver to work on the underpart of the front hood—the luggage compartment lid. What looked like a narrow metal strengthener running around it turned out to be a flange. He unscrewed the horseshoe-shaped length of it, and when he lifted it out I saw that it supported a false bottom to the hood, a very thin plate the shape of the hood itself, and on the plate were several copies of *Het Parool.* So the hood was not the usual piece of stamped metal but two pieces with a couple of inches of space between them. Certainly enough space to store a considerable amount of currency in the area from the curved narrow tip over the front bumper to the broad section below the windshield.

Kees lowered and raised the hood. "There's also a spring action built in. No matter how much weight in our secret compartment, the lid goes up like a feather. A lovely job, right?"

A lovely job in every way.

My first drive in my new toy was to the railroad station where I delivered Kees. It was, as he remarked jovially, the least I could do, since by delivering my car to Bruges he had been forced to stable his in Amsterdam. On the way to the station, he explained procedure.

I was to make a phone call to a London number the first of every month from wherever I happened to be. Any response on the answering device was the signal to report to a certain London garage exactly two weeks later. The code phrase to the attendant when I drove in was "The motor knocks" but in Dutch. The code response should also be in Dutch, "Turn it off, please," and when I got that precise response I would simply depart the premises on foot and pick up the car there the next morning. Did I have all that straight?

"De motor klopt," I said.

"Maar zet hem af, alstublieft," said Kees. "And then bye-bye until tomorrow."

"And if he doesn't answer that way?"

"Drive right out and phone the same number immediately. I can't see it happening though. The arrangements have been worked out too carefully."

"I hope so. And after I pick up the car the next day—all loaded up, I suppose—where do I make delivery?"

"There are eight possible locations on the Continent, two in North Africa." He handed me a sheet of paper. "This a numbered list of addresses and the vital phone number. The man in London will give you a bill for car repairs, and all you do is match the number on his bill with this list. For example, two pounds on the bill means the merchandise goes to number two on the list. Simple?"

"So it seems. What if I have a real breakdown on the road while I'm loaded up?"

"Just phone the London number, and someone will show up to tow you to the nearest safe garage. During those times you're making a run with a payload, that phone will be manned twenty-four hours a day. Any other questions?"

"My payments."

"Yes, I wondered when we'd get to that." He motioned at the instrument panel. "In that compartment after the final delivery each trip. In gulden. After all, as a Dutch national you would be carrying most of your money in that form, wouldn't you?"

"I would." I swung the car off the highway and pulled up before the station. "And," I said, "since everything is so flawlessly automated, there's no reason for any of us to meet each other again, is there?"

Kees grimaced. "All business, aren't you? Not a bit friendly."

"All business," I said.

Someplace in the south, Anneke had said. Somewhere in the sunshine.

It was four-thirty now. Tomorrow at this time she would be dabbling her toes in the Mediterranean.

She was at a corner table in Oscar's eating place when I walked in, seated with a trio of teen-age girls, all wearing the same blue berets and short capes so that Anneke in their midst looked like their schoolmistress. The most voluble of them was wearing thick horn-rimmed glasses and had just reached that point in her young life where, when I seated myself beside Anneke, she hastily snatched off the glasses, almost dropping them in the process.

"*Mijn man,*" Anneke told the company by way of introducing me, then said to me in English, "They're all from England but go to Saint Ursula's School here. Beryl, Kathy, Sarah. We met at the movies next door. *Queen Christina* with Greta Garbo."

Saint Ursula's School? Sarah? But what a wonderfully small world this was. What a delightfully small town was ancient Bruges.

Sarah Leewarden turned pink as I stared at her, and I remembered my manners. "Did you like the picture?" I asked.

"Oh, yes," Sarah said. "And John Gilbert was perfectly beautiful. Did you ever hear of him?"

"I did."

"What about the car?" Anneke asked me.

"Parked around the corner. We'll eat, *mijn Christina,* and then drive off into the sunset."

Beryl and Kathy giggled. Sarah frowned at me. "You aren't really old enough to know about John Gilbert firsthand. I mean, you couldn't have seen his films when they first came out."

"No, but I have seen some of them. *Monte Cristo, He Who Gets Slapped—*"

"Lon Chaney was in that one," said Sarah, and right she was. "You pass with honors," I told her.

"Oh, her head's stuffed with all that sort of movie thing," Beryl said. "Really encyclopedic."

"Her mother's an actress," said Kathy, the smallest of the company. "Emmaline Bell. Do you know about her too?"

"Yes."

"You do?" Sarah said, lighting up.

"Emmaline Bell," I said. "Plays roles in the West End very stylishly. Does film parts too. Always a standout."

"Oh, yes." Sarah looked like Joan of Arc hearing the voices. "She's a great actress."

"She is." Then I did a mental double take. "*Queen Christina.* Do you mean the Sisters at school let you see pictures like that?"

They all looked at each other furtively, and it was Anneke who said, "Well, there's an arrangement with the Mini-Bioscoop where they're allowed in if a teacher's with them. I was elected teacher."

"Last time," said Beryl wickedly, "it was Sarah's mother."

"Beryl!" said Sarah.

"Well, it was, wasn't it? I don't see why it must be so frightfully secret even with people who have nothing to do with the school."

Sarah rose from her seat. "Really, that's quite enough of that. And we must be going." She nodded at Anneke. "And we do thank you for helping out. You'll forget what you heard here, of course."

"Didn't hear a word," said Anneke.

When they were out of the door Anneke leaned forward and gave me a proper kiss of greeting. "Now, *mijn man,* where are we going in our pretty car?"

"South into the sunshine."

"Duty or pleasure?"

"Pleasure."

"That's the way to do it," said Anneke.

I t was almost three months later
—New Year's Day in faraway Istanbul—when I got my first call to
duty. Everything worked precisely as Kees had foretold. On the
scheduled day I pulled into London, parked Anneke in a bed-and-
board off the King's Road, and hunted out the garage in the East
End that was to serve as my depot.

It was on Brick Lane, a shop with just enough room for one
compact and the man in charge, because this turned out to be a
veritable Goliath. Inches taller and broader than me, he had hair
cropped in the Junker style, the stub of a cheroot screwed into the
corner of his mouth, and a moonlike face with the kind of pug nose
that offers a view up its nostrils.

"De motor klopt," I told him, racing it to show how it *klopt,* and
he said with a broad grin, *"Maar zet af, alstublieft."*

That was it. I cut the motor, departed, and when I returned the
next morning there was Goliath with the same grin, apparently the
same stub of unlit cheroot in his jaws, and with the bill waiting. I

had memorized Kees's list so totally that the numbers on the bill instantly translated themselves into my destinations. A double play: London to Zurich to Milan.

"Tot ziens," I politely said as I pulled out of the garage, and he gave me a friendly flip of the hand. *"Tot straks, jochie,"* he said, which "See you later, pal," I took to mean that I'd probably be back for a repeat performance. The real meaning came clear when I drove into the Milan garage at the end of my run. The Zurich stopover had gone according to rote, a lackadaisical youth swapping the code phrases with me there and taking over, but here in Milan was Goliath again.

"Just checking to see that all went well on our maiden," he said. "Jago's the name. And it looks like we've put a winning team together, friend."

So it looked. The next day, when I picked up the car, Jago was on hand to wave good-by, and there in the dashboard compartment was an envelope with my five thousand gulden in it.

So for the newly affluent van Zee and his lady there was a waterfront hostel in Capri and then the Greek islands until spring showed up, and with it another call to duty and another replenishing of funds.

A winning team playing an easy schedule every few months that year and the next and the one that followed, and, as far as I could see, going its winning way as long as various fat-cat corporations felt compelled to pay bribes to keep the shareholders happy.

Anneke was never told that my business was to transport merchandise, not messages. Those few dangerous minutes whenever we crossed a border would be made even more dangerous if anyone so transparent had reason to look guilty when the inspector approached. And if she sometimes wondered about my line of work, she never allowed questions about it to come to the surface.

What did more and more come to the surface was a yearning for motherhood. This would pop up at odd times and lead us into unsatisfying dialogues. How did I feel about the idea, she would ask. Fine, I would truthfully say. No, how did I *really* feel about it? *Lieveling,* I would say, if that's what you want, it's what I want. No, Jan, I want to know how *you* feel about it, especially if it means settling down.

That was the rub.

Or was it?

Playing house with anyone else would have been out of the question. With my Anneke, well, since she was what my life was about, since she—partner, friend, admirer, lover—was what made sense out of chaos, it was something to think about.

"Ik wil er nog eens over denken." A fine old Dutch phrase, "I'll think about it." And that, as Anneke understood, was where the discussion ended.

Until Rome. Until that morning when we were seated on the Spanish Steps watching the world circulate below us in the Piazza di Spagna and Anneke abruptly said, "I think I'm pregnant."

A conversation stopper if ever there was one.

"Are you sure?" I asked.

"I'm two weeks overdue. That never happened before."

"You think the pill let you down? That's hard to believe."

"I know." She looked ready to cry. "But I haven't been taking the pill. And I never told you I stopped taking it. It's been the same as lying to you."

"All right, so maybe you're pregnant. I'm all for it."

"Now you're being kind. You would be. That only makes it worse."

"Look," I said, "the one thing you're not to do is indulge in any guilt *kletskock.* The sensible thing is simply to get a test taken. Otherwise, you could be wasting a lot of emotion on a false alarm."

"I thought of that. And there's a very nice free clinic near where we live. If you went there with me—"

"Why a free clinic? We have enough money for our own doctor."

"An unmarried mother walk in on one of those old Italian doctors? Can't you see him looking down his skinny nose at me? No. The girls in our building told me this clinic is different. They treat you like a human being there."

La Clinica Gratuita In Trastevere, a few minutes walk from our place on via Bassi, was indeed different. It had been installed in one of the ancient tenements on the block and had been designed and decorated, it seemed, so that one would have a sense of being in living quarters, not a medical factory. And, considering that I was putting my Anneke in their hands, those in charge looked alarmingly youthful, although not as young as most of their patients. The view I got of those patients in the waiting room suggested that an epidemic of pregnancy had struck most of the teen-age females in Trastevere within the past nine months, few of whom took any joy in it.

When Anneke emerged from the examination she looked as joyless as the rest of the company. "They said to come back in three days, and they'll have the report ready."

"If you want your own doctor—"

"No. They're very kind here. Now let's just go home please and not talk about it until we see what the test shows."

It was a long three days. It was further extended by the time I had to sit in the clinic's waiting room while Anneke was off with her doctor. Finally she reappeared and gave me a brief nod. There was no mistaking its message.

"Good," I said. "But what took so long?"

"I was talking to the counselor. Now she wants to talk to you. Alone."

"About what? Look, I'm in no mood for medical lectures. What I have in mind is a celebration lunch and then a drive out to Ostia for a swim."

"That can wait. Please talk to her, Jan."

"There's nothing wrong with you, is there?"

"No. I'm healthy as a cow. Now please. It's down the hall to the last room. Signorina Cavalcanti."

Cavalcanti. That put me back in time to another Signorina Cavalcanti, the one who lived in luxurious Parioli far from lowdown Trastevere, the one with the raging head cold who had refused to let me celebrate that long-ago New Year's Eve in her bed. Bianca Cavalcanti. A girl with a real flair for the melodramatic.

I opened the designated door at the end of the hall and found myself staring at Bianca Cavalcanti.

What was the schoolgirl dream she had once confided to me? Some day David Shaw would come storming up on his white steed, and she, no longer buxom and runny-nosed but slender and glamorous, would be swept off to the Happy Ending. Well, slender she now was, but that was about all of the dream that had been cashed in. The glamor part of it she had missed out on entirely. The honey-colored hair was carelessly thrust up on top of her head in a washerwoman's knot, there were dark patches of fatigue under the eyes, the whole face looked drawn. Beautiful in a way—Florentine beautiful like one of those portraits in the Uffizi from Lorenzo's time—but very distinctly the face of a tough-minded, overworked woman just a scant year behind me on the way to a thirtieth birthday.

As for David Shaw in his shining armor on a white steed, here was blue-jeaned, broken-nosed Jan van Zee with his Volkswagen and his pregnant Anneke.

"Come in, come in," Bianca said. "You are Signor van Zee?"

"Yes."

She flashed me a smile of honest amusement. "Well, nobody's going to bite you. I suppose Anneke's told you the good news?"

"Yes."

The room was very small, the one chair available to me was across her desk, much too close to her for comfort. The desk itself was a clutter of books and papers, empty cups, and overflowing ashtrays. "A cigarette?" said Bianca, scrabbling through the mess and coming up with a pack.

"No, thank you."

"Well then." She pointed at the tattoo on my arm. "What is that? A tulip and a knife?"

"Yes."

"And what does it represent?"

I had long ago worked out a standard answer to this. "A warning. He who hurts me must be hurt."

"Very masculine," Bianca commented drily. She lit a cigarette and studied me through its smoke. "Haven't we met before?"

"This is my first visit to your clinic, signorina."

"But it seems to me—"

"My very first visit." I found myself fighting down an insane compulsion to tell her who I was. To break the spell, I said sharply, "You wanted to speak to me about Anneke. Is there something wrong with her?"

"Anneke." She seemed to be fighting her own spell. "Well, emotionally, there is some trouble there. You see, when she was told the news her immediate response was to inquire about an abortion. Yet at our first interview she had told me she planned the pregnancy. In my experience, it's usually the father's attitude that leads to such a reaction. Anneke feels her only loyalty is to you. Your rejection of the child therefore—"

"Wait a moment. Did she tell you I didn't want us to have a child?"

"In effect, yes."

"Then in effect, signorina, she's all wrong about it. I will be delighted to be the father of Anneke's baby."

"Oh?" Bianca lit a fresh cigarette from the butt of the first one. "Well, you certainly failed to communicate this to her."

"Then I'll now communicate it to her." I started to rise, but

Bianca held up a protesting hand. "Wait, please. The girl desperately wants to bear your child, and at the same time she's terrified that this may somehow estrange you from her. That's why there was the talk about abortion, why there's so much emotionalism on her part right now. But if she had a convincing assurance of your devotion—"

"She will have, signorina. My list of priorities is very small. Anneke happens to be the only item on it."

"So? That does make you a rather unusual man in these parts. One rarely hears that kind of talk around here."

"Perhaps not." There was no longer any hint of recognition of me in those eyes. It emboldened me to say, "And you seem to be a very unusual young woman. Attractive, obviously well-bred, and here you are in this office in the middle of the slums. But what brought you here, signorina? The need to make a living, or a passion to save pregnant girls from their cruel lovers?"

She turned red. "It so happens, Signor van Zee, that my brother is a doctor—a gynecologist—and he and some associates were concerned about the rate of abortion in this district and the treatment of young mothers, especially unmarried ones, in the public institutions. They founded this clinic, and I'm in this office because I'm an accredited therapist. Does that satisfy your curiosity?"

"It does."

"Then if you'll call Anneke back in here, we three can—"

"No. I'll attend to her myself, thank you."

I left abruptly. She was quite a woman, this grown-up Bianca, no fool on any count, and no one to play hide-and-seek with about my identity. Quite a woman.

I attended to Anneke as soon as we were outside the building. "You really are an idiot, aren't you?" I said in a way which she correctly interpreted as love talk.

"She told you everything?"

"At least everything you should have told me."

"I tried to, Jan. Only you so much hate talk about the future. You can't see your face when that particular subject comes up, but I can."

"All right, I promise there won't be any more faces like that. Meanwhile, how about rounding out the family picture with a wedding? Has that thought ever crossed your mind?"

"No." Anneke shook her head violently. "I don't want us to be tied to each other by a foolish piece of paper. I want it just the way it is."

"*Ach, de jongelui,*" I said in a fair imitation of her imitation of Hendrick Spranger.

Lovely, mindless, sun-filled days in Naples. On Capri's cut-rate waterfront. In Split. In Dubrovnik. Lovely nights too, for that matter.

The crisis was over, the baby well settled into place beneath that still-flat belly, and Anneke glowed with its presence. Glowed clear green some mornings, retching with sickness, but cheerfully accepted this as a small price to pay for the impending miracle.

In Dubrovnik, December first, I made the required phone call to the London number and learned that I was back in business. In London, two weeks later, I deposited Anneke in the usual bed-and-board off the Kings Road and drove across town to the garage.

Jago, the Man Mountain, shook his head when I got out of the car and said, "See you tomorrow."

"Not tomorrow, chum," he said. "It's right now."

"You mean you'll plant the goods in the car right now?"

"No, you'll pull out empty right now, but you'll be loaded up in Zurich day after tomorrow. The night after that it's Luxembourg, and they'll unload there. At night, remember."

"That's a switch."

"For good reason." He gave me a big wink. "This is for a new customer. Pulled off a really fantastic fiddle in America. Got away with a million dollars, they tell me. I wouldn't be surprised if there's a little extra for us when payday comes, handling a load like this."

So it was back to the b-and-b in Chelsea to pick up my ever-understanding girl who, without a question, simply tucked herself into the car, and from there to Zurich. The Swiss attendant there who responded to the password and relieved me of the VW was yet another of those sleepy-eyed, pimply youths who came and went over the years. Recruited for one-time duty only, they suggested that the garages themselves were open only that occasional day when I had to report to them.

Then, finally, northward through Germany on the last leg of the tour with my million-dollar cargo, and now thinking at least as cannily as Mijnheer Baar, I decided to forego the shorter run through France and hold to the roundabout German route right up to Luxembourg. Extra mileage, extra time, but one less frontier to cross, notably the French one. French customs officials, it had been my experience, were one and all suckled on bile.

I did currency conversion in my head as we rolled along. A million American dollars came to about two and a quarter million Deutsch marks. *Godallemachtig,* one little bang into that trunk rattling along ahead of me, and there would be enough paper money strewn over the highway to have half *Mitteleuropa* out for it with pitchforks and baskets.

So I was glad to see, after we completed the northeast run to Karlsruhe and turned northwest straight for Luxembourg, that the traffic was thinning steadily with nightfall. By midnight, as we approached the border crossing, I had almost no company on the road at all. Only one steady customer a fair way behind and very distinctive because one of his headlights was dimmer than the other and would now and then blink as if giving me friendly encouragement in the otherwise pitch darkness.

The crossing into Luxembourg was easy, the customs man seeming almost as sleepy as Anneke who was out cold, and he good-naturedly gestured at me not to wake her when I handed him our passports.

Now it was pitch blackness again, the emptiness of open fields all around me broken only by sleeping towns, and it was coming out of Grevenmacher, on the home stretch to Luxembourg city itself, that I again picked up those distinctive headlights behind me. But now—chilling logic whispering to me that while I had reason to take a roundabout route it wasn't likely anyone else shared that reason —that flickering headlight no longer seemed so friendly.

Then, for the first time, the lights started moving up fast. I came down on the gas hard, but I was badly outmatched. The car, a big one from what I could make of it in the darkness, drew alongside the VW, deliberately crowding it over on the shoulder of the road, steering me straight into a stand of trees, and there was nothing left to do but jam on the brakes.

The other car came to a stop at an angle that cut me off from escape half off the road. Then a figure, its face concealed by a ski mask, rapped a gun barrel against my window, and since the only choice offered me was whether I wanted to take my medicine with the window broken or unbroken I released the door lock. The door was pulled open, the gun was jammed into the side of my head. A hand, a slender boyish hand, reached across me to switch off the VW's lights and to remove the ignition key.

Anneke must have been sound asleep through it all. Now she stirred and said with bewilderment, "What's happening?" and I said to her, *"Gevaar. Beweeg je niet.* Don't speak. Don't move."

We sat like that as someone emerged from the big car and went to work on the front end of the VW. The lid of the luggage compartment went up, a searchlight beam probed around, and at last— though it couldn't have been more than a few minutes—the painful pressure of that gun barrel against my head was gone, the big car was gone, and I was left sitting there with the thought that since one careless move might have had my brains spattered all over Anneke things could be worse.

On the other hand, they could not be much worse.

"*Lieve God,*" said Anneke irritably. "The lunatics. All that just to steal some second-hand clothing."

I dug out my searchlight, and with Anneke for company, went around to the luggage compartment. It was still packed tight with our belongings, but the false lid was lying on the roadside. On it were the gasket and the car keys. Polite hijackers, at least.

Anneke was looking through the stuff in the compartment. "I don't think they took anything at all," she said with surprise.

I left her to it while I dug out a screwdriver from my tool kit, trusting to luck she'd let it go at that, but I was out of luck this night. She had to wield the searchlight while I, my hands made awkward by the cold, fitted the false lid back into place and screwed the supporting gasket under it.

"So that's it," she said. "A place to hide something in. And now that I know this much, Mijnheer van Zee, you will please tell me the rest."

"All right," I said, "it was currency. Those business trips we make now and then are to pick it up and deliver it."

"A lot of currency? It must be, the way they're paying you."

"It is. In this case, it was worth a million dollars American."

"A million?" Anneke said, stunned. "And those hoodlums took it all?"

"You don't see any of it left, do you? But those weren't ordinary hoodlums. This had to be an inside job, and the ones at the Zurich end are the only ones who could have pulled it off. That was a big mistake on their part. The man behind this operation, this money transport business—"

"That one with the bad karma?"

"That one. Well, he knows who his Zurich people are. So the faster I get to Luxembourg and pass the word along, the faster he can track them down."

"Then," said the logical Anneke, "why are we standing out here in the cold just talking about it?"

It took twenty minutes to reach the city, the clock on the tower over the railroad station marking one A.M. when I pulled into the Place de la Gare. I parked before the least prepossessing hotel in sight, and Anneke said, "Not the youth hostel?" The hostel—l'Auberge de Jeunesse among the hills and valleys of the north side of town—had always served as our abode on previous visits.

"No. I'll need a phone handy for personal calls, and the hostel's too public for that. And the garage where I have to leave the car isn't far from here. Transportation is dead this late at night, but I can walk back here from the garage easily."

The lobby of the Hotel Rhea looked distinctly second class, our room one flight up overlooking the square was shabbily third class, but, as the notice on the bedroom door stated, the place was rated first class, at least by Luxembourg standards. Anyhow, the only first-class feature I required was the phone on the night table, the private bath with scalding water jetting from its faucet being lagniappe that Anneke willingly seized on. I left her to her bath while I drove the car a few blocks north and across the bridge over the railroad tracks to the garage on the rue des Trevires.

In line with company policy, the boy who opened its door in response to my banging on it was no one I recognized. He had a fire going in a steel barrel that did nothing to temper the bitter cold of the garage but did provide enough smoke to make my eyes water as soon as I pulled the car into place.

"De motor klopt," I said according to ritual

"Maar zet hem af, alstublieft." Local talent as usual. The harsh way he pronounced it, it sounded more Luxembourgesch than Dutch.

I got out of the car. "The man in charge," I said. "When will he be here?"

"I don't know."

"But he must have told you when."

Now he looked alarmed. "Come back tomorrow night. The car will be fixed then. That is all."

I walked back to the hotel, on edge with the thought that every minute's delay meant another mile's head start for the hijackers. Anneke was still in the tub. *"De première classe, n'est-ce pas?"* she greeted me. "Did you see the man? What will he do about getting the money back?"

"I didn't see him. I'll try him by phone. I should have done that the first thing."

The time it took to rouse the hotel's switchboard operator didn't do my nerves any good. Finally I gave her the London number and heard the connection being made. Up to now on those calls I made the first of each month all I had gotten from the other end was either dead silence, the signal to hang up and take another month's leave, or a toneless mechanical voice informing me that the number was out of service, the signal to report for duty. Now for the first time I heard a living, unrecorded voice. "Yes?"

"Trouble," I said.

"What sort of trouble?" Uninflected English in a muffled tone. Probably Leewarden.

"A hijacking," I said. "Twenty minutes out of Luxembourg city. The whole load was cleaned out."

"Damn!" It was pretty surely Leewarden. "Will you be able to take a phone call within the hour?"

"Yes."

"Your number?"

I gave him the number, and that was it. One hour, I surmised, would be the time needed to get the executive heads together and chart a course of action. An hour did the trick. The phone rang, and when I picked it up the same voice said, "Where are you now?"

"In Luxembourg city."

"The address?"

"Never mind that." With the address, whoever was supposed to unload the VW over on the rue des Trevires could drop in on me here without warning, and I wanted no such company while Anneke was on the premises.

The man at the other end took his time digesting my rebuff. "Very well. But where is the car now?"

"In the garage."

"Then be at the garage tomorrow noon. Precisely twelve. Is that clear?"

"Yes."

"Meanwhile stand by the phone for any change of plan. Stay close to it at all times. If there is no call, just be at the garage at noon." Click.

After that, sleep was hard to come by and then hold on to. We were up early, had our breakfast—tasteless rolls, pallid coffee, and plastic-packed blobs of chemically manufactured jelly—served in the room, and then sat at the window watching unlovely downtown Luxembourg come to life in the Place de la Gare while I waited out the time until noon or until the phone rang, whichever came first.

A few minutes after ten, there was a knock on our door. "The maid, monsieur–'dame. For your breakfast tray, please."

I opened the door.

It was indeed the maid, and, behind her, looking absolutely delighted to see their old friend van Zee, were the foreman of the works and the general manager.

Jago and Kees Baar.

The maid left with the breakfast tray, and Jago shut the door behind her. The room, not large to start with, shrank to telephone booth dimensions with Goliath standing there, his back against the closed door.

Kees gave my cheek a friendly pat as if to rouse me from my stupor. "Oh, come," he said, "you didn't really think it's that hard to locate an address once you have the phone number for it, did you?"

I said, "You could have saved yourself the trouble. I would have been at the garage on schedule."

"Of course." He took in Anneke and said to her, "Juffrouw Anneke, right? Three years ago in Amsterdam. That gaudily decorated houseboat. You were the young lady tending the infants there." He shrugged deprecatingly. "One of my small vanities. I never forget a name or a face."

I said to him, "The young lady has no part in our business, Kees. So if you don't mind—"

"No." He shook his head at her. "The young lady will remain seated where she is." Then he turned to me, his face now stony. *"Wat is er misgegaan?"*

"What went wrong? Ask your Zurich people."

"My Zurich people?"

I said, "I was followed from the garage in Zurich by a team who knew what the merchandise was and where it was hidden. The way it happened—"

"Yes. Exactly what did happen?"

I explained in detail, but with a growing feeling that my inquisitor was not impressed by the explanation. "Interesting," he remarked, "that you should have entered Luxembourg so far north. A great waste of time, wasn't it? To what purpose?"

"To stay clear of the French customs men."

"Their manners displease you? But of course, when one has such delicate nerves—"

"Don't give me that, Kees. I just happened to know how much money I was carrying this time out."

"Yes," Kees said drily, "you did, didn't you?"

"Look," Anneke said, "he's telling the truth. I was there. I saw it."

"So." Kees leered at her. "And here we have an eyewitness. How fortunate for our Jan."

"That's enough, Kees," I said. "You're being a fool about this. If I took that money, would I drive straight into town here and arrange to meet with you?"

"A good question. Run and try to hide—but how long would one enjoy the use of the money then?—or boldly present himself to his associates and say, 'You see? The fact that I stand before you proves that I couldn't have doublecrossed you.' A very clever device. All one needs is sufficient nerve to test it."

"You do me too much credit," I said.

"I doubt it. So now you will seat yourself next to the lady, both of you keeping in mind that you are under Mijnheer Jago's personal supervision, while I take inventory."

He did an expert job of taking inventory, combing the room inch by inch. He finished with the bathroom, from which came sounds of further probing, and then rejoined us. He slapped away dust from

108

the knees of his trousers. "They don't take their housekeeping here very seriously, do they?"

"I suppose not," I said.

"Well." It was the old Kees back again, all amiability and smiles. "So it seems that you're still one move ahead in the game, Jan."

"Godallemachtig, Kees, you've seen for yourself—"

"I have. So now let's get down to business. The money in question amounts to almost a million American dollars. Really a marvelous coup. False checks drafted by computer against the treasury of the city of Los Angeles in America, paid over to a nonexistent company that banks in Switzerland. But since several people were involved in the coup and lay claim to a share of the profits, I cannot afford to be profligate. What I offer you for the return of the money is five percent of it. Fifty thousand dollars. How does that strike you?"

"It would strike me fine," I said, "if I had the money. I don't." Making it as casual as I could, I started to get to my feet, measuring the distance between Jago and me. The next instant there was a small automatic in Kees's hand, no less mean-looking for its size. It was aimed squarely at Anneke's head. I was briefly suspended there, halfway between sitting and standing, and then I sat down again.

The gun remained on target as Kees addressed me. "You mean that five percent is not enough. A little bargaining is in order. However, my partners, who are gathered at the garage, insist that five percent is their limit. What we will now do is adjourn to the garage to continue negotiations. Of course, en route, for the Juffrouw's sake, you will not attempt anything foolish."

No one was in attendance at the garage when Jago pulled the car into it and parked alongside my VW. In the storeroom upstairs, two men stood close to an electric heater, trying to extract what warmth they could from its orange-colored glow. One was Simon Leewarden. The other, as sour-faced as I last remembered him, was Yves Rouart-Rochelle. In trim black overcoat, black homburg, and white silk scarf, he might have just left the Bourse for this gathering.

He looked at Kees, who gave him a negative shake of the head.

"Comprend-il ce n'est pas de la rigolade?" Yves demanded in tough Parisian. Then, taking notice that Leewarden looked blank at this, he shifted to English. "I asked if this fool understands the

seriousness of what he is trying to do," he told Leewarden. Then to me, "Do you?"

"What I'm trying to do," I said, "is have you all understand that I'm as much a victim of some unidentified hijacker as anyone here. The young lady even more so. And since she's several months *enceinte* and in no condition for all this fuss, I think she should be allowed to leave the proceedings."

Yves's lip curled. "The way I view it, the presence of this vulnerable young lady should impel you to come to terms at once. Consider that she may have to suffer the punishment for your madness."

I said desperately, "Yves, I was followed from Zurich to outside Luxembourg city. I was forced off the road there by two people wearing ski masks. One of them, from the look of his skinny hand, might have been the juvenile delinquent I dealt with in Zurich. That's all I can tell you."

"Not quite. Where did you hide the money?"

I could see what was coming, and I poised for a move. And suddenly there was that gun in Kees's hand again. And again aimed, not at me, but at Anneke's head, six inches away. *"Dat mag je geen ogenblik denken,"* Kees warned me.

Anneke screamed as Jago pulled off my jacket and shirt. That earned her a length of cord around wrists and ankles and a dirty cloth as gag. Then Jago lashed my hands behind me and tied them to a bracket in the wall. He took his time relighting the stump of dead cheroot in his mouth and in removing his coat. Then he went to work on me, always aiming at the body. When I finally doubled over he grabbed my hair to straighten me up again. He was, from his expression, enjoying the exercise thoroughly.

"Wait," Kees told him at last. "The girl must be chilled to the bone. How about warming her up a little?"

Jago moved toward Anneke. As she cowered away from his upraised hand I managed to find my voice. "Stop it! I'll tell you where the money is."

They all came to attention. "Indeed?" said Kees. "Or could it be you're playing for time, my friend?"

"No. I had a room ready near the garage in Zurich. After I drove away from the garage and before I picked up Anneke, I planted the stuff there."

"And the address? The room number?"

"Not yet. First let the girl go. Then I'll take you there."

Leewarden said, "Well, we could settle for that," but Yves shook his head. "I don't trust him." He jerked his thumb at Anneke. "She's what loosened his tongue this much. Let her go, and he can forget how to use it again."

"All right," Kees said, "then the logical move is to return to Zurich and verify our friend's story. That's easily done."

Yves gnawed his lip, considering this. "But we travel together. All of us."

"All of us," said Kees. "After dark. No use making the cortege too conspicuous."

D

arkness came too soon.

A late dinner of bread and cheese, then we were conducted downstairs to the garage where Kees designated seating arrangements in
the two cars. Despite all the room in Yves's big Buick, Yves and
Leewarden would have it to themselves. And despite the discomfort
Jago suffered when he was wedged behind the wheel of the VW, that
was the spot he was assigned, Anneke at his side, while Kees and
I occupied the back seat. In the car Anneke was released from her
bonds but I was not.

We moved off through the back part of town past Bonnevoie
cemetery—a reminder, as if I needed any, of the menacing future—
and into the Route de Thionville. Still some traffic this time of the
evening, but the gaudy taillight display of the Buick offered a beacon
easy to follow.

My mind raced in circles. As far as I could calculate, the dangerous time for Kees would come at the French border. My hands
would certainly have to be untied just before we reached it, then we

would be required to pull up and show passports. So this was the time for me to order Anneke out of the car. Just tell her loudly and clearly to get out while the *douanier* was hovering close by.

And then?

I mentally sweated out every conceivable possibility of *what then* as we moved steadily southeast, passed the outskirts of Mondorf-les-Bains, that Luxembourg version of luxury spa, and headed into a black and traffic
less region beyond, on our way toward Schengen and the frontier. The red bars of the Buick's taillights held steady a hundred yards in front of us, and then Kees leaned forward, sighting at what could be made of the roadside in the illumination of our headlights. "Slow down," he suddenly said, and Jago obediently slowed down.

In the distance, the Buick's taillights continued to recede then also slowed down. Obviously, Yves was keeping an eye on us, adjusting his pace to ours.

"There." Kees pointed. "In that opening between those trees."

The car lurched off the road into the opening. It crawled a few yards, dried twigs crackling beneath the wheels, and came to an abrupt stop, its lights fixed on absolutely nothing ahead, although there was something below. A deep gorge, even deeper, it seemed, than the Vallée de la Petrusse that cut through the heart of Luxembourg city.

"You and your friend understand," Kees said to me, "that when we arrive at the border you will both behave with great discretion. Now we will rearrange ourselves to avoid complications. Jan, as proprietor of this vehicle, will take the wheel. I will be seated beside him. Jago and the young lady will move back here. And"—he displayed the gun—"this will be an unseen but overwhelming presence."

Jago surveyed the back seat. "I'll never make it."

"You will. And it's only for a short time."

My hands still bound, I was ruthlessly hauled out by Jago. It was his turn now to take the place I had occupied, and his getting into it was like the swollen cork of a champagne bottle being driven back into the bottle. Meanwhile, the gun in Kees's hand was indeed an overwhelming presence.

When Jago was settled into place Kees leaned through the open door to take stock of him. "Well, how is it?"

"It could be better," Jago said, "but I'll survive."

"Will you now?" said Kees, and the sound of the gunshot was like a dynamite blast going off inside the car. Jago's head bounced back against the seat, came forward a little. Slowly it slid sideways until it rested on that huge shoulder, the unblinking eyes staring at me through the window. I was incredulously fixed on those eyes when what must have been the gun butt hit me a sledgehammer blow on the skull.

I came to, seated in the car, draped over the steering wheel, aware with slow-dawning, head-splitting awareness that Anneke was seated next to me, drooping forward in an approximation of my position, and that my hands were at last unbound. And finally, and much too late, that the car was in motion, gaining speed as it rolled toward the gorge. There was a stench of gasoline in my nostrils, a flickering light around me, a wave of heat suddenly scorching my back, and as the car tilted over the edge of the gorge while I hopelessly jammed my foot down on the brake, I had just enough command of my wits to know that Kees Baar, whatever his reason, had supplied the gasoline and flame.

Down we went, the car bounding over obstacles, fast picking up momentum, the heat from the spreading flames almost unbearable now, and still, idiotically, I kept jamming my foot down on the useless brake. Then we slammed hard into some obstruction, the door on my side sprang open, and I was hurled through the opening, like something released from a slingshot, into a sloping carpet of wet leaf mold. I hit it on my shoulder, skidded along it, then rolled over and over down the slope to be brought up short by a thicket.

I heard the car hit the bottom of the gorge, heard the explosion, saw the glare of it, and the dimming of the light as metal and flesh burned steadily. I couldn't bring myself to look around at it. But from where I was, deep in soggy mold, camouflaged by thicket, I could look up at the crest of the gorge and see by the light of the flames behind me a figure standing there. Kees Baar. As I looked, two other figures joined him. From the length of white scarf against black coat one was Yves Rouart-Rochelle, so the other had to be Leewarden.

It was Yves alone who started down the slope, scrambling and sliding, and, as he came, bellowing in anguish, *"Non! Non! Non!"*

Then he must have seen there was no going further downhill

without danger—in fact, there was no use going downhill at all just to view that pile of burning metal and the ashes in it—so he stopped where he was. The two others made a chain of clasped hands to reach down and help him back to level ground.

All three together again, they stood looking down at the scene for a little while and then went away.

I lay there. The fire incinerating the wreckage flickered lower and lower, finally becoming a dull glow that I could see reflected in the rivulet trickling through the gorge. The slightest move was agony, but, as in that terrible Paris wintertime years before, the chill eating into every cell of me soon began to numb other physical pains. Even so, the sodden mold I was half buried in showed no signs of frost, which meant that possibly I wouldn't freeze to death before sunrise.

Too bad.

Because death—the falling asleep and never waking up again—was the sweet and comfortable and necessary way of coming to terms with the knowledge that there was no more Anneke. I had ingested her into my being so completely that just the thought of living without her was as horrifying and implausible as the thought of dragging myself through life with my belly ripped open and my organs and entrails bloodily hanging from the open cavity. My Anneke a handful of ashes? Impossible. Incomprehensible. If I could bear the pain of the effort and call her name, she would come to me. I filled my lungs as best I could and feebly called her name. Called it louder. Called it again and again, and in a sort of delirium waited for those warm ashes to swirl upward and take form as my woman. They didn't. I had created a small, perfect universe for myself out of this woman, but now it had been blown to dust by His Satanic Majesty and a pair of assistant demons.

Kees Baar.

Yves Rouart-Rochelle.

Simon Leewarden.

It had been Kees who had hijacked that million dollars, had made the false case against me, had brilliantly disposed of all evidence against himself, so that his partners would never know the truth.

No. I didn't want to die.

I had an overpowering reason to live until all accounts were settled. With only the scorched clothes on my back and very little money in my pocket I might not seem a proper adversary for that trio, but I had one asset that was beyond all price.

I was dead.

And Kees Baar, Yves Rouart-Rochelle, and Simon Leewarden had been witnesses to my death.

I opened my eyes in a panic. Gray misty daylight, a ravine in some unfamiliar stretch of emptiness east of Mondorf-les-Bains, west of Schengen, a stench of burnt cloth in my nostrils, a sound of approaching footsteps. A man moved toward me, gaunt, white-haired, in rough clothes and with a shotgun under his arm. He stood over me, the twin barrels sighting between my eyes. "Can you understand me?" he said. The language was Luxembourgesch with a strong French flavor.

"Yes."

"I heard the noise last night, but no use trying to make it here in the dark." It was not an apology. "You have business around these parts?"

"No."

"Papers?"

I painfully tried to reach into my pocket and had to give up. "My wallet," I said. "You'll have to get it out."

The gun remained sighted between my eyes as he got out the

wallet and went through it, thumbing through the scanty assortment of banknotes—Dutch, West German, British—and then examined the passport. "Dutch?" he said.

"Yes."

"But you like to travel empty roads late at night, it seems, and with all kinds of money in your pocket. Now let's have it. What were you trying to do, run some stuff across the line and the police got too close?"

I said nothing, just stared at him.

"Don't be a fool, Dutchman. You can trust me. The name is Delange. Joseph Delange. I live two kilometers that way"—he pointed south of the ravine toward the French border—"and there isn't another house near mine. And the doctor I can get you knows how to keep his mouth shut. So let's have the truth. You're in the trade, aren't you?"

I didn't have to ask if he was. The look and sound of him, that ready gun, the questions about the police indicated that, like many another who lived within a stone's throw of the border—any border—he had at least a finger in the smuggling trade. "It wasn't the police who ran me off the road," I said. "You don't have to worry about them. It was my partners who did the job on me."

"That happens." The gun swung away from me. "You're too much of a load for me to carry. I'll be back in a while with a horse."

He returned after an hour with a swaybacked old cart horse, and then, myself shakily riding pillion behind him, we made our way along the narrow stream at the base of the gorge through a woods and out into the open, naked fields. A barnyard, a conglomeration of pigs and geese, and then a stone farmhouse with a sagging roof, a telephone line looping across the fields to it the only sign that this was still the twentieth century.

A room of my own under the eaves. Into bed at last, half dead from the journey. Two kilometers. Three would have finished me off for good.

The doctor, it turned out, was a veterinarian who took an illegal turn now and then at handling human trade. In appearance and speech he was another Joseph Delange. "Nothing broken. Eat and sleep, that's all. Time will make all the repairs."

Sound advice, no doubt, but each day I ate unwillingly, trying to force down the meals Joseph carried up to my attic room, and each night I slept badly, endlessly raging at myself for the weakness that was keeping me from my mission. The images of Mijnheer Baar and Monsieur Rouart-Rochelle and Mr. Leewarden were always there with me in my room, the toothy smile of Kees Baar more real than the encouraging curve of the lips Joseph gave me when I managed to get some food down.

Joseph was no fool. One day he said to me, "Not sleeping, eh? And shouting nightmares as soon as you close your eyes. You know, that time I found you, you let slip something about your partners. I think that's what's doing it. I went through it myself."

"How?"

"It wasn't partners in my case, it was the police. The French police, the scum of the earth. They caught my son on the other side of the line with a case of cigarettes. A lousy five hundred francs worth of cigarettes. He tried to get away, and they ran him down in their car like a chicken. Killed him on the spot as neatly as if they'd put a bullet through his head. An accident, that's how it went on the record. I didn't sleep after that either. It took me two years to hunt down the driver of that car and get him where I wanted him. Two years. Then the *garrotte*. A nice shiny piece of piano wire around the neck. I could have used the knife, but no, the *garrotte* gave me the time I needed to whisper my son's name in his ear before he went. After that, I slept."

"The *garrotte* is too quick," I said.

"Then choose anyway you want as long as you can get away with it. Believe me, until it's all over life isn't worth living. How many of those partners were there?"

"Three," I said. "Big shots, all of them, living the good life. And I've already worked out what must be done to them. Two aren't worth the killing; just taking away the good life will be enough. Taking away everything that makes it worth living. The third is a different case. A fox, that one. A rabid fox. And he must be driven back and forth like an animal until he's ready for the killing. A very slow and painful killing."

"Three of them," Joseph said. "Quite a handful. The danger is that when you move against the first one, the others take alarm."

"Not the way I plan it. The trouble is that I need money to attend to it properly."

"Your money is still in your wallet," Joseph said. "Every penny of it."

"I'm sure of that. But I'm talking about a great deal of money, maybe twenty or thirty thousand francs. Enough to provide me with a certain style, give me freedom to move around readily. But that's not your problem."

"The *garrotte*," advised Joseph. "Find your fox and do with him as I would. When you've got your strength back I'll show you just how it's done."

He was, for all his grim look, the soul of kindness. I finally made it down the stairs on wobbly legs and unable to help with the outside work, I undertook to be a scullion and cook and housekeeper again, putting my heart into it. Joseph took notice of the order emerging in his home from the encrusted accumulation of years. He nodded approval. "My son was like that. Always neat and orderly. And a good cook too when he tried his hand at it. You're like him in many ways."

And when at long last I did have the strength to go outside, wearing the son's long-stored-away clothing, to work the other end of the crosscut saw, swing an ax, apply myself to carpentry and masonry work, although my mind was always off on my mission, Joseph said, "I've been thinking. If you want to make your home here—"

"Is there money to be made here?"

"Not the kind you talked about. No, if you mean we might turn a fat profit overnight moving some stuff across the line, there isn't anything doing in that right now. There's a fat trade in drugs coming down from Luxembourg city, but I have no part of it. For the rest—"

"So," I said, "I have to go where the money is."

Where the money is. Sweat it out on the docks or truckloading platforms, scraping together pennies until I had the capital I needed? Foolish, considering how eternally long it would take and the state of raw nerves I was in. Hit a bank? Go for broke with one big heist? In the final desperate analysis, it might come to just that.

Then, what I found my mind turning to again and again was the old man in that house on South Bay Shore Drive in Miami. My grandfather. A man with a lot of money in the bank. And maybe with a trace of the old affection for me still in him.

Make it a loan. Call on him as a borrower, not a beggar. And what were the odds that I would be turned down? Too good. All right, worry about that when it happens.

I made dinner the day of decision, working myself up to the moment. At dinner I said to Joseph, "There's someone who might lend me the money. But I must use the phone for a long-distance call. It won't cost you anything. The one I'm calling will either refuse the call or pay the bill for it."

After dinner, he always sat by the stove and read his paper. But the phone was in the kitchen, so now, tactfully, he gestured at it after downing a last slice of cheese, and then took himself off to the living room.

I couldn't remember the phone number, so there were maddening negotiations with the Luxembourg phone service before the connection was made. A collect call to Miami in the United States of America? I had the feeling that it was the first time in history such a strange demand had been made of the service.

Then from four thousand miles away I heard a woman's voice acknowledge in Spanish-flavored English that this was Mr. Hanna's home. Of course, the housekeeper. It might even be the same Mrs. Galvan out of my childhood. "An overseas call," the operator said to her. "Collect. From Mr. David Hanna Shaw. Will you accept the charges?"

The answer was an excited flurry of Spanish, then a long silence. Suddenly there was another voice on the line. An unfamiliar male voice. "Collect?" it said. "David Shaw? Yes, I'll accept the charges."

I had made contact. But with whom?

"Look," I said, "I'd like to speak to Mr. Hanna."

"You the one who says he's Shaw?"

"Yes. Who is this?"

"We'll get to that." It was a tough, no-nonsense growl. "First I've got some questions for you. You want to answer them, okay. Otherwise just hang up and forget it."

"You mean I'm supposed to identify myself. All right, I can tell you—"

"Let's stick to the questions. Like about Mrs. Hanna's bedroom here. What was always on her dresser? The big item."

"A jewel case. Red leather with a—"

"No. Something besides that."

Besides that? I wasn't prepared for this kind of test. Finally it came to me. "A photograph. In a gold frame. My photograph, taken when I was a kid."

"Maybe. Meanwhile, suppose you tell me how that kid in the picture is dressed."

"In an evzone costume. That fancy Greek military outfit."

"And who took that picture?"

"The family chauffeur in Athens. His name was Ray Costello." Then it dawned on me. "Costello, is that you?"

"That's who it is, Shaw."

"Then how about putting my grandfather on the line?"

"What? You mean you don't know about him?"

I did as soon as he said it. "Dead?"

"Last March. Coronary. And if you don't know about it, how come this call?"

"I need some money. That's all right. I'll try somebody else."

"Hold it!" It was a roar of panic. "Whatever the hell you do, Shaw, don't hang up that phone. There's a will, understand? I just put in six months all over Europe trying to locate you and tell you about it. So whatever you do, don't cut out again, or you'll really screw up the works."

"A will?" I said. "And I'm in it?"

"In it? For Chrissake, it's all yours, Shaw! The whole load! Ten million dollars after taxes! You hear me?"

I heard him.

God, how I heard him.

A messenger come to tell an avenging angel that at last he was fully armed for total destruction.

THE
EMPEROR OF
SQUARE NINE

Part III

Costello showed up forty-eight hours later, courtesy of Air Bahama, Miami direct to Luxembourg, and then a rented car. I had told Joseph that, miraculously, one of my ventures had turned up a big winner, and that the American connection would be coming to settle with me. When Costello hauled himself out of the car it was evident from Joseph's expression that this American met all expectations. A tough one, plainly. And, from that sun tan and those clothes, extremely prosperous. Obviously a man high up in the rackets the way all rich Americans were.

Costello gingerly made his way across the snowy crust to the door, and I opened it to him. "Van Zee?" he said, as he had been instructed to say, and I said, "Yes," and he said, "Well, it's been a long time, Davey, hasn't it? Now how about a drink?" The voice was that mix of drawling redneck and hardboiled New York found no place on earth but in Dade County, Florida.

I took him inside and made introductions and saw to it he had his drink—half a glass of contraband cognac that he took down like water—and then we were left to ourselves by the fireplace in the living room where a proper fire had been kindled in honor of this visitor.

I saw him sizing me up closely. I said, "Still wondering if I'm really David Shaw?"

He shrugged. "Your mother gave me a hundred bucks that day to have some pro photographer take your birthday picture up on that Parthenon place, and that's what I told her I did. If you'd ever let her know different, I would have caught hell for it. That means you and I are the only people anywhere who know I took that picture myself."

"Smart."

"Not as much as you some ways," he said. "After you ducked out of college I put in a year trying to track you down and never got a lead past Orly Airport."

"On whose orders?" I said.

"Your grandpa's. You don't think it was your father, do you? He's the same, by the way. Same wife and all as last time you saw him. Just ten years older. Anyhow, a few months ago I tried tracking you down once more on the estate's say-so and crapped out again."

"Why you?" I asked.

"Because I was the one J. G.—your grandpa—trusted to get things done the way he wanted them done. His one worry was that if you didn't show up sooner or later after he was gone, your mother could claim the estate. Meaning the guy she's married to could."

"Still Periniades?"

"Still him. And what's kept him out of court about the will so far is that J.G. had all the dirt on him filed away where I could pull it out if I had to. Swindles he worked in Italy, payoffs to government people there—enough to land him in jail for a long stretch. And Periniades knows that. So now all you have to do is get home and collect the jackpot. I've got your van Zee ticket here. You sure your passport's in order?"

"Yes. What about my draft status?"

"Hell, J. G. took care of that long ago with one call to Washington. You never did know much about him, did you? Or how he handled things?"

"No. But I'm beginning to get the idea he was quite the wheeler-dealer."

"He was, Davey. When he snapped his fingers the biggest politicians and fat cats in the state rolled over and played dead. And why? Because he knew where all the bodies were buried. That was my job, finding out where they were buried."

"His right-hand man," I said.

"A lot more than that. Near the end when they ordered him into the hospital and he didn't want to go I moved in with him, right there in his bedroom, and I tended him hand and foot until the end. I didn't have to, but I did it. That's how I felt about him. I think you missed a hell of a lot by walking out on him."

"Possibly."

"For sure. And now that we're talking so nice and open, I'd like to know exactly what you did trade him in for." He looked around the room. "For this?"

So there it was. As he had taken my measure, I was, with single-minded purpose, taking his, and more and more I liked what I saw and heard. I had already planned vengeance against Kees Baar and company. Here in Ray Costello I saw the proper agent to help carry it out.

Ten years before, Costello had lost me at Orly. Now, in undramatic and bitter detail, I took him past Orly into the world of Madame Chouchoute, of Kees Baar and *Les Amis du Bon Évangéliste,* and right up to the present.

He heard me out to the end with no show of emotion. Then he said reflectively, "A wife, so to speak, and a kid. J. G. would have gone for that all right. He was a lonely man after your grandma was put under the ground."

"I know the feeling," I said.

"I guess you do." He gave me a sharp look. "But you didn't let me in on all this just so I could send you a sympathy card, did you?"

"There are three men who have to be settled with, Ray."

"I can see that. So you just give the cops all the information they need without ever letting them know where it came from. I'll show you how."

"No," I said. "It's not police business. Only mine."

"Jesus, Davey, the way you make that sound—"

"Because I had all the time I needed to think about it. To know what had to be done and how it must be done. And after you called me about the inheritance I had a funny thought about it. That everything in my life was actually preparing me for this mission. Making me the perfect instrument for it. There's nothing after death, Ray. No hellfire waiting for Baar and Leewarden and Rouart-Rochelle. So if accounts are going to be settled, they're assigned to someone right down here on earth. For all I know, I was handed that job the day I was born."

"For Christ's sake, are you serious?"

"As I said, Ray, I've had time to think about it. Now I'm ready to move on it, and I want your help in that. I don't have to tell you that money is no object."

"Good," said Costello. "Then strictly between us I'll tell you how to move on it. There are some people around Miami who'll take care of anybody you finger if the price is right. One of them owes me a big favor. If I make contact with him—"

"No," I said again, "it's too quick and easy that way. Anyhow, Baar is the only one I've marked for killing, and he's all mine. The other two have women who mean a lot to them. Leewarden a daughter, Rouart-Rochelle a wife. They have to learn what it feels like to lose the woman you've invested your life in."

"Look, when it comes to hurting a couple of women who have no part of this—"

"The women won't be hurt, Ray. Take my word for it. In fact, they'll wind up rich and happy. So will you, if you go along with me."

"Meaning?"

"Meaning name your price."

Costello picked up a poker and rammed it into a smoldering log in the fireplace. He watched the flames flicker along it, then turned back to me, narrow-eyed with speculation. "What if this never works out the way you figure?"

"It will."

"All right, whether it does or not, I'll give you one year at two grand a week, tax free. That means one hundred grand guaranteed. And an expense account, no questions asked about it. One year, and that's it."

"I don't have anything to pack," I said. "We might as well get moving right now."

Potent traces of my grandfather's clout still lingered in the Florida air. First report had it that Dr. Isao Kimura's Clinic for Cosmetic Surgery in Palm Beach had a waiting list so long and distinguished that there was no way of being serviced by it for at least a year. But once I established my credentials as the J. G. Hanna grandson, I was promptly invited to become a client by Dr. Kimura himself. He examined my interesting nose and the tattoo on my forearm, studied the photographs of me extracted from my grandmother's album, and assured me that I would, without difficulty, soon be restored to my original self.

The clinic was a far cry from *La Clinica Gratuita In Trastevere.* On thirty landscaped acres were a medical building, the doctor's residence, a scattering of cottages for convalescents, a sauna, and a swimming pool bordered by cabanas. Cottage C, my home away from home, was a luxurious four-room suite, fronted by a flagstoned terrace, all of which was surrounded by a high, privacy-enforcing fence of bamboo palings.

The charge for this, excluding medical costs, was five hundred dollars a day, and the payment of my bill each week gave me occasion to comprehend the seemingly incomprehensible: that living at this rate made no dent in my inheritance. Clinic, Costello and all, I was richer each day when I woke up than I had been the day before.

This information had come from Owen Bibb, executor of the Hanna estate and president of the South Florida Merchants Bank, an institution founded by the late J. G. Hanna. As soon as I was back in the old house on South Bay Shore Drive, Bibb had showed up in the company of a watchful pair of lawyers. Carefully not addressing me by name, he explained that he had in hand the vital documents of David Hanna Shaw, most notably his birth certificate on which was imprinted the infant's foot- and toe-prints. Now if I had no objection to undergoing this test before the assembled witnesses—

Not very cordially, I removed shoes and socks and bore with Costello until, after some messy failures, he came up with the required goods which the delegation then bore away. Two days later, Owen Bibb returned, a now very respectful bank president, this time accompanied not only by the lawyers but also by the bank officer who had been handling the estate and was prepared to render an account of it. Miller Williams was the name of the bank officer, and the account he rendered from page after page of inventory took up most of the afternoon. After that there were papers to sign, a ream of them.

When I had signed the last one I said to Bibb, "I understand from Mr. Williams that up to his death my grandfather was a member of the bank's board of directors."

"Yes. As majority shareholder he would be."

"And now," I said, "I'm majority shareholder."

He saw what was coming and didn't like it. "Well, yes, Mr. Shaw, and if you wish to nominate someone for the board—"

"Myself," I said.

"Mr. Shaw, banking is an extremely complex business, and when important decisions must be made—"

"Myself," I repeated sweetly. "And I'd like an emergency meeting of the board to settle that immediately. As for making decisions, Mr. Bibb, I'm sure I can rely on your good advice. I don't see why I shouldn't have the same confidence in you that my grandfather had."

That he liked. "I worked hard to win that confidence, Mr. Shaw. Yes, I'll take care of the matter at once. You can count on it."

Costello saw the party out. He returned to me wearing a broad grin. "Putting down bank presidents now," he remarked. "You learn fast, don't you?"

"So does Bibb. What do you know about that Miller Williams, Ray?"

"Him? I'd say strictly a company man."

"Personal life?"

"I can check it out tomorrow. Why?"

"If he's as unimaginative and conscientious as he looks, I want him on my payroll. Can you see what he'll add to the act when we hit Europe?"

"Not bad," said Costello. "I'll look him up."

He reported back the next evening. "Like I figured, a straight arrow. Forty years old, fifteen of it with the bank, neat, clean and sober. Only big thing in his life was when his wife walked out on him last year. No scandal. It probably made her sleepy just looking at him."

"Fine. Arrange a leave of absence for him with Bibb and sign him on as my business manager. It ought to be happy news for him."

But it was not altogether happy news for Miller Williams, a man not at his best facing the unexpected. "A movie, Mr. Shaw? To be made in Europe? But film production is an extremely soft area of investment. Are you sure—?"

"I'm sure, Miller. I've been dreaming of this project for a long time. But I'm green as grass about financing film production, and that's why I want you on the job."

"Truth to tell, Mr. Shaw, I don't know too much about the industry myself."

"Understood. But we're not hopping over to Europe tomorrow. You'll have time to put together whatever information you need."

So the day before I entered Dr. Kimura's clinic, David Shaw Film Productions, Inc. was born, with D. H. Shaw its president, Raymond Costello its secretary, and Miller Williams, somewhat to his own surprise, its treasurer.

During its period of birth I finally began to get control of my nerves. Slowly, very slowly, I learned the mastery of that inwardly shuddering, twitching sense of impatience which, much of my waking time, made me feel as if I were being flayed alive, the skin being stripped from me by a dull blade, inch by inch. It was a sort of triumph of mind over emotion, this business of forcing myself to recognize that the instruments for my mission had to be forged precisely, and in the process there could be no speeding up of clock or calendar.

But of course there was no need to speed them up. I was the agent of a destiny charted for me. And knowing that, I had to know that nothing could ever happen to Baar, Leewarden, and Rouart-Rochelle that would cheat me of the pleasure of attending to them my own way.

They would be all mine whenever I was ready to drive the knife into them.

I came out of surgery into a bed in the clinic's medical building. Eventually, face masked by bandages, arm fixed against my body so that the newly grafted skin would not be endangered, I was moved to Cottage C, there to put in the time needed for complete restoration. Finally all the bandages came off, and I looked into the mirror. Beardless, pale, and with that discolored patch of grafted skin on the forearm, but, over all, not bad. Distinctly ten years older than the David Shaw I had last seen in any mirror, and to judge from the set of the lips and the lines of the face, they had been a hard ten years.

So to work.

In the cottage wall was a safe, and in the safe, besides Jan van Zee's passport and driver's license, was a package of writing paper and notebooks. These, and the flight bag to lug them in, were the only purchases I had made in Luxembourg city before Costello and I enplaned there. Letters had to be written on paper that was uniquely for sale in the Low Countries, because sooner or later someone might be driven to examine that paper closely.

I put in two weeks at the job, four or five hours a day, tearing up as much as I salvaged until I was satisfied with my handiwork.

The letters were from Jan van Zee to David Shaw.

They were in a competent though sometimes stilted English, occasionally flavored by the literal translation of a Dutch phrase, and were written in the angular van Zee script. Before attending to the actual writing, I tediously drafted a calendar for the past few years, the first date on it that day when Berti van Stade's column about me appeared in *Het Oog Amsterdam*. I then entered under their approximately correct dates the memorable events in the life of J. van Zee up to near his demise—second demise, that was, considering that the first had taken place in the English Channel ten years before —and once I got this far I found it easy to recall less memorable events and chart them in proper sequence.

The letters themselves varied in length. Some contained only a few lines simply answering a question directed at van Zee by Shaw. Others offered detailed accounts of the daily life of van Zee interspersed with recollections of his checkered past. Almost all contained some mention of financial transactions. *The 200 dollars American now received at the office of American Express.* And *Thanking you for the 100 dollars American.* And once, irritably, a brief note entirely devoted to the subject. *By agreement you must provide money as needed. Send now the 500 dollars or there is no more agreement.*

Anyone interested in adding up all those numbers would find that the total came to twenty thousand dollars. A logical figure, because it seemed that Shaw, a would-be movie producer, was purchasing the right to use this autobiographical material as the basis of a film. In a short note of recent date, van Zee addressed himself to the delays in this project. *You write me the film-making will start soon. Last year it was the same thing. Will it be the same five years from now? Also I do not like that title* The Last Hippie. *One who works hard for his money when he must is not a hippie. This title is what we know in Dutch as* kletscock.

Obviously a testy fellow, this van Zee

I brought Costello the collection, and he went through it carefully. "Sounds like this guy had total recall," he said. "Anyhow they look good. I'll take care of having the copies made."

His bedroom in Cottage C was our office, and he had gone to work there as soon as we checked in, scouting out a reliable investigative agency in Europe and turning it loose on the list of names I submitted. From its address—Avenue Matignon in Paris was distinctly high-priced—the agency was not one of those B-picture deals with a French Sam Spade working out of a shabby office. And its business card suggested wide-ranging efficiency.

"DETEC"

UNIVERS AG. SURVEILL.

CONSTATS—PROBL. DIVERS

PARIS–BRUXELLES–GENÈVE–LONDRES

Four offices, well-located for my mission. Most important, the first report to come in was reassuring. The information on Yves and Vahna appeared accurate from what I already knew of them; no big deal putting together this material. But the news that Monsieur Simon Leewarden had just disposed of a house in Bruges and was now the weekend occupant of an apartment on Avenue Louise in Brussels occupied full-time by his daughter Sarah and a housekeeper was exactly the kind of news I was ready to pay for.

Of Kees Baar no word yet, an omission that worried Costello more than it did me.

"He's got that million in cash to play with, Davey. What's to say he isn't already holed up in Rio playing with it?"

"Not what," I said. "Who. Yves Rouart-Rochelle. That million, and how to find it, must be on his mind day and night. And he expects it to be on Baar's mind too. If Baar suddenly dropped out of sight, it would make Yves highly suspicious. That's no way to enjoy your money, with Yves tracking you down to confirm his suspicions. Baar will stay close by and in touch with him for a long time to come."

"Most people wouldn't have nerve enough to play it that way, Davey."

"Kees Baar isn't like most people, Ray. Remember that when this thing starts developing, or you're in for some nasty surprises."

Now, along with the van Zee letters to be xeroxed, I gave him additional names for his list. Marie-Paule Neyna, last described by Kees as operating Leewarden's porno film factory in Copenhagen; Madame Chouchoute who, after all, had provided my introduction to Kees; and someone I knew only as Renaudat, the operator who had hired the pair of thugs to hijack merchandise from Marie-Paule and me in Marseille those ten years ago.

Costello handed me the report on this trio along with the copies of the van Zee letters. Marie-Paule was still operating the factory. Madame Chouchoute's place was still a landmark of rue Houdon in Montmartre, although Madame herself was rarely seen and was reported very ill. As for Renaudat, according to Detec's findings, there were several so-named in Marseille, all very respectable. However, on the police record of three years before was an entry regarding the murder of a Robert Renaudat, a felon with several convictions and known to have been involved in the drug traffic.

So much for that side of the Atlantic.

On this side, I turned my attention to the recruiting of a proper entourage for D. H. Shaw, film producer, when he would make his entrance on the European scene. Miller Williams, hard at work mastering the art of motion-picture financing and at the same time attending to my personal accounts, offered substance to any entourage, but, as I explained to Costello, more was needed to put on a proper show.

"Makes sense," said Costello. "Did you ever take real notice of our friend Harry on the job?"

Harry. A big, good-natured blond twenty-five-year-old, Harry was an inobtrusive presence in Cottage C, its maître d'hôtel, housekeeper, repairman, valet, and therapist. Naturally, since this was Florida, land of sunshine, the initial process of providing me with a proper tan was done indoors by lamp. Harry spotlighted my newly repaired areas, timer in hand, then expanded his range until slowly, slowly, he obtained the desired effect, a flawlessly even tan, head to toes, front and back. Now there was no detecting the incision along the nose, the patch of grafted skin on the arm.

Harry even provided me with eye-filling entertainment his days off duty when, while I was sunning on my terrace, I would observe him turn up with a female companion to share with him the temporary use of a cabana and the pool. It was never the same girl, but it was always a lissome beauty.

Finally, out of curiosity, I asked him where he had struck this mine.

"Stewardesses, sir," said Harry. "If you'd like me to arrange something—"

"Not now, Harry. I'll let you know when I feel the need."

"Any time, sir."

And once Costello put the bug in my ear, I could see that Harry was made-to-order entourage material. Harry, as a member of the party abroad, attending to the luggage, the dining arrangements, the wardrobe. Harry, in livery, chauffeuring the limousine. Van Zee might have preferred a Ferrari roadburner, but, as Costello advised, this was the very reason why the president of Shaw productions should be the chauffeured limousine type.

I approached my prospect roundabout. "You seem handy in all departments, Harry. Where did you pick it up?"

"Yachting, sir. Mr. Charlie Schoonover's *Saraband.* I signed on as cabin boy, then made steward, then just about everything else. And Mr. Schoonover liked things done by the book."

"Suppose I asked you to sign on with me?"

"For what, sir?"

"I'll be going to Europe to produce a film. You'd take care of me there the way you do here. Double whatever you're getting here, plus expenses. Interested?"

"Ready to go, sir," said Harry.

Strategy dictated the choice of the next recruit. Among the additional names I had submitted for Detec to work on was that of an old school friend, Jean-Pierre, Monsieur le Comte de Liasse, and the report on him that came back was intriguing in its possibilities. Head of prosperous De Liasse Electronics in Paris. More important, unmarried and very much a ladies' man. In fact, the French press had several times given scandalized notice to his *affaires.*

Harry, of course, would be the one to help me capitalize on the possibilities.

"Harry, didn't you tell me you could arrange female companionship for me whenever I was interested?"

"Yes, sir."

"Well, I'm interested now, but not precisely in that sense. I'll be shooting most of the picture in France and Holland, and since I don't speak Dutch or French it would be handy to have someone around who can. Say, someone on the order of those ladies you bring around here."

"Speaks French and Dutch, sir? I'll put it on the grapevine."

It took only a week for the vine to produce the requisite grape. Small and exquisite, *café au lait* in complexion, with slanted eyes of emerald green, and silky, raven-black hair. Her name, Harry said as he made the introductions, was Grete Hansen.

"Grete Hansen?" I said. If you wanted the antithesis of the Scandinavian, this daughter of the tropics was it.

She gave me a languorous smile. "Papa was Swedish, Mr. Shaw. Mama was a local."

"Of what location, Grete?"

"Saint Maarten in the Islands. That's Dutch. And next door is Saint Martin which is French. I get along fine in both languages."

"And right now you're a stewardess?"

"Inter-Caribbean. But if what Harry told me is true—I mean, you are going to make a movie, aren't you?"

"I am."

"Then I'd rather work for you." Again she turned on that languorous smile, wetting her lips for better effect. "You know, I photograph very well. Any chance I could get a part in your movie, Mr. Shaw?"

"At first glance, Grete, I had the feeling you could. So with that settled, may I assume you're now on the payroll?"

"Sure." Without invitation, she strolled into the cottage. I followed, but Harry, evidently sensitive to nuances, remained behind. Grete coolly surveyed my bedroom, took stock of the kingsized bed. "If you want me to move in right now," she said, "most of my things are out in Harry's car. He can bring them right in."

During the years with Anneke, I had taken no other woman to bed. The temptation was sometimes acute, but weighing it against the least chance of losing my woman I refused to take the chance. And since her death, the temptation was not there at all. Now, suddenly, here it was again.

As it very soon turned out, Grete and I did not make an inspired pair of lovers. Illogical as it was, a sense of guilt in me had a chilling effect at the wrong moments, and while my bedmate occasionally showed herself capable of an inspired effort, she was usually more dutiful than otherwise. What she lusted after—and she made no pretense about it—was a place in movieland. Stardom. She actually used the word now and then, and when she did she took on the expression that another woman might have at the peak of orgasm. She was in her way as single-minded as I was in mine, and to that extent at least, she was a proper member of the team.

Even Costello, at first concerned about an arrangement which put an outsider so much in our midst, finally admitted that as long as I didn't openly reveal my true mission to her she'd never get the picture. Catlike in so many ways, it seemed that Grete was wholly uncatlike in one vital respect. There wasn't a drop of curiosity in that beautiful, egomaniacal head.

So there now remained only one member of the cast to sign up before we took the show on the road: a professional movie-maker, someone with proper credentials but generally unemployed. To solve the problem, Costello turned to a West Coast investigative agency for a list of prospects. He presented the list to me with relish. "You'll never guess who's down here. An old friend of yours from college. Guy name of Oscar Wylie."

There the name was. Oscar himself, the old movie buff and nose breaker. According to the report on him, he had so far produced a few TV commercials and had directed one film which had sunk without a splash. *Hot Wheels.* An epic of young motorcyclists, definitely not starring Marlon Brando. He was also sweating out alimony payments to two ex-wives and was rated on various computers as a poor credit risk.

"You wouldn't know it," Costello said, "but after your mix-up with him in college, J. G. bought him off for a lousy two grand. I was going to cross his name off the list when I saw it, but then I thought what the hell it might give you a laugh, so I left it there."

"Good. Because he's our man."

"Wylie? Somebody you had trouble with? Why him?"

"Because we're not really making a picture, Ray. Which means we're making a fool out of anyone who signs on for this job. If Wylie's the one, it doesn't matter. Just agree to his price and get his signature on a contract."

"Easy."

"And I want a print of that cheese he turned out. That *Hot Wheels.* There must be a screening room somewhere in Miami. Book it for my use the day after I'm out of here."

"No biz like show biz," said Costello.

"So I've heard. Anything new from Paris?"

He had the latest telexed reports from Detec in his pocket. "Lee-warden's kid goes to school in Brussels. Parochial school, uniforms and all. Frenchy's wife just took a two-day holiday in London with a lady friend, same as she did last week. Some shopping, mostly casino action. But the financial stuff about Leewarden and Frenchy comes up interesting."

"How?"

"Leewarden's got more bills than income. Frenchy is mortgaged up to the eyeballs. Got a lot of paper out at some banks. Promissory notes. Might go to a million francs, which is around a quarter of a million dollars in real money."

"I want that paper," I said. "Those banks will probably be glad to dump it cut rate, but I want it whatever it costs. Put Williams on it. Have him set up a dummy outfit to do the buying."

Costello nodded wisely. "I get it. Leverage. Very big leverage."

"Very big. But Yves must have some heavy money coming from somewhere with a wife like that to support."

"So?"

"The more I think about it, Ray, the more I'm ready to bet that he's been partner all along in whatever Baar set up, including that airlines kickback racket. He's probably been getting most of his income from it."

"Could be. How much of an income?"

I said, "My cut came to between eight and ten thousand a year for a few easy deliveries. And I was only a handyman."

"A ten percenter," said Costello.

"A one percenter at most. I was probably paid out of petty cash."

Costello did some mental arithmetic. "So," he said, "there's still a hell of a lot of dough coming through that pipe line. And you want to plug up the pipe line. But how?"

"Tell Williams I'm taking a flyer in the market. He's to get me a hundred shares each in some airlines operating between the States and Europe. And North Africa. Here's the list of them. No questions. Immediate purchase at the market price."

"What does that do for you?"

"It makes me a concerned shareholder."

142

"You're kidding, Davey. You really look to turn that van Zee stuff over to those outfits?"

"Only selected sections of it, all names deleted. And only to the chairman of the board. The man where the buck stops."

"So then the pipe line starts to dry up." Costello paid me the compliment of a broad smile. "Pretty," he said. "If it works."

"It will. Get Williams on it right now. And don't forget about signing up Wylie."

Oscar didn't sign up all that easily. I was already back on South Bay Shore Drive, fully repaired, when he phoned me from the Coast. Having pinballed down the machine for ten years without lighting any lights or ringing any bells he was plainly uneasy about this sudden rescue from oblivion by an old enemy. "If you don't mind my asking, Shaw, why me?"

"Because, Oscar, what you put into *Hot Wheels* is what I want in my picture."

"You saw *Hot Wheels?*"

"I not only saw it," I told him truthfully, "I have a print of it here."

"You have?"

Uneasy or not, he was being offered a handsome producer-director contract by someone who plainly admired his talents. It was enough.

He showed up in Miami as soon as the contract was signed, the same skinny, sharp-nosed Connecticut Yankee. I led him to his room and made talk about his masterpiece *Hot Wheels* while he was stowing away his belongings. When he had everything in Oscar Wylie apple-pie order I handed him the précis of *The Last Hippie* I had worked up, along with Grete's translation of the article Berti van Stade had done on Jan van Zee. I explained what they were. "Now read them, Oscar, and tell me what we've got here."

Oscar wasn't the fastest reader in the world, but eventually he came to the end of the last page. "Well," he said, "I can see why *Hot Wheels* grabbed you. Same thing going about the rebel without a cause. Same feel to it. And we've got an edge here I didn't have with *Hot Wheels* because this van Zee is an actual person."

"He is. Which brings up a problem."

"A problem?" said Oscar warily.

I said, "I was doing the tourist bit in Holland three years ago when somebody brought this article to my attention. It struck me that here was material begging to be filmed. A story that would show, through a young drifter named Jan van Zee, a life style already dying out. I finally met him, and we made a handshake deal. He wasn't going to sit down and write any autobiography, but he would send me letters regularly and get everything into them, past and present. In return, I'd supply him with money whenever he needed it. When I felt I had all the material I needed we'd go into production, and he'd collect a final payment then."

Oscar was fully on guard again. "All handshake?" he said. "Nothing signed?"

"It was a case of doing it his way or not at all. Now for the problem. A few months ago I let him know I was ready to start production. I haven't heard from him yet."

"Haven't heard? But, Dave, you can't even—"

"I know," I said solemnly. "No signature, no production. But he'll turn up. That'll be my job when we get to Paris next week, locating him. Meanwhile, you'll be shaping up this material for a screenwriter. And while you're at it, Oscar, there's something to keep in mind. The young lady I introduced you to downstairs—"

"Grete?"

"Grete. Well, she's slated for a part in the picture. I'll leave you to work out the best way of handling that."

That did it. Gone was all wariness forever, because here was the explanation to the mystery. Dave Shaw wasn't the first monied citizen to invest in show biz out of lust for a lady. Oscar came close to leering at me. "You can count on me, Dave."

"I knew I could. By the way, how are you on publicity? Can you give the production a big build-up in Europe before we even land there?"

"I hate to sound my own bugle, Dave, but when it comes to PR I'm very heavy. And we've got a beautiful handle here. Not only this hippie material, but the search for the mysterious author himself. And there's Grete for cheesecake. By the time we hit Paris we'll have a red-hot campaign cooking there."

Costello, in our strategy session that night, said, "How did it go with Mister Wonderful?"

"Headed in the right direction and rolling fast."

"Good. And that's not all that's rolling fast. Frenchy booked into a hotel in Brussels for overnight. He and Leewarden had supper there. In the middle of it, a third party sat down with them."

"Baar?"

"Sorry, but this one was strictly American. Name of Gardiner Fremont according to the hotel register."

"He might be a go-between for some airlines, telling them the heat is on."

"Not from what the agency man took down of their talk. Listen to this." Costello squinted at his notebook. "Frenchy said, 'Dead, both of them. And they were the only ones who knew where they hid it.' Then Fremont said, 'I'm a computer expert. That means I have a very logical mind. I tell you I don't believe it.' "

"And then?"

"Then Frenchy started to say something about bad judgment—the Detec man thinks it was that—but Leewarden piped them both down because they were getting too loud." Costello gave me his cat-that-ate-the-canary smile. "Are you thinking what I am?"

I said, "What else is there to think? That million dollar check-forging swindle on L.A. was set up by computer. Fremont has to be the one who worked that computer."

"And here he is," said Costello, "come to collect his cut and thinking he's getting the double-cross. Anyhow, I already told the agency to have somebody on him night and day. If Frenchy and Leewarden steer him to the Dutchman, we go right along with him."

"In that case," I said, "it's time to start pulling some long-distance strings."

In the dossier on Jean-Pierre de Liasse, the ever-efficient Detec had provided a series of phone numbers including that of the Château de Liasse at Chaumont, the family estate where I finally reached Jean-Pierre. "David Shaw?" he said. "But of course! Monsieur Stampfli's! The genius at football. My God, but it's been a long time."

"It has. But I suddenly remembered I owed you some money. I wanted you to know you can expect repayment very soon."

"You owe me money?"

"A hundred francs. For one secondhand bicycle."

He laughed. "But that machine was in terrible shape, dear friend. I was swindling you outrageously."

"Then I regard the debt as cancelled. But I will be in Paris day after tomorrow, Jean-Pierre, and I did want to see you for old time's sake."

"Delighted. I planned to be here at Chaumont a bit longer—a few days of holding mama's hand, you understand—but I'll gladly cut that short. And you'll be my guest at my apartment in Paris. You'll find it most comfortable."

"Kind of you, Jean-Pierre, but I'm with some business associates, and I've already arranged for all of us to be at the Meurice."

"Business, hey? Well, business or not, we'll have time with each other. Yes. So delighted."

No more than I.

O scar delivered the goods.

There were reporters and press photographers waiting at the airport in Paris, not many, but enough to indicate that here might be a celebrity in the making. There was a VIP lounge set aside for the interviews. At the sight of the first camera aimed in her direction, Grete put herself on full, seductive display, and the press took to her immediately. Beneficiary of reflected glory, I was then given the treatment ordinarily reserved for a Bergman or Fellini.

Our entrance into the Meurice was at least as impressive, and, most gratifying of all, upstairs in my suite I found waiting a magnum of Dom Perignon '66 with card attached. The card bore the elaborate crest of de Liasse. Its message read *Will you share this evening with me to celebrate your arrival? Please call at once.*

Good. Better than good.

The *pied-à-terre* on Avenue Montaigne was a luxurious apartment largely dedicated to stereo equipment. I remembered Jean-Pierre as lean and sardonic. I discovered that while he was still trim of figure, he was, unbelievably, maudlin about the old school days. For his part, he was taken aback when I asked that we converse in English, my French having rusted badly after years of disuse. But once over these hurdles, we got along as if we were in fact dear old friends.

We covered school days at length, and then Jean-Pierre said, "Your mother. How is she?"

"All right, I suppose. I rarely see her."

"Ah, well. Of course you wouldn't know I was in love with her from the first time she visited you at the lycée, would you? No, don't smile. It was quite serious as far as I was concerned. What moonstruck animals boys can be. When she divorced your father I actually dreamed that some day I might tempt her into marriage, never mind the grotesque discrepancy in age. After all, I could offer her a title. Women, you must know, are strangely susceptible to titles."

"Dear mother," I said. "Madame la Comtesse."

"Amusing, no? But not to my mama, dear old snob that she is. To her, the indescribably boring world of the aristocracy—that dreary index in the *Almanach de Gotha*—is all that matters. She wouldn't admit under torture that what she lives on are the proceeds of a commercial enterprise."

"Well," I said, "from an outsider's view, the *aristo* does inhabit a highly glamorous world. I note that as an expert. Glamor happens to be my business."

"Your film business, you mean. Yes, you made quite a splash in the newspapers this morning. But is all that true? I refer to the young Dutchman who was writing your screenplay and mysteriously disappeared before completing it."

"All true, unfortunately."

"Too bad. But at least you are involved in work which has, as you say, a certain glamor. That girl, now that we're on the subject. The one photographed with you. An adorable little beauty, isn't she?"

"She is," I said. It had taken a long time, but here we were at last.

"Yes," said Jean-Pierre. "Ah—I suppose that between you two there is a rather special arrangement?"

"None at all." We looked at each other with complete understanding. "An adorable little beauty," I said, "and extremely susceptible. I'm sure she'd be overwhelmed by an introduction to Monsieur le Comte."

"I'm pleased to hear that. Now if you will only—"

"But," I cut in, "you have the advantage of me in one large regard. I've never met your mother. Never even gotten a glimpse of her world. To me the *Almanach de Gotha* remains a book with tightly closed covers."

"Indeed?" He considered the implications of this. "My dear friend, if what you seek as film-maker is a close view of the *ancien régime* in modern dress, I'm afraid you're in for a dreary time of it."

"Perhaps. But the film-maker's needs—especially in dealing with *cinema vérité*—"

Jean-Pierre nodded wisely. "Yes, I thought that was it. Well, God willing, Mama may be in an amiable mood next weekend. She'll be in Paris then for one of her terrible *salons*. If you—and the young lady—have no other plans for that afternoon—"

"None."

"Then you shall receive an invitation to attend. I trust I'll see you both there." He raised his glass. "Now a toast to old friendships?"

"And new ones," I said.

A slow news week evidently.

Reuters and some other news services picked up the van Zee story as an entertaining tidbit and spread it far and wide. Now, with journalists feeding on journalists, there were more interviews, and Grete was aglow, gathering newspapers from all corners of the Continent, setting up her own press-clipping service.

Oscar, on the other hand, was disgruntled. "I've got stories planted in damn near everything printed this side of Siberia," he complained, "and still no sign of your wandering boy. It makes rough going, Dave, when I work over that material of his wondering what happens if he never shows up."

"Oscar," I said, "if you've worked over that material, you know he's subject to criminal charges in half a dozen countries. That means he's going to move very carefully, make sure there's no trap being set for him before he shows up. But he will show up."

"If you say so, Dave."

"I do. How's Williams making out with his cost estimates?"

"Well, for a guy who's new at it, he showing a real talent for this business. He's already set up meetings with some French film people who can give him an inside look at production costs here."

"Good. Stay with it, Oscar."

My suite was for this kind of by-play. Costello's room adjoining it was for serious business. Here, with Detec close by, he could watch the pieces move around the board on an almost hourly basis and record the moves on the growing stack of index cards he kept locked away in his desk drawer. If Yves publicly dined in company, Costello had a description of each member of it before the check was paid. If Leewarden had a lengthy conversation with someone in Piccadilly, Costello had the description of that someone soon after. No description, however, matched the one of Kees I had given the agency. And the reports on Gardiner Fremont indicated that after his meeting with Yves and Leewarden he had simply holed up in a *pension* in Brussels and seemed to have no contact with anyone at all.

Costello said, "That means he never did buy Frenchy's story about van Zee hijacking the money. And since the Dutchman is top man of the gang, Fremont is probably waiting for him to show up and pay off."

"That makes two of us," I said.

I went through the stack of index cards again and again, trying to piece together patterns from them, and sometimes this made for a gnawing frustration. Vahna Rouart-Rochelle, for example, whether during her weekly London expeditions or at home could never be found alone in the presence of any male other than her husband, could never be charged with sending out even a ripple of scandal.

"If she made one little slip," I told Costello, "that's all I'd need. I could move right in on her."

"She probably figures one little slip means she gets her arm broken by Frenchy. Or worse. Give up on that angle. Work out some way of getting at her through the London trips. Those gambling holidays of hers. That's probably happy time as far as she's concerned."

Sound advice, if the lady continued playing that unexpected role, the faithful wife.

On occasion, a report offered encouragement. Most gratifying during this bad time was one from far away. A phone call from banker Owen Bibb in Miami who, as my agent in the matter, had lately been receiving urgent messages from various airline executives. All the messages struck the same note. My concern as shareholder about certain illegal practices engaged in by the company was now being investigated. Immediate correction of the problem was assured.

"So the squeeze is on," Costello said. "No more kickbacks. For all we know, Frenchy and the rest of them are feeling it in the pocket right now."

"Probably."

"So," said Costello, "considering that you're holding a quarter of a million dollar's worth of Frenchy's notes, how about asking for full payment of them right now?"

"I have to get to Vahna first, Ray. She makes up the payment that matters."

"It's too complicated that way, Davey. You're trying to fit a lot of odd pieces together all at the same time."

"They'll fit," I said.

And, as I saw, going through those index cards again and again like a riverboat gambler trying to foretell the deal coming, there was material here which provided neither frustration nor encouragement but only a large blank. There was the original report on Chouchoute noting that she was very ill and generally out of sight, and nothing more.

I pointed this out to Costello. "Doesn't Detec still have a man on her, Ray?"

"No need. They've got one of her girls on our payroll. The head girl. She'll report quick if anybody like the Dutchman shows up there."

"What's her name?"

"Avril. No second name. Just Avril. Our contact man with her is a guy name of Schefflin. Why? You figure on meeting with her?"

"Her boss," I said.

I timed my arrival at Chouch-
oute's for precisely noon. Much might have changed over the past
ten years; perhaps Madame's waking time had not.

A grimy young man answered the door, all hair, mustache, and
dark glasses, the latest model Jean Lespere. *"Que voulez-vous?"*

It was shrewd of him to suspect that I was too well turned-out to
be a customer for this level of entertainment. I smiled engagingly.
"I'm sorry. I don't speak French."

"No? I say what do you want."

"Avril. A friend sent me."

Chacun à son goût. He opened the door wide and motioned me
in, not briskly and cheerfully as Jean Lespere had once done it,
giving the client full value for his money, but indifferently. Viewing
my surroundings with a professional eye while he trudged upstairs
to rouse Avril, I had the feeling that no one since my time had
properly scrubbed and polished these premises. And what about that
early springtime chill in the air? Undoubtedly, the furnace had gone

out again, the ever-cranky grates collapsed into the ash pit. The one small improvement I could mark was that the pair of girls sprawled at ease in the waiting room seemed to be younger than the girls I remembered here. Or, on second thought, was I that much older?

This year's Jean Lespere hailed me from the head of the stairway, and I made my way up to the door he indicated. Avril's room was already prepared for business, the traditional bowl and stack of towels in evidence, and Avril, a buxom redhead, was ready for action in men's pajama tops. " 'Allo, *bébé,* " she said cheerfully, advancing on me.

I waved her off. "Do you speak English?"

"A little. If you speak slow."

I said it very slowly. "A man named Schefflin works for me. Do you understand?"

She nodded with instant comprehension. "I watch, I tell the others to watch, but no van Zee. No *Hollandais.* "

"Then just keep watching. But right now I want to talk to Chouchoute."

"Impossible. She is sick, you know? Ver' sick."

I had the bribe ready. I handed it to her, and with deliberation she examined the thousand-franc note front and back. "A gentleman," she said. *"Vraiment. "*

Decent in robe and slippers she led me up to the top floor. For a moment as we left her room I found I was doing the leading but caught myself in time. A knock on the door, and there was Madame's voice, shrill with the familiar bad temper. *"Entrez! Entrez!"*

Chouchoute was propped up in bed, a breakfast tray before her, newspapers scattered all over the coverlet. In whatever sunshine could filter through the dirty skylight she looked like a yellowed, mummified image of her old self, but the eyes were very bright as they fixed inquiringly on me and then angrily on Avril. *"Et qui est-ce qui ce type-là?"*

"Un Anglais, Madame. Un brasseur d'affaires. Il ne parle pas Français. "

A Britisher. A wheeler-dealer on a large scale. Non-French speaking. I listened poker faced to this description of myself, but could see no reason for playing the bilingual game. Madame, as I well knew, had an excellent command of basic English.

I said to her, "I've heard that you speak English."

"I speak what I wish to speak."

"Right now," I said, taking out my money clip, "English would be most profitable to you."

This time it was two one-thousand-franc notes. Madame seized them with a bejeweled claw. "And so?" she said.

"Ten years ago," I said, "a young man named Jean Lespere worked here for you. He was also called Janot. Do you remember him?"

"Yes. An ugly brute. And starving out there in the streets until I gave him honest work. Then what does he do? One day he steals the money I keep here and runs away."

"No, he did not steal your money and run away. What happened was that you sold his services to a certain man. The man who supplied you with drugs." Madame strained to sit upright, then fell back against her pillow. *"Va-t'en!"* she snarled at Avril who was taking all this in, mouth agape. *"Va-t'en, salope!"*

It was the old snarl again, one not to be denied. Avril departed with a slam of the door. Madame narrowed her eyes at me. "Who are you?"

I pointed at the newspapers around her. "Somewhere there you may have read about me. The name is David Shaw. I'm American, a maker of motion pictures. I had an arrangement with a man to write a story for a motion picture, but now he's disappeared. He was your Janot, Madam."

"My Janot?" She scrabbled among the newspapers. "It's here. You are the one with *la belle négresse,* true?"

"True."

Her face clouded. "But wait. You say Janot. But in the paper it was not somebody French."

"That's right. The man you sent Janot to gave him a Dutch passport, so Janot became Jan van Zee."

"Yes, yes, that is the name. But I did not sell his services. It was a kindness to him."

"That's not important," I said. "All I want is the address of the man you sent him to. Kees Baar. Any address where I can meet him and ask him how to find Janot. Have you seen Baar lately?"

"Seen him? No."

"Heard from him?"

She took too much time deciding on the answer. "No."

"Madame—"

"No." She weakly shook her head from side on side on the pillow. "I have no strength left. Go now. Tell Avril to come to me."

No use pushing this further. She had weighed her answer and would stay with it. And from the waxy look of her, the hard breathing, she really had used up what little strength remained in her. But she had, no matter her intentions, fortified my conviction that Kees Baar was not far away from here.

When I pushed open the door to depart I almost banged it against Avril's head. "She wants you," I said.

Avril swung the door shut. "She will wait, *hein?*" Then very sourly, "Why did you give her so much money? She will never live to spend it, you know?"

"Never mind that. Did Schefflin tell you to look through her mail?"

"No."

"Well, do it with any letter coming to her from another country. Then tell Schefflin what they're about. I'll arrange extra payment for that, understand?"

"Yes. But do you know she sold this place? When the new one comes—"

"The new owner?"

"Yes. She was already here to see what it was like. She will soon be here again, even before Madame is dead. When she is I do not think I can help you any more."

"Do you know her?"

"A stranger. I think there will be trouble when she comes. Ver' thin, you know?" Avril pursed her lips and drew her face down. "And with a face like this. It looks to me a type worse than Madame. Not one to play tricks on."

"Too bad," I said. "Then let's just hope that Kees Baar shows up here before she does."

"**S**old the place?" Costello said. "Well, she sure as hell got a pile for it, because I never yet knew a whorehouse that wasn't a gold mine."

It gave me a picture of Madame's almost lifeless yellow claw grasping my bank notes. And flung over the chair beside the bed, a corset that would now go twice around what was left of her. I said, "What concerns us is that she knows more about Baar's whereabouts than she's telling, and there's not much time left for her to tell it. A lot depends on Avril. Make sure Schefflin understands he's not to bargain with her. Whatever she wants for worthwhile information, she gets."

"The whole agency knows that's our policy."

"All right then. Did they have anything to report since this morning?"

"One item," said Costello. "They checked out that woman who goes along with Frenchy's wife on those London trips. It's a Mrs. Max Denoyer. Seems she's Frenchy's sister."

"And watchdog."

"That's the size of it. When the women go shopping in London the sister-in-law doesn't buy, and when they're in the casino she doesn't bet. But she's always right there. If you want to get to the wife in London, you'll have to figure out some way of getting around the watchdog."

"When the time comes," I said.

"I'll leave it to you. But talking about watchdogs, when you went to look up old lady Choochoo you didn't take Harry along, did you?"

"No."

"That's a fact. Because right after you left he was in here picking over my clothes for the valet service. Which was not very bright of you, Davey. Nobody is so big and tough that a thirty-eight slug can't cut him right down to size."

"Not in this case, Ray. There's one thing all of them must have on the mind. If anything happens to Mister Shaw from America, his collection of van Zee letters is likely to wind up with the police."

The salon of Jean-Pierre's mama, the dowager countess, was held in her town house on the Île Saint-Louis, that picturesque bit of real estate in the middle of the Seine. Grete and I made a strategically late entrance among the company, and Grete, playing the chaste damsel on my orders, was enough to set the already overheated Jean-Pierre back on his heels. *"Incroyable,"* he murmured at the sight of this vision.

Upstairs in the grand reception room, however, we were received with considerably less warmth. No great surprise. This was not merely High Society, as Vahna Rouart-Rochelle must have resentfully put it to her nonpedigreed husband, it was the Highest, hence the only one for a daughter of Siamese nobility to attain to, never mind her plebian marriage.

By the time we came to the dowager countess, I knew I had my work cut out for me. Jean-Pierre's mama was tall, handsome, snowy haired, and with the hard eyes and tight lips of one always in command. There was no rise in the temperature as Jean-Pierre imaginatively set forth my credentials—my family among the foremost in America, my father once an honored envoy to France—and, in fact, there was even a further drop in it when, in answer to the direct question from my hostess, I explained that at present I was engaged in the making of a motion picture.

"Indeed?" the lady said with distaste.

"Yes. It will portray what's happened to a world which once existed—that happy world our ancestors bequeathed us and which modern generations have shattered into fragments. Have you ever felt, Madame, that today we're living in a second Rome, the barbarians already inside the gates?"

The hardness of Madame's eyes was softening. "Who of any breeding would not feel this, young man?"

Peripherally, I saw Jean-Pierre and Grete receding from us hand in hand. It was an encouraging sight. "Madame," I said, "one may expect an American to approve this new barbarism, but—forgive me —so many of your own countrymen seem to share this approval. Or is that too harsh a judgment?"

"No, no." Madame now had my wrist in a tight grip. She drew me down beside her on a settee. Someone imposingly white-bearded approached us and addressed her, and she irritably waved him away. "Young man," she said to me, then shook her head in self-deprecation. "But my son informed me of your name. David, is it not?"

"It is."

"Then let me tell you, David, I know that contemptible breed you must have encountered in France. All descended from those pawnbrokers who bought their titles from the scandalous third Napoleon. What is more—"

After that, all I had to do was listen.

When Madame and I made our farewells she suggested that if, despite the press of my work, I could manage a visit to the château at Chaumont, I might find her ancestral home worth the viewing.

"I'm sure I would, Madame. But do I have your word that you'll accept my hospitality in return?"

"I am not often in Paris, David—an unbearable place really—but yes, I feel we have much to discuss with each other. I trust he'll forgive me for saying it, but I wish my son were more like you."

Downstairs, Jean-Pierre, a proprietary arm around Grete, said to me, "You know, my mother seems quite infatuated with you. How the devil did you manage that?"

"By letting her know the truth," I said. "That I'm quite infatuated with her."

The Rolls was parked on the embankment side of the street, Harry, in decorous gray livery, already holding its door open when Grete and I crossed over to it. He saw us seated, then got behind the wheel.

"Hold it," said Grete. She pointed down the block and said to me, "That's Jean-Pierre's car. The little red one."

"Very nice."

"Yes. Well, there's something I want to get straight with you, only I don't know how you'll take it."

I said, "Jean-Pierre invited you to dinner this evening. So far you haven't said yes or no. If it's yes, he'll find you waiting in that little red car."

"Close," said Grete. "But it's more than dinner. His mother has this big place in the country. He thinks that while she's in town here he and I could drive out and have a weekend there. But I don't know how you feel about it."

"How do you feel about him?"

"I like him. But not as much as getting into the movies. So if you say no, that's all there is to it."

"Then all I have to say is that from now on you'd better have your own room at the hotel. When do you expect to be back in town?"

"Monday morning, Jean-Pierre said."

"Make it Sunday night. Because early Monday, Oscar and I are going to Brussels on business, and I want you along."

I watched as she went down the street switching those hips in the glare of the Rolls's headlights and saw Jean-Pierre leaving the house to join her even before she reached his car.

Pawn had taken knight, no trouble at all.

Early Monday morning Costello joined me for coffee and a final briefing. He handed me a slip of paper. "On top is a café address in Brussels. You pick up our agency man there, and he'll take you to the school and point out the kid. How old would she be anyhow?"

"Sarah? About sixteen."

"Old enough to have her own opinions about this, but that's your problem." He pointed at the paper. "Her mama's down there too. Emmaline Bell. Macclesfield Street, London. A couple of cheap rooms over a Chink restaurant."

"Money troubles?"

"Last show she was in closed six months ago. And she's into her law firm for a thousand pounds. Bills she ran up going to court about the kid. I've got copies of the bills if you want them."

"No need. Just copies of the van Zee letters."

"All ready and packed," said Costello.

Grete, looking as if she had put in a hard weekend, slept in the front seat of the limousine through the entire trip. Oscar, in back with me, talked most of the way, starting with the question of why we were embarked on this expedition. "All right, so van Zee mentioned the kid in those letters, she might still have contact with him, it's worth checking out. But a part in the picture for her, Dave? Why?"

"Authenticity."

"The documentary quality? Look, Dave—"

"I like the idea, Oscar."

He recognized his master's voice. "Well, if you feel that way about it—"

We held close to schedule. At twelve-fifteen we picked up the Detec agent at his café and were at the school with time to spare. It was on rue Melsens, a weatherworn building next to an even more weatherworn church.

Harry and the agent took their positions on the sidewalk, and when a covey of uniformed girls spilled through the school door I watched the agent point out our mark to Harry and depart. Harry, cap in hand, moved toward a girl and addressed her. Sarah Leewarden had grown in inches, apparently without adding an ounce to that narrow frame. The elongated look of her and the lank blond hair reminded me of those illustrations of Alice in Wonderland after she had shot up in height above her surroundings, except that this Alice wore thick eyeglasses.

She seemed bewildered by what Harry was saying, then aimed the eyeglasses in the direction of the limousine. I opened the door. "Miss Leewarden?"

She walked over and stooped to get me in focus. "Yes?"

"I'm David Shaw, Miss Leewarden. Of Shaw Film Productions in the United States."

"I'm very pleased to meet you," she said mechanically.

"And it's a happy meeting for me. This gentleman is Oscar Wylie, the film director. The young lady is Miss Grete Hansen who'll appear in the picture we're now making."

Oscar grunted his greetings, Grete turned to nod hers. Sarah disregarded Oscar; she seemed transfixed by the sight of Grete. "Grete Hansen." Her voice rose. "Grete Hansen? But you were in the newspapers here!" Those nearsighted eyes returned to me, the light of wonder in them. "You're that David Shaw, aren't you? The one searching for the missing writer."

"I am. And to explain your part in the search, I'd like you to read this." I reached out to hand her the van Zee letter, then indicated that there was room on the seat beside me. She was tempted but shook her head. "Thank you, but I'll read it here, if you don't mind."

As soon as she started reading her face turned pink. When at the very end she looked startled, I knew that the meaning of the signature had penetrated. "Van Zee," she said. "The writer you're looking for."

"Right."

"But I didn't realize—I mean, when we met he just called himself Jan."

"But you do recall that meeting."

"Oh yes." She shrugged broadly. "But the rest of this letter—the impression I seem to have made on him. I don't know how. Really, I was such a kid."

"That's your opinion. Obviously, he found you an extraordinarily mature and perceptive kid."

Oscar leaned forward. "Look," he said to Sarah, "what it comes down to is whether you can give us any lead to him."

"I'm afraid not. I only met him that once."

"Oh, fine," Oscar said sourly. He looked at me. "Well?"

I glanced at my watch. "Thoughtless of me," I said to Sarah, "taking up your lunch hour this way. So, although Mr. Wylie and Miss Hansen must now get back to their hotel, I'd like you to be my guest at lunch. Your helping me find van Zee is only part of the reason I'm here. You see, since his brief contact with you was so deeply meaningful to him, Mr. Wylie and I want to make use of it in our film. And, if possible, with your playing the role of the younger Sarah. Right, Oscar?"

"It was a thought," Oscar acknowledged ungraciously.

Sarah looked from one to the other of us. "Me?" she said.

"Yes. Can we discuss it over lunch? The chauffeur will drop us off any place you choose."

"Across the street," said Sarah in a daze. "I mean, that's where we all go to eat."

Downstairs across the street turned out to be noisy and crowded, but upstairs there was comparative quiet. I ordered *poulet rôti,* the national bird of the Low Countries. Sarah ordered *gauffre Bruxelles* and was delivered a waffle sheathed in crystallized sugar and piled high with whipped cream and syrup. She abstractedly put away a spoonful, still clutching the letter in her other hand. "Please," she said, "I really don't understand about your wanting me in your movie. Are you serious about that?"

"Completely. After all, van Zee wrote that you dreamed of becoming an actress. And that your mother is Emmaline Bell. In professional circles she's regarded as a marvelously talented actress. I'm sure she'd be enthusiastic about your getting a start in her profession this way."

"But she has nothing to say about it. And my father—"

"Yes?"

"Well, there was a most awful divorce, and the court awarded me to Daddy—I mean, they made Mummy look dreadfully tawdry and unworthy—and now he's quite rabid on the subject of show business."

"But you're not a child any more. You should have some choice of career, shouldn't you?"

"I know. And I did so want to go into the performing arts. But who's to pay for what I want? Mummy certainly can't." She looked panicky. "Look, if Daddy suspected I was sitting here with someone in films—"

"Then he mustn't ever suspect. Now tell me something. Are you in touch with your mother?"

"Well," Sarah said uneasily, "it's a most desperate secret, but once a month she comes to Brussels and we meet here in the central library."

"The library? A pretty conspicuous place for a secret meeting, isn't it?"

"I suppose. But then I can tell Daddy truthfully that I was in the library. Anyhow, Mummy and I stay out of sight in the stacks and just talk."

"And you get along well with her?"

"Oh yes. She's a darling."

"All right. Now listen very carefully. If it could be arranged for you to move in with your mother on short notice—and with a contract from me that would help settle all financial problems—

would you have the courage to make that move?"

"A contract?" Her fork, a piece of waffle harpooned on it, remained poised midway to her mouth. Then she set the fork down and clasped her hands in agony. "Oh God, yes, I'd want to do it. But I couldn't. Don't you see, there's that court order—"

"I give you my word it won't be any obstacle."

"But what if I can't act? All I've done so far are school plays."

"That's my risk."

"And there's Daddy to consider. I'm not sure you'll understand, but he's frightfully dependent on me in some ways. And all this is so sudden really. Must it be settled right now?"

That strained face across the table from me. That syrupy mess on the plate before her. That was what she had been feasting on three years ago in the little restaurant in Bruges. And suddenly here was Anneke beside her, Anneke proudly saying *"Mijn man"* as I drew up a chair next to hers, slipping her arm through mine, delighted that now I had—clever Jan—obtained a car and would soon be taking her south to the Mediterranean sunshine.

Here she was, and even though I knew there was no longer any Anneke, that all that was left of her was a handful of ashes nurturing a stand of trees in a Luxembourg valley, I could feel her arm pressing hard against me while a horrid stench of burning cloth and flesh rose to my nostrils, choking me.

"What is it?" Sarah said in alarm. "Are you ill?"

"No, no. I'm all right."

"But the way you look—"

"Pressure, that's all. My line of work invites it. Like this matter of your signing a contract with me."

"Yes, that. Really, I must have time to think about it."

I controlled the impulse to grab those narrow shoulders and shake them until her head rattled. Instead, I reached out my hand and rested it on hers. She gave a little start, and again there was that surge of color to her cheeks. "I'm sorry," I said, "but I've got an enormous investment in this picture and every day's delay adds to it. Every hour, in fact. So you have to decide right now. Say the word, and tomorrow morning I'll be in London making the necessary arrangements. Otherwise—"

"Arrangements? What arrangements are those?"

"First," I said, "I must have your decision."

Sarah drew a deep breath. "You know, I've never in my whole life had the chance to decide on anything important to do with me."

"Now's the time," I said.

I made it to my hotel on Grand' Place on foot and found a message waiting. Telephone M. Costello in Paris, s.v.p.

Costello wasted no words. "How did it go?"

"Fine."

"London tomorrow?"

"Yes."

"All right, now here's Williams with something to tell you. I'll get back on the line after he's done."

Miller Williams sounded apprehensive. "Well, Mr. Shaw, about those shares you held in transatlantic airlines—"

"Held?"

"That's what I must explain. A little while ago—bank opening time in Miami—the brokerage department there called me. Both *The New York Times* and *Wall Street Journal* had stories this morning about federal action being planned against every one of those airlines whose shares we hold for paying illegal rebates to travel agencies."

"I see. Well, if you've put in a sell order on that stuff, Miller, you did the smart thing."

Over the line came what I took to be a heartfelt sigh. "I'm glad you feel that way, Mr. Shaw. Now here's Mr. Costello."

A few moments later, Costello said to me, "I had to get him out of the way. Are you alone?"

"Yes."

"Maybe. For all you know, a certain Dutchman could be leaning against your door right now."

I said impatiently, "What's on your mind, Ray? Let's have it."

"Sure. Gardiner Fremont is dead. The hard way."

"What happened to him?"

"Well, he's been holed up in Brussels there with Detec guys on him around the clock. Last night about eleven, the man on him— Chiasson's his name—sees him come out of his boarding house and get into a cab. He follows along and they wind up in a neighborhood —wait, I've got it down here—Chaussée de Mons. You know that section?"

"Yes. A warehouse district."

"That's it. Anyhow, the cab stops in front of an old warehouse, Fremont goes inside, the cab waits. After awhile, the cabbie goes in and then comes running out yelling for the cops. It seems Fremont walked into an elevator except the elevator wasn't there. He landed on the bottom of the shaft all busted up. The cops combed the building and couldn't find anybody there, so they put it down as an accident. You and I know different, don't we? Especially since there's a back way out of that building."

"But what makes you so sure it was Baar? What about the other two?"

"All accounted for. No, Davey, this was the Dutchman's job. That means he was close to you last night and he still could be. I want to be there too. So hold off on the London trip until I am."

"What do you plan to do when you're here? Stand around and look menacing?"

"That might not hurt, Davey. This baby is a killer. And whether or not he's worried those van Zee letters might go public, you're crowding him hard."

"Stay where you are, Ray," I said and replaced the phone on its stand.

I pulled off my shoes, then switched out the room light. Silently, I made my way through the darkness to the hall door and flung it open.

Nobody.

At least, not yet.

Piccadilly Circus. Shaftesbury Avenue. Theaters; cheap eating places; electronic musical instruments; porno shops; porno movie houses, the gaudiest of them featuring *Danish Delights* which, from its title, might be a Leewarden production turned out at the Copenhagen works by the multitalented Marie-Paule Neyna.

A right turn, a snail's crawl through traffic for two blocks while I tried to stop my mind from racing through the moves of the game about to be played, and at last, thank God, here was Macclesfield Street. No parking place in sight, so Harry double-parked. It was noticeable that passing drivers, no matter how loudly wrathful about this obstruction, gave the Rolls room to spare in passing it.

Emmaline Bell's flat was two flights up a rickety stairway that smelled of cooking oil. The woman who opened its door was in bulky sweater and slacks. About forty, with tight little coppery curls close to the head and an amusing face.

"Miss Bell?"

"For better or worse." The voice was surprisingly deep. "Is that your car down below? That loverly, old-ivory number?"

"I believe it is."

"Well, I'm sorry to report there's a bobby standing there preparing to do something about it."

"That's all right," I said. "The chauffeur'll take care of it." I handed her my card and she scanned it nearsightedly. "Film Productions, Incorporated," she recited. "What beautiful words. Film magnates are always welcome here, especially the solvent. You are solvent, Mr. Shaw, aren't you?"

"Very."

"Good for you. That isn't true of all your colleagues, you know, and I'm the girl with the half-healed scars to prove it." She stood aside to let me in and with a broad gesture motioned me to an armchair. "I trust that handsome attaché case contains a script with an Oscar-winning part for me?"

"Sorry, Miss Bell. My business here concerns your daughter."

Her face went white. "Something's happened to Sarah?"

"Not at all. She's fine. You have my word on it."

"Then what—?"

"Look," I said, "do you recall a news item about a million-dollar production that's bogged down because a young Dutchman has turned up missing? Something you might have read lately in the trade papers?"

"Young Dutchman?" She pressed her fingertips to her brow. "Wait. I think so. An untutored genius of sorts? There's supposed to be a vast search going on for him?"

"There is a vast search going on for him. I know, because as producer of that picture I happen to be leading it."

"Seriously?"

"Very seriously, considering the amount of money I've invested in the production. Getting down to cases, the missing man—his name is Jan van Zee—has already been paid a large amount for his story material. My mistake was in giving him final script approval. And now that I'm ready to roll—"

"No van Zee. But what does Sarah have to do with it?"

I said, "All the van Zee material was in a series of autobiographical letters he sent me over the years. Sarah popped up in one of them, and yesterday I had a meeting with her about it. Not in the company of her father who so far knows nothing about this. The reason for that bit of evasion, I think, will interest you."

"There, Mr. Shaw, is the understatement of the century."

"I know what you mean. And I'll let the van Zee letters do the explaining." I handed her the packet. "The first one tells of a chance meeting between Sarah and van Zee three years ago. All the others concern her father. Take your time with them."

I kept an eye on her as, hunched over on a rump-sprung couch, she did her reading. Her concentration on those pages was so fierce that after awhile it didn't seem likely she knew I was there.

When she was finished she remained in a brown study. "All clear now?" I said, to bring her out of it.

"I don't know. Are you sure this stuff about Simon is true?"

"Every word."

"But it's incredible. Dear God, if you'd seen that man stand up in court and tell the world of my pathetic little *affaire,* of the menace this made me to my daughter—Mister Simon-Sanctimonious-Lee-warden with his porno films and smuggling and God knows what else—and not only the court believing he was the unsullied little prig he seemed to be, but damn it, I believed it too!"

"Now you know better," I said.

"But too late!" The deep voice vibrated with outrage. "That poor kid. All those years of his hypocritical bilge. Now she's not even a kid any more. There's no way of ever making up for it."

"But there is," I said. "And you still haven't heard the whole story. I have an agency on the hunt for van Zee, and the evidence it's turned up points in one direction. Going by that evidence and by the last letter I ever received from van Zee—it was written in Zurich just before he was to start on a smuggling trip to Luxembourg for your ex-husband and his partners—well, I'm now convinced that he was done away with."

"Murdered?"

"Yes. As he himself put it, he had learned too much about the operation. And this Luxembourg run offered them a perfect opportunity to get rid of him."

"And you really believe Simon had a part in that?"

"Yes."

"But why come to me? Isn't this police business?"

"It will be as soon as I piece together the final bits of evidence.

That's what this is all about, Miss Bell. Until I met Sarah, I planned to swing the ax and let the chips fall where they may. After that meeting, I realized that I didn't want any of those chips to land on her."

"Oh God, no. I didn't think of that."

"I did. And so far, Sarah knows nothing about any of this."

"So far." Emmaline frowned at me. "That doesn't sound very promising. You mean that sooner or later—"

"No. Not if she'll leave her father right now and come live with you. Under those conditions it's possible she'll never know the worst about him. And once she's under your wing, I'll feel free to take action against him. Under any conditions, I must take action quickly, and I intend to."

"I understand that. But have her leave him without telling her the truth? Not only will Simon do anything to prevent that, but there's her own feelings to stand in the way. She knows she's the one human being on earth he's devoted to, and that makes her dreadfully defenseless against him. But"—Emmaline tapped a finger on the packet of letters—"if I were to confront Simon with these—"

"He'd promptly take off for parts unknown," I said. "With Sarah."

"Would he?" She weighed this. "Yes, I suppose he would."

She was at the point where I wanted her. Eyes teary, hands fluttering, she was ready to grasp at any straw. I said, "But what if I told you that when I spoke to Sarah yesterday she made it plain that she's now ready to make the move, never mind how her father felt about it?"

"She told you that?"

"She did. So now, Miss Bell, it's all up to you. It's very simple really. Tomorrow, at twelve-thirty, Sarah will be waiting outside her school. You'll arrive there in that ivory-colored job now parked below, with my chauffeur at the wheel. Tomorrow evening, you and Sarah will have dinner together in this apartment."

Emmaline looked dazed. "But Simon—"

"I'm meeting with him tomorrow. After that meeting, he'll be completely out of the picture. Take my word for it, there won't be any court action, any difficulties at all for you or Sarah."

"But it's all so incredible!"

"Not at all, if you leave everything to me."

"The return from Brussels?"

"The car and driver are yours until you're back here. To make sure you're on schedule getting there, you should leave for Brussels right now. A hotel room there has already been reserved for you overnight. The chauffeur knows exactly what's to be done and how it's to be done. So much for that side of it. But there is a side of it you may find a bit uncomfortable."

"Yes?" Emmaline said.

"Naturally, I lied to Sarah about my motive in all this. I told her that since she had made such an impact on van Zee, I wanted her to play a part in the film. In fact, wanted her under contract to me. That not only settled the question of my motives but helped solve another problem."

"Which is?"

"The matter of money, Miss Bell. Sarah's coming to you without dowry, so to speak. It'll cost money to keep up with her."

"I'll manage, thank you."

"Don't be a fool," I said. "Just swallow your pride and settle for your daughter's well-being." I handed her the check and accompanying letter. "That, should Sarah raise the question, is in payment for her services whether or not they're called on. It's made out to you, of course. And my signed letter of agreement. It doesn't matter that it's neither legal nor binding, since it's for Sarah's mental ease only."

Emmaline looked at the check. She looked at me. "Ten thousand pounds?" she said incredulously.

"It's worth at least that much to me."

"But ten thousand?" She was not, however, thrusting it back at me. "At least let me offer you a drink in return for it."

I went down the stairs two highly emotional drinks later, and Harry leaned through the window of the car as I approached. "All set, sir?"

"All set. She'll be down very soon."

"Yes, sir. I'll phone you tomorrow right on the dot."

If he said he would, he would.

Walking through Soho on my way back to the Berkeley Regal, I suddenly found myself in the throes of that schizophrenia which, given enough impetus, would come on me now and then without warning. That uncertainty about whether I was David Shaw or Jan van Zee or both or neither. It was so acute now that when I skirted the familiar little park and saw a trio against its railings, two heavily bearded, youthful males, one wild-haired, stringy, very youthful female huddled over a well-remembered ritual—it might have been painted by Cézanne and titled *The Lighting of the Joint*—I would not have been surprised to find, if I looked closer, that one of the males was Jan van Zee.

The *crise d'identité* faded as I got clear of Soho, passed away completely when I reached Berkeley Street. But I still had a surprise coming. In the hotel lobby there was Costello seated near the entrance.

He saw me and came to his feet with an effort, the ruddiness of his face replaced by a sallow gray-green, the eyes bleary. "I couldn't get into your room," he said. "Let's get up there quick so I can lay down."

"Stoned or hung-over?" I asked.

"Neither. It's that goddam English Channel. How'd it go with the kid's mama?"

"As planned. She and Harry are on their way now."

I convoyed him up to the suite and saw him stretched out on the bed in Harry's room. It was after pulling off the first shoe against his feeble protest that I realized why he had taken the boat-train instead of a plane. A fistula showed on the stout calf beneath the trouser leg. When I hauled up the cuff I saw a holster strapped to the leg, a gun butt protruding from it. Boarding a plane, the metal detector would have sounded that out.

I unstrapped the holster and held it up before him. "Sorry to say if you're not going back by boat, you'll have to get rid of it."

"I know. I'll dump it before I take the plane because I'm sure as hell not getting back on that boat. I'll dig up another gun in Paris now that I know where to dig."

I locked the gun in his bag. "Meanwhile," I said, "how's the opposition doing?"

Costello showed a flickering sign of life. "One in particular. You told that Avril at Choochoo's to look into any mail coming from out of the country, right? So there was a letter from Copenhagen. Marie-Paule Neyna. Your mission lady from way back. Now guess who the new owner of that whorehouse is?"

"Marie-Paule?"

"None other. She's taking over next month and she expects Choochoo out by then. Dead or alive, I guess. You know, Davey, that's a big money deal, not the kind you'd figure for hired help like Marie. And the Dutchman was not only Choochoo's connection in the old days, he now has a million bucks in cash to play around with. How's chances he's the new owner and Marie is just a front?"

I said, "That would mean he's trusting her with his money."

"He could be."

"If he is, Ray, they're a lot tighter little team than I ever suspected."

"Then maybe they are," said Costello.

He was still asleep when I woke early next morning, so, not to disturb him, I had breakfast downstairs in the dining room and then did St. James's Park. A typical springtime day for London, scudding clouds with patches of Wedgewood blue showing among them, spatters of rain alternating with sunshine. I had brought the remnants of my breakfast toast, and on the footbridge where Anneke used to feed the untrusting sparrows she patiently lured to her outstretched hand, I now fed them.

When I got back to the hotel Costello was at breakfast. He said with his mouth full, "I just checked with the agency. Leewarden's in his office now, and he'll be there until one. When do we leave?"

"We?"

"I'm coming along for the laughs," said Costello.

That was one way of looking at it.

Noontime Oxford Street was, as ever, solidly packed with shoppers, and it took an effort to work our way through the crowds to the storefront marked *Leewarden Tours, Ltd.* Inside, a girl at the counter said that Mr. Leewarden's office was upstairs. "Expecting you?" she asked, picking up a phone.

"Just possibly. Tell him it's Mr. Rouart-Rochelle."

I started upstairs, Costello on my heels, before she made her call. When I pushed open the office door Leewarden was standing behind his desk, the same bald, middle-aged Bertie Wooster Leewarden. An outraged Bertie. "I thought I made it plain—!" he snarled, and then got the full view of his company. "Who the devil are you?"

Costello pushed the door shut behind us and leaned back against it looking grim. "My associate, Mr. Costello," I said. "I am David Shaw."

"But that name you gave my girl—"

"Yves Rouart-Rochelle?"

"Whatever it was." Leewarden was trying to pull himself together and not doing too well at it. "I don't know anyone by that name. Don't know you, for that matter. And I'm not interested in whatever game you're up to."

I dropped the packet of letters on his desk. "Evidence to the contrary, Simon. Exhibit A. Read them."

"I don't see why."

"Because if you don't, they'll be mailed at once to the Los Angeles police. By now Los Angeles must have found that it has a million dollars less in its bank account than it should have. It might like to know why."

The shot hit dead center. Leewarden sagged into his swivel chair and picked up the packet. It was fascinating to watch him apply himself with growing horror to page after page of his own story. He wound up a sweating lump of misery.

"Blackmail," he said bitterly. "Film producer, the newspapers said. But blackmail is the game, isn't it?"

"No."

"Oh, there's a load of cod's-wallop," he jeered. "Then why bring this stuff to me? Why wasn't it brought straightway to the authorities?"

"Because the newspaper stories were right, Simon. I've got a few hundred thousand sunk in this van Zee film. Without him, it all goes down the drain. And the authorities can't seem to locate him. I think you can."

179

"Then think again, because I don't know where the devil he is."

I said, "What about the gent who seems to be the brains of the act? Kees Baar? Tell me where to locate him, and maybe he can come up with the answer."

"Locate him? Nobody locates him. He comes and goes as he damn well chooses, and where he is in between I don't know."

I said, "For a man involved in large-scale crime, you don't know much, do you, Simon?"

"That's very sharp of you, Mr. Shaw. I don't know anything. And since I'm done with operating on that side of the fence, what would you say to just packing it in with me? I have a feeling that for your own good reasons you're not all that anxious to make this a police matter anyway."

"My own good reasons. That intrigues me, Simon. Now what could those reasons be?"

He was growing bolder. "Well, what do you have to show to the police really? A stack of letters from some Dutch crackpot? It would just be his word against mine, wouldn't it?"

I reopened the attaché case and drew out the folder prepared for this moment. "Exhibit B. A detailed report from the detective agency I put on the case. It seems that one of their men—no crackpot either—was back to back with you at dinner in Brussels when you and Yves and an American named Fremont had a meeting there. Fremont made painful demands. Very soon after, he met death by violence. Can you see how gratified the Brussels police would be by Exhibit B? Look it over, Simon."

He didn't want to, that was clear. But ashen-faced, his hands trembling, he couldn't keep himself from picking it up and examining it. Then he placed it carefully on the desk. "What a bloody mess," he whispered. He shook his head numbly. "What a bloody mess it's been from the start. If the banks had only seen me through—"

"The banks? What did they have to do with it?"

"Nothing. That was the bloody trouble. When I hit the rocks financially they all refused me a loan and I had to go elsewhere. And the man I went to put Baar on me."

"Baar loaned you money?"

"He loaned me nothing. He got me to use the travel agency for smuggling. Tourist parties go through customs easily, see? And it worked very nicely for a while. Then when customs tightened up because of all this terrorism around he set up the porno film thing in Copenhagen. You're in the film business. You know those cans marked *Undeveloped Film. Do Not Open.* Well, it looked like a foolproof way of moving the stuff. Then that got risky too, so Baar found this mechanic who could rig up a car that was safe against any search."

"Jago."

"That's right. Jago. And van Zee was taken on to do the driving. But if anyone had known he was writing it all down just to turn an extra penny—"

"Twenty thousand dollars so far," I said.

"Thirty pieces of silver is how I see it. But the question is what happens now. All I can say is I'm out of the racket for good, and unless you want to be bloody righteous about my past sins, you can say good-by to me and let it go at that."

"Except for one thing." I had him chained to the post, the kindling piled high around him. I thrust the torch into it. "Your daughter."

"My daughter? What the bloody hell does she have to do with this?"

"A great deal. I don't think you're a proper father for a kid like that. And if your courts get a look at these letters, they'd have to agree with me about it, wouldn't they?"

He gaped at me. "Where do you have the right to talk like that? What do you know about my kid?"

"I met her two days ago. Took her to lunch in fact. But if you're worried that I let slip any of your little secrets to her, rest assured I haven't."

"Oh? And I'm supposed to thank you for that? Well, all I'll thank you for is keeping your distance from that girl from now on. A long distance, understand?"

I nodded understanding. "When it comes to Sarah you're not to be trifled with."

"That's it, Mister. Try it, and you'll soon find out for yourself."

"You mean," I said, "you're challenging me to turn you over to the police?"

The bravado oozed out of him. He hunched forward trying to read my face. "Cat and mouse, that's your game, isn't it? But why? For God's sake, just tell me why?"

"For Sarah's sake. What with one thing and another, Simon, I've decided that she's best off with her mother."

"*You've* decided?"

"Yes." I glanced at my watch. "Any moment now," I said, "you'll be getting a call from Sarah. That's to notify you of her change of address."

"I don't believe you!"

I disregarded this. "Now listen carefully, Simon, because if you make one little slip during that call, Sarah will be told the whole dirty story of her loving daddy. It's as simple as that. That means you're to let her know you understand her decision to change homes, it's probably better this way, good wishes and farewell."

He looked like a fish just out of the water, his mouth opening and closing in an effort to bring out the words. Finally he did. "My ex-wife put you up to this, didn't she? And you went for it because you're soft on that bitch. Well, I'm not going to—!"

"Yes, you will," I cut in pleasantly. "And nobody put me up to it. But if you can tell me why Jan van Zee dropped out of sight so completely and where he is now—"

"I swear I don't know!"

"Well then," I said, and as if on cue the phone rang. I snatched it up before Leewarden could. "Mr. Shaw?" said Harry.

"It is."

"Everything's A-O.K., sir. We're back at the hotel now. Miss Leewarden's right here."

"Good. Put her on."

I held out the phone to Leewarden, and he grasped it as if trying to squeeze it out of shape. "Sarah?" He sagged so far forward that the mouthpiece almost rested on the desk. "Yes?" There was a long silence from him, while from the phone came the sibilance of the voice at the other end. "Yes," said Leewarden at last. "Yes, I understand . . . Yes . . . No, it isn't as if it were a stranger . . . Yes, that's it, I suppose. Take care of yourself."

He sat back staring at the wall, the phone still in his hand emitting a loud hum. All devoured by the flames now. The only thing left of him was that croaking voice. "Five years." He looked at me, not really seeing me. "Five years of being bloody father and mother and everything else to her. Tomorrow she won't remember who I am."

"Possibly," I said. "And don't try to remind her of it, Simon. No communication from your end, because I won't take that kindly. Do you understand?"

"Yes." His voice was barely louder than that incessant humming from the phone. "Why don't you clear out?" he said lifelessly. "Just clear out."

In the hallway Costello said to me, "Feel better?"

"Yes."

"The way he took it," said Costello. "Any chance of his going out of that window?"

"No. I think that as soon as he pulls himself together he'll be on the phone with Yves, spilling this whole thing. Or possibly Baar."

Costello shook his head. "He's stupid if he does anything like that. He has to know they'd only start wondering how much he told you."

"Yes," I said, "they would, wouldn't they?"

Harry reported back to the Berkeley Regal in the early evening. "Went smooth as silk, sir," he said in answer to my question. "That Miss Bell is sure a likable lady, sir."

"She is. By the way, Mr. Costello's taken your room. You won't have trouble lining up another, will you?"

"No trouble at all, sir."

There never was, with Harry.

When I walked next door I found Costello at the phone. He said into it, "Hold on," then said to me, "Williams in Paris. He just now got an invitation for you from the royalty."

I took the phone. "Miller, is that invitation to the Château de Liasse?"

"That's right, Mr. Shaw. For the coming weekend."

"Then call there and accept it on my behalf. And let them know I'll be bringing a young lady. Now I want some information. What's the value of those Rouart-Rochelle notes we hold?"

"Well, the face value is two hundred and forty thousand. Dollars, that is. But there's accumulated unpaid interest that brings it to about three hundred thousand."

"All right, call in those notes first thing tomorrow. Immediate payment in full demanded, no holds barred."

"No holds barred, Mr. Shaw? I don't—"

"That means, Miller, that if Mr. Rouart-Rochelle doesn't make payment at once, I'm starting court proceedings against him next week. Let him know it, and, if the question comes up, you can also let him know who I am."

I put down the phone, and Costello said with relish, "Poor Frenchy. The smuggling racket busted, Leewarden in his hair, and now the sheriff's coming down the road to foreclose on the old homestead."

"What was that about Leewarden?"

"I just got word from the agency that he hopped a plane and walked in on Frenchy an hour ago. Which makes him as stupid as he looks."

"And Vahna? Any signs she'll be showing up here tomorrow?"

"That we won't know until the morning. If she sticks to her weekly routine, she will. But moving in on her might be tricky. Remember, this is no sixteen-year-old kid itching to get into the movies. And then there's the watchdog. The sister-in-law."

I said, "What do you have on the watchdog?"

Costello flipped through his index cards and extracted a few from the deck. "The Frenchy file." He scanned the cards. "Madame Max Denoyer. Was Yvonne Thérèse Rouart-Rochelle. No known connection with any of Frenchy's rackets."

"How about her husband? What's his line of work?"

"Insurance. Commercial and personal. He looks to be a straight arrow though. Clean all the way. You want a set of the letters to show him?"

"No, you just gave me a better angle to work on. That is if Vahna and Yvonne show up here tomorrow."

They did.

At ten the next morning, the pair took a plane for London. At noon, they registered in the Berkeley Regal. Midafternoon, I went down to the Unicorn Club in the bowels of the hotel to obtain my membership card.

The manager of the casino had evidently checked out my credit rating after my application was in. "A bit early," he beamed, "but if you'd like to be shown around—"

"I would like that."

At this time of day, the club offered a vast, thickly carpeted, heavily draped desolation. Inside its entrance, a dining area, a few waiters arranging settings. Beyond that, a display of gaming tables, one of which was attended by a couple being dealt blackjack. Roulette, I had gathered, was Vahna's game. I drifted over to the trio of roulette tables and took note that each bore a small card indicating the minimum stakes at it—50p—£1—£5. From Vahna's reputation, it seemed likely that when I came down in the evening I'd find her on that stool close by the croupier of the five-pound table.

At nine in the evening, the Detec man trailing her phoned up that she had entered the casino. At nine-thirty, I found the lady on the stool nearest the croupier of the five-pound table. At her elbow, obviously not taking part in the proceedings, was seated a thin, hard-featured, gray-haired little woman who had to be the duenna. When I fitted myself into the narrow remaining space beside her where she provided a barrier between her charge and me I saw with a sudden queasiness that Madame Denoyer bore a distinct resemblance to her ferret-faced brother Yves.

Vahna herself was still the exquisite Siamese doll of ten years before. Nothing showed in that flawless face as she made calculations on the chart before her and—so tiny that she had to stand on a rung of her stool to do it—reached out to scatter chips over the table with calculated abandon.

I watched the action for awhile, then held out a hundred-pound note to the croupier's cashier. "Color?" he said.

I leaned toward Madame Denoyer. "What does he mean?"

"He wishes to know the color you prefer to play. The checks. So there will be no confusion."

"Oh. Thank you." And when the cashier, now calling me sharply to attention, said, "Color, please?" I said anything lucky would do and, stacking the chips before me, again leaned toward Madame Denoyer. "This is my first time at it," I told her, "and I see you're not betting. Would you mind very much giving me an idea of what it's all about?"

Up to now she had looked bored to death. Now she came to life and, sotto voce, gave me a quick course in combinations and odds. At its conclusion, I said, "But it seems you can't do much betting on all those combinations with only a handful of chips, can you?"

"True. But at that table where the stakes are lower—"

"Might I have the pleasure of your company at that table?"

"I am sorry, but I am with this lady." She indicated the preoccupied and hardworking Vahna. "My—what is the word?—*belle soeur*. The wife of my brother."

"Sister-in-law. Oh well, in that case—"

Madame Denoyer's eyes opened wide as I detached two thousand pounds worth of very new and crisp bank notes from my money clip and exchanged them for chips. I remarked to her, "As they say in my business, it takes money to make money. The business, by the way, is motion pictures." I offered her a card from the gold-trimmed Mark Cross wallet. "The name is David Shaw."

She acknowledged the introduction with a dip of the head. "Madame Max Denoyer. Yvonne Denoyer."

"So pleased. But Max Denoyer?" I frowned. "Somehow I know that name."

"It is not an unusual name, Mr. Shaw."

"I suppose not." I considered the far wall of the room briefly then clapped a hand to my forehead. "I have it. Max Denoyer. On the rue de Rome in Paris."

Madame looked startled. "The rue de Rome you say?"

"Yes. My company is producing a picture in France, and of course a great deal of insurance is required. I have someone investigating some French agencies right now. I'm positive that one of the names on his list is of a Max Denoyer at that address."

Madame rested a hand on my arm. "I have a surprise for you. This Max Denoyer is my husband."

"You're joking."

"I assure you I am not." The grip on my arm tightened. "Forgive me for asking, but you have not yet made arrangements for the insurance?"

"No, not yet."

"And will you be in Paris soon?"

"Within a day or two." Madame's face brightened, but it clouded over when I shrugged regretfully and said, "But I'll only be on my way through to answer an invitation to a weekend house party out of town."

"Ah," said Madame, "but this urgent matter of the insurance where my husband could be of such help—"

"It'll have to wait. You see, the invitation is from a dear friend I wouldn't dare let down. Possibly you know her. Henriette de Liasse?"

"No," Madame said shortly, then did an almost comic double take. "Henriette de Liasse? La Comtesse de Liasse?"

"The Countess. Yes. She seems to regard me as a member of the family, so the weekend must be hers. And I don't really know if I can get back to Paris afterward."

I allowed Madame to unhappily digest this while I did some heavy betting on a series of losing combinations. I also allowed her to observe that I was paying very little attention to the wheel and a great deal to the profile of her lovely charge who, hard at work on her chart, was off in a world of her own. According to Kees Baar, the little lady with the chart was a fanatic worshiper of such authentic *aristos* as the de Liasse clan. If he had been wrong about that—

I placed my lips close to Madame Denoyer's ear. "You know, your sister-in-law is a remarkably beautiful woman. In my business one sees almost too many beautiful faces, but hers is absolutely unique. The star quality, we call it."

Madame's nostrils dilated. Glum the moment before, she was now plainly delighted to find this fish still on her line. "I must tell her that, Mr. Shaw. She will be pleased by the compliment."

"I hope so. And I've been wondering—if you won't think it rude on such short acquaintance—whether you two ladies would mind joining me at dinner now?"

"I should be pleased. As for Madame Rouart-Rochelle"—she cast a hard look at the oblivious Vahna, then said to her in French, "Pay attention a moment."

"Well?" said Vahna without raising her eyes from her chart.

"This expensive-looking type next to me is in a position to throw Max some highly profitable business. An American making a film in France." Her French shifted from genteel Faubourg Saint-Honoré to machine-gun Faubourg Saint-Denis. "He and I are already as thick as thieves, and now we're invited to dine with him.

He's got eyes for you, so I want you at the table. I put myself out enough for my precious brother with these wretched expeditions. I feel his wife owes me at least this small favor."

"Does she?" said Vahna. "And can you imagine how Yves would feel about this small favor?"

"Never mind that. This man is an intimate friend of the de Liasse family. He actually spends weekends with them at the château. Doesn't that interest you?"

It did. I sat there, the uncomprehending innocent, as the lady turned to get a full view of me. After due consideration, she smiled at me, a little curl of the lips which barely showed the edges of small, very white teeth. "How do you do?" she said graciously in the carefully modulated English of Henry Higgins's Eliza.

At the supper table—very little supper and a great deal of champagne—we all became thick as thieves together, and in the end a glassy-eyed Vahna opened her soul to me. Therein I saw the *Almanach de Gotha,* the society columns in glossy monthlies, and a bitterness that the lady's forebears—princes of the blood in Thailand —received small tribute for this in the barbaric Western world. She was not so drunk that she came right out with it and demanded to know how I, a lowborn American, should happen to be the pet of those whose lineage extended back to Charlemagne, but there were moments when she came very close.

I commiserated with her, I offered sympathy and wine in equal measure, and then I came out with it. "About this weekend at Chaumont," I said, "well, I've been wondering. I'm supposed to bring a young lady with me—no doubt to make a proper number at the table—but I've been so busy at my job I haven't thought to invite anyone yet."

"Yes?" said Vahna encouragingly.

"Forgive me, David," Madame Denoyer cut in. She turned to Vahna and said in French, "This is now going too far. You know Yves would foam at the mouth at the mere idea."

"Would he?" said Vahna, and there was that little smile again, but somehow chilling in its effect. "But you're the one who forced this handsome stranger on me. Could you deny that to Yves?"

"Let's not threaten each other, Vahna. Let's talk sense. I'll make a deal with you. Just arrange that our friend here delivers you to my apartment Monday after your weekend in Chaumont, so that Max can talk business with him then and there. Do that, and I'll do what I can with Yves."

"I can try. But what if I fail?"

"Look how our friend here is mooning at you. You can't possibly fail."

They both looked at me.

"Well," I said brightly, "can we get back to my question now? That little matter of my inviting someone to accompany me to Chaumont?"

Madame Denoyer reached out and patted my hand. "How rude of me to interrupt," she said. "Do tell us more about it."

The dreams, never bad in themselves, always made for a bad awakening. Again and again Anneke would become part of them, we would be together, and, strangely, never in a nightmarish situation. There would sometimes be surrealist episodes, but nothing that ever gave me the feeling of danger. But the awakenings were always a disaster, bringing each time the stunned awareness that there was no Anneke, there never again would be an Anneke.

Costello knew this and understood it, and his way of counteracting it whenever he woke me was to plunge immediately into the business at hand, deliberately snatching me past those bad minutes into wide-awake consideration of our strategy and tactics. He did this at noon, bringing me out of my sleep by gently poking my shoulder, and, as soon as I opened my eyes, by saying, "How'd you make out with her last night?"

"She'll be leaving with me Friday afternoon for Chaumont."

"Quick work. There's also news from the Paris end." He sat down heavily on the edge of the bed. "Nine o'clock this morning, Williams met with Frenchy about those IOU's. Sweated him good. Put in American money, the best Frenchy can offer right now is a hundred grand. For the remaining two hundred he wants a lot of time, but Williams kept saying no. Then Frenchy came up with something real interesting. He asked how about taking the house there as collateral until the two hundred G's is paid off."

"Williams didn't agree to that, did he?"

"No," Costello said with satisfaction, "our boy knows what he's doing when it comes to this kind of thing. He left it at that and went to records to check the title. And what do you think?"

"It's mortgaged right up to the chimneys."

"No mortgage at all. But Frenchy doesn't hold title to it. It's his wife's. His wedding present to her."

"Meaning," I said, "that if he wants to cash in on it, he has to get it back from her."

"Uh-huh. Any chance of that?"

"None," I said.

"Are you sure?"

I said, "She got half stoned last night and let her hair down. I heard enough to be sure about it. Incidentally, when Williams was talking to Yves did my name come into it?"

"You said it could, so it did. Frenchy wanted to know who was squeezing him for payment, so Williams told him. Which must have handed him a real jolt."

"Tomorrow he gets another," I said. "His wife isn't keeping her social success from him. She's letting him know about the big weekend before we leave for the château."

"Your idea?"

"Yes. The sister-in-law wanted to rig some kind of cover-up, but I let them know this could lead to a scandal involving the countess herself. That was out of the question."

"Poor Frenchy. You put him in the pot to stew and then hand him a ladle and tell him to baste himself."

"I wish to hell it was poor Kees Baar," I said. "Still no lead to him at all?"

"Possibilities. For one thing, Leewarden's standing by in Paris." Costello, the perfectionist, referred to an index card. "Hôtel Mazarin, rue de Vaugirard. For another thing, last night an old girl friend of yours, name of Marie-Paule Neyna, took the train from Copenhagen to Paris, and right now she's fixed up with a room in the same hotel. That puts the three of them in town together. They could be waiting for the Dutchman to show up and organize them against this weirdo Davey Shaw."

"Are you rating Marie-Paule as a full-fledged partner?"

Costello took his time lighting a cigar. He exhaled smoke through pursed lips. "When you were on their payroll, Davey, you settled for being hired help. But suppose Marie didn't? Does that make any sense?"

It suddenly made such sense that I could only stare blankly at its implications.

"Well, well," said Costello. "I seem to have struck a nerve."

"You have. When that money was hijacked all I could make of the one holding the gun on me was a skinny hand like a kid's, so I've been assuming it was some kid Baar cut in on the deal, risky as that was. But put everything together and it could have been Marie-Paule."

"I don't think it could have been," said Costello. "Put everything together, and I think it had to be."

I returned to Paris to find David Shaw Productions, Inc. in disarray.

Where, demanded Oscar, was this screwball van Zee? If the idea was to get the show on the road—

Miller Williams, anguished at the thought of refusing ready cash, argued that I must consider accepting the initial hundred thousand dollar payment from my debtor. Then, if a schedule of further payments could be drafted—

Grete, on her way to dinner in décolletage down to her navel, stopped by just long enough to ask what was being done about the publicity lately. Where were the photographers now? The only thing she had gotten the past week was a brief mention along with Jean-Pierre in some scandal sheet. Not that Jean-Pierre was happy about it, because the way things were with all his uptight relatives—

It was Yves Rouart-Rochelle, of all people, who provided consolation. I was sharing a whiskey nightcap with Costello when the phone rang.

"Mr. Shaw? Mr. David Shaw?"

There was no mistaking that soft and sibilant voice. More than once I had had the thought that if Yves were ever reduced to his essence, he would certainly emerge as a black mamba.

"Yes?" I said.

"I am Yves Rouart-Rochelle. I am sure we do not need elaborate introductions to each other."

"I'm sure we don't."

"Now I must meet with you. I can be at the Meurice within half an hour."

"Sorry, not tonight. I'm getting ready for bed now."

"Then tomorrow morning." A sharpness crept into the voice. "As early as possible. I leave the arrangements to you."

"I see. Has Madame Rouart-Rochelle told you that at four tomorrow afternoon I'm to drive her to the Château de Liasse for a weekend stay?"

"Yes." Yves bit it off hard. "She has."

"Fine. Then I'll arrive at your home a bit earlier for our meeting. That way, neither of us will suffer any inconvenience."

"Ah," said Yves as if he were struggling for air, "so you choose to be openly insulting, is that it?" His phone banged down hard enough to hurt my eardrum.

I put down my phone and sat there watching it.

"What happened?" said Costello.

"He hung up. I seem to have hurt his feelings."

"That's the good news. How about the bad news? Are you sure you didn't blow the chance to meet him?"

"Wait," I said.

The phone rang. I let it ring a few more times before I picked it up. "Yes?"

"Tomorrow at three," snarled Yves. "At my home."

Well before the hour Harry laid out the wardrobe for my weekend, packed my bags, and saw to it that I was wholly presentable. It struck me that Harry, having been informed that our destination was the château of a certified, blue-blooded countess, was giving every indication that he was at least as much a social climber as Vahna Rouart-Rochelle.

It was a maid who opened the door of the Rouart-Rochelle home to me and then scurried upstairs to bring the word to the master.

I was kept waiting awhile—a test of nerve?—and then here was Yves, a small, somberly clad thundercloud. He looked acutely ill. Haggard, with dark patches under the eyes, a pronounced wattling of the jowls, and shrunken into his clothes as if, despite that pot belly, he had suddenly lost considerable weight. "Mr. Shaw," he said, not offering his hand.

And then, prematurely, here was Madame coming down the broad staircase, the loveliest of Siamese dancers descending the temple steps, the weight of a luxurious sable coat lightly borne by one slender arm, a Vuitton jewel case in that childlike hand. "My dear David," she said, far more joyously than the occasion required.

Yves wheeled on her in an eruption of hard-boiled French. *"Votre beau mâle, hein? Ça n'a pas de nom!"* which in recklessly describing me as her glamor boy and the situation he confronted as unthinkable instantly wiped the smile from his wife's face.

She stopped short midway on the staircase. In French she addressed her husband as chillingly as she might address a servant who had stepped out of line. "Pig! You will speak respectfully to me in my own home! *My* home, do you hear?"

So Costello and I had both been right. Yves must have demanded that his wife return his wedding gift of this property to him, and, plainly, she had no intention of doing it. Now he wore the expression of a man who had raised his hand to chastise an errant kitten and discovered it had turned into a tiger.

Madame, having disposed of him, turned a smile in my direction. "My dear David, my husband has advised me that you and he have arranged a private talk. I will wait in the car as long as you require," and with that she completed her alluring descent of the staircase and was gone.

The sound of the door closing behind her roused Yves from his stupor. "A private talk," he said to me. "Yes."

The room he led me to was strictly business. The one picture on its walls concealed a safe. Yves removed a set of papers from the safe and planted them on the gleaming mahogany surface of his desk. At a glance, either the copies of the van Zee letters I had left with Leewarden or copies of the copies.

Yves dropped into the leather-quilted swivel chair behind the desk and waved at the chair facing him. "When you first arrived in Paris, Mr. Shaw—when the name of Jan van Zee appeared in the newspapers—I entered into an investigation of you. Now I must admit that the results of it bewilder me. You are enormously wealthy, of good family, the director of a distinguished bank, and, as I have good cause to know, you have entry into the highest social circles. You have come here with reputable associates to make a motion picture, so you are, in fact, a businessman engaged in a proper enterprise. Yet your methods"—he clapped a hand down on the letters—"suggest that you are much more intent on a savage persecution of me and my associate Leewarden than on any mere search for your missing author."

"Do you seriously believe that?" I asked with polite interest.

"I do. For example, your government is now examining certain dealings between transatlantic airlines and tourist agencies. You inspired that action, did you not?"

"Yes. But, of course, as a concerned shareholder."

He stared at me, drumming his fingers on the desk. "I cannot play games with you, Mr. Shaw, because these letters give you all the advantage of me. What I will do is provide you with information about van Zee that even the letters do not. After that, we will be in a position to strike a bargain."

"And the information?"

"To put it simply, van Zee was assigned to transport a million dollars in currency from Zurich to Luxembourg. The temptation was too much for him—he was a liar and thief at best—and he disappeared en route to Luxembourg with the money. I am sure none of us will ever see him again. That is the truth of it."

"Is it?" I said. "You realize, of course, what's likely to happen to you if I don't believe your version of the truth."

"Naturally, I understand the possibilities!" His voice rose. "Exposure of those letters would be disastrous to me. Even now, without that, you face me with ruin. Any serious attempt to collect the full amount of my notes will bankrupt me. More than that, it will be enough to end what is left of my marriage. Certainly I understand all this. And that is why I have every reason to speak the truth. Believe me, if I could produce van Zee for you, I'd gladly do it. Is it your idea that the threats you aim at me would enable me to perform a miracle I cannot possibly perform?"

I put on a sympathetic face. "There's no arguing with logic, is there? Well then, what if I settle for a lesser miracle? Kees Baar might have some helpful information about van Zee. Where do I find Baar?"

"I have no address for him. And even if you met with him, he could tell you no more than I can. I beg you to accept that fact. Only in that way can we come to terms with each other."

"I see. Any particular terms?"

"Yes. I offer you a hundred thousand dollars in part payment on my notes. Within a year, I will make full payment of the remainder. Since you must have purchased the notes at discount, you stand to make a handsome profit by exercising a little patience. What could be more fair?"

"And if I accept these terms?"

"Then, Mr. Shaw, we go our own separate ways. Madame will deplore the change in her plans for this weekend"—with unbelievable resilience he was getting more and more smoothly confident as he went along—"but, alas, these things do happen. After that—well, I see no reason why you and I need have any more to do with each other."

I gave him time to take comfort from that thought, then shook my head. "No."

"No?"

I said, "I'll accept payment of the hundred thousand, but for the remainder I had something else in mind. As you remarked, I do have entry into the highest social circles. And I've been looking for suitable accommodations in which to entertain my friends in those circles. This handsome building would serve the purpose admirably."

Yves looked bewildered. "This handsome building is my home, Mr. Shaw. And it is not for sale."

"I don't want to buy it. All I want is the rental of it for a couple of months. And at a very generous price. One hundred thousand dollars a month."

He gaped at me. "A joke?"

"Not at all. My offer is entirely serious. All you have to do is be off the premises by the time I'm back in Paris on Monday, and the two hundred thousand dollar balance of your debt is cancelled. What could be easier than that?"

He was darkly suspicious now. "So much for so little?"

"Monsoor," I said, doing him the courtesy of trying out his own language on him, "why question the offer? It's a much pleasanter solution to your problem, don't you think, than the alternatives? The legal proceedings that assure your bankruptcy? And, inevitably, the exposure of your colorful career?"

He flinched. "Unfortunately"—he sounded in pain—"most unfortunately, even taking your offer at its face value, the problem cannot be solved this way. You see, this building is Madame's property. Her wedding portion, which she cherishes with a passion. She would never consent to leave it under such conditions even for a short time."

"Of course not. It would be insulting to suggest she do any such thing."

"What? But you just said—"

"Only that *you* were to be off the premises. For that matter, I won't be using them very often myself. Now and then, simply to provide the proper ambiance for a dinner party. Madame, who will remain in residence, may be pleased to serve as hostess on such occasions."

The silence grew so intense that I became aware of his hard breathing. "So that's it," he whispered.

"That," I said, "is it."

Yves rocketed out of his chair. *"Mais non!"* he shouted wildly. *"Non! Non! Non!"* smashing his fist down on the desk to punctuate every repetition of the word. Once before I had seen him in this kind of hopeless fury as he watched a car below him in a Luxembourg gorge become a sheet of flame. It was painful remembering that scene, but the pain was eased a little by witnessing his performance now.

I said, "Even with my limited French, I gather you're refusing my offer."

"To sell you my wife? You find that amusing?" A trickle of saliva dribbled from the corner of his mouth. "In all my life—!"

I cut this short. "Where are you hiding van Zee?"

"I have told you—"

"—a pack of lies. As soon as I showed up in Paris you hid him away somewhere. Why not? A man who probably drinks too much, takes drugs, talks too easily. Not the kind of man you'd want reporters flocking around, is he?"

"No! I swear I told you the truth about him."

I stood up. "Very well. If that's the way you want it—"

"Wait, wait!" I waited while he faced me, digging a hand through that slick black hair. "The truth," he finally said. "But you will not like it."

"I'll take my chances on that."

"He is dead."

"Van Zee?"

"Yes. He stole the money and hid it somewhere in Zurich. Then he drove to Luxembourg and told us he had been robbed by people on the highway. We were taking him back to Zurich when he attempted to escape us. He seized control of the car and in the darkness he drove it off the road. It was destroyed completely. He died in it."

I said incredulously, "He stole the money—a million dollars—and hid it in Zurich, then drove all the way to Luxembourg just to tell you it was gone? And you really expect me to believe such nonsense?"

Yves held his arms wide in supplication. His face was very pale, the sweat showing on it. Then he let his arms drop to his side. "No," he said lifelessly, "who could believe such a monstrous chain of events if he was not witness to them?"

"Nicely put," I said. "And now that we've reached agreement on the essentials, my friend, let's sit down and attend to the details."

As the car moved out into the street, Vahna said, "I know what Yves wished to talk to you about. His one concern was to make the worst of our friendship, was it not?"

"No. It seems he's facing some business problems which—but forget that. I shouldn't be saying it. I'm sure he wouldn't want me to."

She arched those narrow eyebrows at me. "Indeed? But you are not the only one to know of his financial difficulties, David. On my arrival home from London yesterday we had a scene that made them very plain to me."

"Then he did tell you he's close to bankruptcy?"

"No," Vahna said in a brittle voice, "he did not."

"Trying not to alarm you, I suppose, because it is an alarming possibility. So, knowing my circumstances, he asked if I would help him out. A matter of a few hundred thousand dollars, just to keep the wolf from the door."

"He asked you for money? You?"

"Yes."

"And I did not enter into the discussion at all? This visit to Chaumont did not disturb him?"

"Please," I said, "we're getting into something so embarrassing—"

She placed a soft little hand on mine. "David, I insist you tell me everything that happened between you two."

"Well"—I brought it out unwillingly—"he did say that he found the relationship—friendship—between you and me intolerable."

"Yes?"

"But that he might manage to tolerate it, if I would help him out financially."

The hand resting on mine clenched convulsively, the nails digging hard into my palm. "*Un ménage à trois, hein?* And you believed my husband really offered you such an arrangement?"

"Vahna, the offer couldn't be misunderstood. Once I agreed to help him out, he said he'd leave Paris tomorrow for two or three months while you remained here."

Again those sharp nails cut painfully hard into my hand. "Then he has gone mad! Completely mad!"

"Possibly. But tell me, in all your years of marriage didn't you ever realize that if he had to choose between you and his money you would be the loser?"

"No. Never. And I cannot understand any of this."

I said soothingly, "But what is there to understand? Nothing out of the way has happened. Yves must leave town for awhile on business. You are spending the weekend with Henriette de Liasse who will be delighted with your company. I am a friend of the family hoping to see it through its difficulties. That's all it amounts to right now, isn't it?"

The darkly glimmering eyes narrowed. "Right now?"

"Yes. Afterward—well, you must know my feelings for you. But if you want to call off this weekend, return home immediately—"

That gave her a start. "With Madame la Comtesse waiting?" she said, lining up her priorities. "Would she not be offended?"

"Perhaps. But if you say the word—"

"No," said Vahna shortly.

She was not much company the rest of the trip, but when we were ushered into a vast sitting room—the fireplace would have been enough to park the car in—and the Countess rose from her conversation with some leading lights of the *Almanach de Gotha* to greet us, the transformation in Vahna was complete. From impassive to radiant, from monosyllabic to fluent.

She had style too. There were about a dozen present, and as we were led through introductions to Madame la Princesse and Monsieur le Duc and so on down the line, Vahna struck a perfect balance between deference and vivacity.

The Countess took notice of this. "Charming," she commented in an undertone, drawing me away from the company. "But, David, much as I dislike reproving you for a gaucherie, I am compelled to do so." She was only half playful about it. "When one receives an invitation such as I extended to you, an unmarried young man, it is not his privilege to choose his partner for the occasion."

"Then I apologize. But there's quite a story attached to this gaucherie."

She gave me a knowing look. "An old and familiar story, I suspect."

"No, this concerns the lady's problems. She's a princess of the blood in Thailand. When she was still a schoolgirl she was married off—actually sold off—to a French businessman there. Yves Rouart-Rochelle. A moneygrubber and a brute. Hates the amenities, hates what he sneeringly calls aristocratic pretensions. Robespierre wasn't the last of that breed, you know."

"How well one knows," said Madame.

"But," I said, "now there's been a separation. She finally made it plain to him how much she detested his vulgarity, he walked out, and that's where matters rest. She's been left without a friend to turn to."

The Countess again gave me that knowing look. "You are not her friend?"

"I want to be," I said innocently, "but it's not easy. She's rigidly moral, afraid that even being seen with me might be misinterpreted. That's why when your invitation came I thought that here at least, where she would be received with understanding—"

"Ah, poor child." Madame looked across the room where Vahna was prettily engaged in several conversations simultaneously. "You must let her know, David, that I may be counted on as a friend."

"I will. That leads me to wonder if, on her behalf, I might impose on your kindness."

"In what way?"

"She's all alone in that huge house of hers in Paris. Really a magnificent old place in the Parc Monceau, but it's like a living tomb. So if she were to arrange a dinner party where you were guest of honor—where, in fact, you decided on the guest list but she would be hostess—would you approve such an arrangement?"

"Impossible, David. You seem to have no idea of the difficulties posed by such an unnatural arrangement. The matter of preparations, the protocol—"

"They could be in no better hands than yours."

"No, your flattery will not overcome my sense of the proprieties. There are some things"—but her voice trailed off, her eyes glazed over, she was evidently having second thoughts. Then she said in a businesslike tone, "If I granted you this favor, could I expect immediate repayment?"

"Anything you ask."

"It has to do with Jean-Pierre. My son, who is of an age to marry and produce for me a grandson bearing the family name, is making himself a scandal because of a certain woman. *Une négresse.* I believe this woman is an employee of yours and subject to your authority. Is that correct?"

"To some extent."

"Very well. Then give me solemn assurance that Jean-Pierre will be promptly relieved of her company—that she will be kept at a distance from him—and I will do you your favor."

"You have my assurance. And my gratitude."

"Very nicely said. And, David"—she held up an admonitory forefinger—"you must deal with this discreetly. Jean-Pierre is not to know my role in it."

"He never will."

"Now," she said brightly, "let us return to the company, or my son will not be the only member of the family regarded as a scandal."

There now remained in this phase of the game only one more piece to move into position.

During an endlessly tedious and nerve-racking dinner, what sustained my hopes of thus moving it into position was the view of Vahna across the table taking notice of the close attention paid me by Madame la Comtesse and finally flashing that special smile at me.

Good friends again? In that case—

At midnight, in the pajamas, dressing gown and slippers Harry had laid out for me before hieing himself off to his own quarters, and assured by the silence in the corridor outside my bedroom that I wasn't likely to encounter traffic there, I made my way down the corridor to Vahna's room.

She opened the door just wide enough to reveal that she was still fully clothed. She recognized my surprise at this and explained, "I sent the maid away. All I can do is walk up and down with the excitement of it. Madame la Duchesse de la Quintinye. Do you know her?"

"Of course. The fat one with the taste for cognac."

"Ah, what a way to speak. She was so kind. She has some chinoiserie among her *objets d'art.* She has invited me to Quintinye to examine these pieces and help determine their value."

"Without fee?"

Vahna frowned. "What is it, David? Does my pleasure in this company offend you?"

"Not at all. In fact, what I've come to tell you is that you are very soon going to give a dinner party for them at your home. A large and grand dinner party. The Countess herself will be delighted to prepare your guest list, explain protocol, help in all details. All you have to do is speak to her about it before we leave."

Vahna looked stunned. "Madame la Comtesse herself?"

"Yes. Look, may I come in? It's awkward holding a conversation like this."

She opened the door wide, I stepped in and closed it behind me. I remained with my back against it while she gave me a demonstration of what she had meant about walking up and down with excitement. She suddenly stopped short before me. "You arranged this, did you not? You asked her to do it for me."

"Yes. I explained your circumstances, your separation from your husband, your loneliness, and she was very sympathetic."

"My loneliness? Yves has not even departed from our home yet!"

"It's only a matter of a few hours now. And," I said pointedly, "you're already very lonely, aren't you?"

Slowly, slowly into those exotic eyes came the light of calculation. That gave way to panic. "But the cost of such a dinner! I have no money of my own. It has always been Yves—"

"Sit down," I said.

As if mesmerized she seated herself on a massive fautueil that made her look even more doll-like. I said, "Now try to understand. Before Yves can get any help from my company he must be down to his last penny. Otherwise, what money he has left—"

"But you said—"

I held up a hand. "Otherwise what money he has left will immediately be claimed by his creditors. To avoid this, he must turn over everything to me. Only then will he get the assistance he requires. Is that clear?"

She gave me a sober little nod. "I think it is."

"Good. My manager will get Yves's check for a hundred thousand dollars Monday morning. It will then be deposited to your account."

"My account? But it is Yves's money, is it not?"

"Was. Now it will be all yours. After all," I observed gravely, "what are friends for?"

The light dawned. *"Formidable!"* she breathed. "A hundred thousand out of your pocket. Five hundred thousand. A million. No matter, if you will get what you want."

"In this case," I countered, "only if you feel I deserve it."

And that, as it turned out, was exactly the right thing to say.

Wherever he was, Yves Rouart-Rochelle must have known what was taking place in his wife's bed that night, and the sense of this —of his being an invisible witness to it—made it as perversely an exciting experience as I had ever shared with any woman in my life.

And it was the same the next night at the Château de Liasse, and the night after.

When I walked into his room Costello, fully clothed, unshaven, and bleary-eyed, was stretched out on his bed, hands under his head, contemplating the ceiling. There was an empty whiskey bottle on the floor beside him.

"Rest and recreation time?" I said.

"Not too much. Leewarden got himself knocked off last night."

"Murdered?"

"Uh-huh. Took a walk after supper, came back to his room, and this morning when the hotel maid walked in there he was, ready for the embalmer. Stabbed to death, but it was made to look like a robbery."

"What about the agency man tailing him?"

Costello shrugged. "The agency guys were watching him, not his room. While he was out somebody got in and was laying in wait for him. And then took off through the window and down the fire escape."

"Kees Baar."

"Who else?" Costello hoisted himself upright and squinted at me through red-rimmed eyes. "You know Frenchy is out of town since Saturday, don't you?"

"Yes. When I brought Vahna back to the house the maid told us about it. Where out of town?"

"Marseille. He leases an apartment there full-time, and he's in it now. The agency's got him staked out good. And little Marie from Copenhagen was at Choochoo's when it happened, so it can't be pinned on her. It had to be the Dutchman." He held the empty bottle to the light, then phoned room service and ordered another.

"Nerves?" I said.

"Some. I don't like this blindman's buff with a guy who kills as easy as that Dutchman. And it's funny how the action always takes place right around where you are."

I said, "I'd rather have it that way. The other way is that he could just pack up his million and head for Rio."

Costello seemed to find bitter humor in this. "That you don't have to worry about. I mean about him packing up the million and heading for Rio. You want to know something? I don't think there's too much of that million left to pack up."

"Why not?"

He lurched to the desk, fumbled through stacks of index cards, and finally came up with the one he wanted. He waved it at me. "Marie, the porno kid."

"What about her?"

"Plenty. That hooker at Choochoo's, that Avril, fingered Marie for our agency guy. She said Marie's the one who's buying out Choochoo. Not only that, she's dealing for another whorehouse on the Pigalle, even bigger and better. And she's already bought out one in Copenhagen. Any one place like that would take a nice bite out of a million. Three of them—and there could be more we don't even know about—means you're really putting your money to work. Marie's the Dutchman's partner, right? So he is not keeping that dough in his mattress. He's investing it."

I said, "All this on Avril's say-so?"

"The agency guy, Schefflin, is one smart old-timer, and he buys her information. So do I. Maybe some ordinary stiff hits for a million and then blows it on high living, but this Dutchman is sure as hell not ordinary."

"No, he isn't. Is Marie-Paule still in town?"

"Still. Another cool one. Probably waiting for Mr. Shaw to drop in on her about van Zee the way he did with her pals."

I said, "Before I do, there's some company business to clear up. Grete's making the Countess unhappy. So Grete's being shipped back to the States."

"She won't like that," Costello warned. "It could be easier said than done."

"Maybe. Anyhow, the same goes for Oscar and Williams. They worked out fine, they gave us the front we needed, but now they'll only be in the way. It's time for them to open our Hollywood branch. Get them all together before dinner, and we'll settle it then."

Costello looked doubtful. "Oscar and Williams, okay. But our girlie? She's got His Highness right where she wants him whether his mama likes it or not, and that means she's got options. And that babe is solid brass all the way through."

"Just call the meeting, Ray."

I was on my way out of the room when an unpleasant thought struck me. I turned and said, "Hell, with Leewarden murdered right after I delivered his kid to her mother—"

"That's right," Costello said. "That's why I was on the phone with Emmaline right after I got the word. She caught on quick. She said when the police come around with the sad news you can depend on her to handle them perfectly."

"How did she take the sad news?"

"With pleasure," said Costello.

I was skimming through Oscar's inept screen treatment of *The Last Hippie* in preparation for the company meeting when the phone rang.

"David, you were right," chimed the little temple bells. "You said I would soon be very lonely. I am lonely now. Would you dine with me this evening?"

"Any place you name."

"*Chez moi.* A dinner for two at home." She timed a pause. "And who knows? Perhaps a breakfast for two?"

"Servants' night off?"

"No. Why do you ask?"

"Because," I said with deliberate intent, "if it isn't, Yves is soon going to learn what takes place between your dinners and breakfasts."

"Good," clanged the temple bell triumphantly. "Eight o'clock, *mon cher.*"

So when I joined the gathering in my sitting room I was not only dressed for dinner *à deux* but had a bag packed for the night to follow. There was nothing for settling raw nerves like the cuckolding of Yves Rouart-Rochelle, and if he were now going to be given convincing proof of the cuckolding by, I hoped, his loyal domestics—

At the company meeting I came straight to the point. Since Jan van Zee would not cooperate in the making of our *cinema verité,* we would simply shoot the picture in the States as an American fiction. It was now Monday evening. On Wednesday morning, Wylie, Williams, and Hansen would fly to Hollywood and set up shop there. I would join them as soon as possible.

Grete who had started off sullen now looked stormy. "Now wait. You can't just tell people to pack up and take off on two day's notice. I'm not sure I even want to go. And I don't have any contract where you can make me."

I said, "The choice is yours, baby. The idea was to try you out for the lead—van Zee's girl friend—and, if you had the talent I think you have, to sign you for a long-term contract. Star billing and all. But if you're not interested—"

"I didn't say that." She was wavering a little. "All I said—"

Whatever it was, it was cut short by a staccato rapping on the door. Costello opened it a few inches, held a muttered colloquy through it, then motioned me to join him in the corridor outside. I did, and he hastily closed the door behind us, indicating that this was not public business.

The tall blonde woman he had been having it out with smiled warmly at me.

"David, sono liato di vedera," said Bianca Cavalcanti.

Bianca Cavalcanti?

Off balance, I struggled to right myself. David Shaw had last seen a buxom and emotional Bianca ten years ago. But Jan van Zee had been confronted by a slender and coolly self-possessed Signorina Cavalcanti only months ago. I wasn't prepared to sort out my identities on such short notice. And there was the language problem, because I could never get away in this case with pleading ignorance of her language.

I held my breath and took the plunge. "But it's Bianca!" I said, *molto Italiano.* "I didn't recognize you. You've changed so much."

"And you haven't, aside from shedding your youth. How strange.

211

I've had the image of you in my mind over the years, and you so much resemble it that it's almost frightening." There was no kittenishness in this. It was her considered judgment of a curious and troubling phenomenon. "But I'm glad we're face to face at last." The magnificent gray eyes darkened. "Your man here did his best to make that impossible. You should tell him to manufacture better lies than he does. A meeting indeed."

I opened the door briefly to give her a view of the company inside. "You see," I said, "there is a meeting."

She looked puzzled. "But those phone calls from your mother about my arrival. I thought you would be prepared for it at this time."

"Phone calls from my mother?" I said in English for Costello's benefit, and looked at him hard.

"Twice last week," he said. "And I didn't mention them, because I know how you feel about having Mama mentioned."

"*Allora.*" I shrugged at Bianca. "That's not far from the truth. For various good reasons."

She nodded. "Yes, your mother has made plain the distance between you two. Over the years she's come to confide in me very openly. But I'm not here on her behalf alone. There's also an amazing coincidence involved. When I saw her last week she had newspaper clippings about you. About your search for a writer, Jan van Zee. David, I met this man only last summer. I was going to call you about it from Rome, but when Umberto suggested I take time off from my work and visit you—"

"Your work?" After all, David Shaw was not supposed to know what Jan van Zee knew.

"I'm a therapist at a free clinic for obstetrics Umberto runs in Trastevere. It was his feeling that with your recent good fortune you might, for old time's sake, donate some of the money the clinic needs. But what I was getting at is that I met this Jan van Zee at the clinic. He came in with a girl—"

That struck a nerve.

"My meeting," I said abruptly. "Too bad. I do want to hear about all this, but those people inside are waiting. And afterward I must leave for a long night's session on some important matters. Where are you staying?"

"I don't know yet. I came here straight from the airport. But I'll find a room on the Left Bank to fit my purse."

"If that's how you want it. My chauffeur is at your disposal." Her crestfallen look had me torn between guilt and anger. "Have you had dinner?"

"No."

"Well, that much I can offer." I turned to Costello. "Miss Cavalcanti can wait in Grete's room until the meeting is over. After that, see that she has dinner in the sitting room here. Then tell Harry to put himself at her service."

I left her like that, bewilderment written all over her face, and rejoined the company inside. Grete did nothing for my mood by stubbornly picking up exactly where she had left off. "All I said was why does the picture have to be made in the States? If it's the same story, I don't see—"

"Look," I said, "we'll be borrowing van Zee's material without his consent. If we shift the locale to the States, change names and descriptions, he can't make claims on me for that." I turned to Oscar who was looking doubtful about this. "Top priority," I told him. "If Grete's cutting out, the first thing you have to do on the Coast is find a replacement for her. And get the publicity buildup started for whoever it is. After that—"

"Wait a second," Grete said sharply. "Did I tell you I'm cutting out?"

"I had the impression—"

"Well, I'm not."

When the meeting adjourned I went into the bedroom to make the necessary phone call. It took time to break through the chain of command at the château but at last there was Madame la Comtesse herself.

"A very brief message," I said. "The young lady will leave in two days for America. She will certainly remain there for a long stay."

"Indeed?" A wise old bird at the other end of the line. "How very efficient you are, David. Will I see you soon again?"

"No doubt at the party Madame Rouart-Rochelle is arranging in your honor, Countess."

"Of course. *Au-'voir* then, until the occasion."

It was not Vahna's fault that our candlelit dinner and the romantic interlude that followed did not come off as they should have. The shadow of Bianca Cavalcanti lay long over me, and an unsettling shadow it was. At three in the morning, with my hostess's sympathetic farewell—*"Vraiment, mon cher,* you must learn that you cannot bring your business affairs to bed with you"—I removed myself from her embrace, and leaving my belongings as assurance of my constancy, I set out on foot for the Meurice, Bianca's shadow maddeningly with me every step of the way.

Odds were that my rudeness had sent her off in a rage, and she'd be on the plane to Rome first thing in the morning. Good. The bad part was the vision of that stricken face before me. Strange that once we were out of our childhood, every time we encountered each other, whether I was Shaw or van Zee, she was left with bruises to show for it.

I considered this in a sort of troubled draydream as I made my way down the deserted rue de Rivoli. My awakening was almost fatal. I was halfway across the rue des Pyramides opposite the Tuileries when there was a wild screeching of tires arcing full speed toward me, headlights blinded me momentarily, and with no room at all to spare—I could have sworn that the fender of the turtle-backed Citroën brushed my jacket as I leaped for safety—I just managed to lunge out of range, landing hard on my hands and knees.

This was not to be a one-shot attempt. There was another screech of rubber as the car backed up like a rocket in reverse and the driver came piling out. Small and slight, the face hollow under gray hair, a black patch over one eye—under the lamplight the effect was that of the skull on a pirate flag—and most piratical was the long-bladed knife in his hand.

As I came to my feet he was almost on me, light glinting along the blade, so I did the only thing left to do, I lashed out with a straight-legged kick that sent him full length into the roadway. Then, aware that others were heading this way—night-walkers, passers-by, coming to see what the action was—I sprinted down the avenue as fast as I could until, winded, I pulled up near the Meurice.

A hired assassin, no question about it, but hired by whom? Leewarden was dead and Kees Baar plainly preferred to do his own killing. Yves? Would Yves risk the threat that the van Zee letters would wind up with the police if anything happened to me?

When I let myself into the suite I saw that Harry had for once been derelict in his duties. A couple of empty bottles of Perrier and a half-filled glass were occupying a puddle on a coffee table, and every ashtray in the room was brimming over with cigarette butts.

I opened the bedroom door and as I walked inside and pressed the light switch I banged a foot against something parked near the door. A valise. And sleeping in my bed, clothed except for her shoes—one was on the bed, the other halfway across the room—was the long-legged, tousle-haired, wholly unwelcome Bianca Cavalcanti, an arm flung across her eyes.

A light sleeper. She stirred, then raised herself on her elbows and regarded me steadily, as if taking stock of me from head to foot.

"Good morning," I said.

"Good morning, Signor van Zee," she said.

Signor van Zee?

I wildly groped for some clue to her insight. An incredibly lucky guess? Information from the only reliable source?

"Did you enjoy a friendly talk with Signor Costello?" I asked, testing her. "He's a great one for unfunny jokes."

"He told your chauffeur to have my dinner served here and then take me where I wished, that was all. He didn't give your secret away."

"My secret? Look, Bianca—"

"David, you told the newspapers you once met Jan van Zee in Amsterdam and had then gone right back to America to study the rebellious young people there. But, you see, your mother informed me whenever your grandfather received a postcard from you over the years, and the postcard was always from Europe. The truth is that during that time, you were living the life you now attribute to someone named Jan van Zee, weren't you?"

"No."

"Don't lie to me!" She got off the bed in one lithe motion, pulled a cigarette from a pack on the night table and lit it, drawing at it short and hard. The ashtrays here, like those in the sitting room, were heaped high with crushed-out butts.

"You smoke too much," I said.

"Nice of you to be concerned. Now can we sit down and talk about this like old friends?"

"Talk about what? Your fantasy that I'm spending my life hunting for myself under a different name?"

"David, the last time we met was in the clinic. Stop pretending it wasn't." She walked across the room to confront me. "You sat across the desk from me—a big, bearded man with a broken nose —and I was tormented by a feeling that I knew you from somewhere. I never lost that feeling. It was the first time the image of any man but the old David Shaw was so strong in my mind. Yet it never struck me until tonight that Jan van Zee—"

I cut in, "So you met van Zee. But to turn that coincidence into a ridiculous theory? I wish you could hear yourself."

"A theory? That a young American student runs away to Europe, changes his identity and becomes involved with some murderous scoundrels who betray him cruelly? That inheriting great wealth, he now lives only for vengeance against them?"

The shock of it left me numb. She took quick pity on me. She pointed at the night table and said wearily, "You left the scenario for your motion picture there. Some of the truth is in it. For anyone who knows you as I do, the rest wasn't hard to fill in."

"And you made it your business to fill it in."

"You invited that," she said loudly. "You're supposed to be desperately searching for van Zee, aren't you? Yet the instant I said I had met him you ran from me!"

I faced her in silence, my mind racing.

"Aspetti," I commanded. "Wait here. I'll be right back."

I knocked on Miller William's door, and when he sleepily opened it I pushed him back into the room not as gently as I might have. "I need some information, Miller. What cash balance do we have in our Paris bank here?"

"About two hundred and forty thousand dollars, Mr. Shaw."

"How much is that in lire? In round numbers."

"Lire. Yes." He went to his desk which was as neatly ordered as

Costello's wasn't and did quick calculations on his pocket computer. "A hundred million lire. Which still leaves a balance of ten thousand." He was eyeing me apprehensively. "Mr. Shaw, do you feel all right?"

"Yes," I said. "Sorry to bother you."

Bianca was in the sitting room when I returned. Her expression matched Williams's. I said, "Afraid I disappeared for good?"

"No. Or perhaps I was. All I know for sure is that I've turned you against me. That's the last thing I want."

"And the last thing I want is anyone persistently meddling in my life."

"Ah, that's unfair. I saved you from making a fool of yourself with Sophia Changouris. Anneke Brun came to the clinic of her own accord. Now I have good reason to be afraid for you. Do you regard such passages as meddling? I don't."

"Except for one thing," I said. "We've become strangers over the years."

"Strangers? You and I? David, do you remember the fat Bianca, the self-hating Bianca, the Bianca intended by her parents to be the empty-headed wife of some foolish young man of their milieu and the adoring mother of his many children? Now look at me. Consider what I am and what I've made of my life. Don't you know who's responsible for that?"

"You mean you're attributing this miracle to me?"

"Listen. After you left me that horrible New Year's night in Parioli I cried until morning. And then I stood before the mirror and designed the changes that were going to be made for you. Only for you. The way I must look. The courage I must develop to stand against the conventional. The career I must enter. All for you. All for the time when we would meet again."

She was serious about it. Florentine tall and beautiful, Neapolitan intense and shining-eyed, certainly a little crazy. I said, "You were that sure we'd meet again?"

"We have, haven't we?"

"Bianca, I'm thirty. You can't be far from it. It's ridiculous to pretend we're still kids together eating ice cream at Tre Scalini."

"True. But I wasn't a little kid that New Year's night when I found that just looking at you made my head spin. And when I was far from being a child a stranger named Jan van Zee walked into my office, and there was that feeling again. A stranger, mind you. You didn't know how I had to struggle against the temptation to touch his hand, to let him know how shaken I was by his presence." She stared closely at my face. "The eyes, that's what it must have been. They were the same eyes. And something about the voice."

I was being hypnotized by this. I shook myself out of it. "You always did go in for the operatic style. It seems worse than ever now."

"Why? Because I'm not ashamed to let you know my feelings for you? But I have a right to. I've won that right. I'm independent in all ways. I live alone on what I earn. I owe favors to no one. I'm as free as any man to declare my feelings."

"*Fantastico,*" I said from the heart. "And in all this have you considered my feelings in the matter?"

"Yes." She had to nerve herself to come out with it. "I told myself that once you understood my devotion you'd have to respond to it. You'd be a fool not to. I believe I can offer you more than any other woman can, if you're man enough to live with it. But I am frightened now because of what you've gotten yourself into. This insane vendetta. And it is because of Anneke, isn't it?"

"Yes. I escaped an accident they engineered. She died in it."

"Ah, dear God. And the child?"

"Never had a chance to be born. Does that change your mind a little about my vendetta?"

She was badly shaken. She stood there uncertainly, then made a helpless gesture. "David, you think you want to make those men pay for their guilt in her death, but it goes deeper than that. It's your own guilt you want them to pay for. You became involved in their enterprise, and you made her your partner in it."

This was too much. It had to be ended right now.

I said, "How much money did you expect me to contribute to your clinic?"

"But that isn't what I—"

"How much?" I said it so sharply that she looked alarmed.

"I don't know," she said. "Umberto thought perhaps a hundred thousand lire. It's desperately needed if we're to continue our work. And the cause is good." Then she added with a sort of defiance, "You must have seen that for yourself."

"I did. So what would you say to a hundred million lire?"

"A hundred million?" she said in stupefaction. "My God, with that amount—"

"But there's a condition attached. I'll give you a check for it on the spot, but you must be on the first plane leaving for Rome tomorrow. In Rome you'll forget everything you've learned about me. Everything. You'll give my mother my regards, you'll tell Umberto I was generous for old time's sake, and that will be the end of it. The money is all yours, but only on those terms."

It took her time to find the words. "You must realize you couldn't have found a more brutal way of dealing with me, don't you?"

"I imagine waking anyone up from a childish dream is always a little painful. I'm sorry."

"I don't want your pity. I just want you to open your eyes and really see me. Look at me, David. Don't you find me attractive?"

"Alarmingly so." I knew instantly, from the brightening of her face, that it had been a mistake to let this slip out.

"And you approve what I've made of my life, don't you?"

"No," I said, "not if I'm the reason for it. As long as you hold to that nonsense you're still living a schoolgirl dream. You're not really what you think you are."

"I don't agree." Whatever she felt, she was now being remarkably self-possessed about it. "Even if I did, I can tell you that it's far more rewarding to live my kind of dream than your kind of nightmare. If I'm still the little girl of the Piazza Navona, what are you? A de'Medici bravo of five hundred years ago?"

"And this kind of talk," I said, "is one reason why you'll be better off in Rome with no remembrance of me. You may find it hard to believe, but here you're a danger to me and to yourself."

"I do find it hard to believe."

That made sense in a way. She had never been properly introduced to Mijnheer X and Monsieur Y and Mister Z. The screen treatment she had read, and which thus identified them, only drew them in bare outline.

I managed to get the file of letters out of Costello's room without rousing him. I brought it back to the sitting room and handed it to Bianca. "Read all this if you really want to see what you're trying to get yourself into. Meanwhile, since I don't have your endurance, I'm going inside to get some sleep. Just wake me whenever you've finished your reading."

220

She weighed the folder in her hand. "What is this?"

"The documents in the case. You have my word for it that everything there is very close to the facts."

In the bedroom, as I peeled off jacket and shirt, I realized that her valise and sandals were growing distractions better put out of sight. When I brought them into the sitting room she was already sunk deep in an armchair scanning a page, an unlighted cigarette drooping from her lower lip. She looked up at me. "Letters from Jan to David?"

"Right. But disregard the dates. They were all written only a little while ago."

I got into bed, angrily wondering if I could fall asleep when I was so aware of that presence on the other side of the door. It seemed extraordinarily foolish that under these circumstances it should be on that side of the door. And, simultaneously, it seemed a gross betrayal of Anneke that I should allow myself any such thought.

I was wakened by a cool hand pressed to my forehead and opened my eyes to bright sunlight and a view of the bedside clock marking the time as a few minutes before eight. Bianca was seated on the edge of the bed beside me, but through the door of the sitting room I heard sounds of activity.

"The chauffeur," said Bianca. "He seems pleased to have so many ashtrays to empty."

"He would be. Have you read all the letters?"

"All. But they suddenly end where you—where van Zee was to take the money from Zurich to Luxembourg. What happened then?"

She listened intently as I answered that at length. Then the hand moved down and came to rest against my cheek. A pleasant feeling, and a dangerous one. She said, "So now it all becomes clear. You're using the letters to show those men you know all about Jan van Zee. That way you can make them do what you want. Which of them is already dead?"

"*L'inglese*. Leewarden."

"You drove the others to kill him?"

"Let them do it."

"I understand. But, David, do you understand that with your kind of wealth you could buy the most clever lawyers—the most powerful friends—"

"As you can see, I don't need them."

"You mean you'd get no pleasure from settling it that way."

"None," I said. "But that's beside the point. Your clinic is the point. Your good works. And the money I'm ready to donate to them, but only according to the terms laid down. Have you decided what to do about that?"

"First answer one question. If I do leave for Rome at once, will you join me there as soon as you can?"

"When I can." It seemed to be the only way of breaking this maddening deadlock. Then—even though Anneke was suddenly sharp in my mind, looking wounded by it—I found myself wondering what it might be like if I were speaking more truthfully than I intended.

"Meglio tardi che mai," said Bianca. Better late than never, words she evidently lived by. She stood up. "I'll wait for you there."

"Bianca—"

"I'll wait for you there," she said calmly. "Meanwhile I'll do it your way."

I was already at breakfast in the sitting room when she emerged from the bedroom, bathed, freshly clothed for the homeward trip, and apparently serene of spirit.

Over our coffee and brioche, we talked. It went awkwardly for me at first, because uppermost in my mind was the realization that ten long years had passed since that disastrous New Year's Eve in Rome, and here I was across the table from a poised and apparently mature female who had spent those years in a handcrafted ivory tower waiting for her knight to come riding up again on his white steed. Talk about Elaine, the Lily Maid of Astalot. Or about pinning your childish and loony faith on an unlikely conjunction of the planets.

So I was jolted to discover that it was more a case of Rapunzel than Elaine, the Lily Maid. A ladder had once been lowered from that tower.

"Umberto's partner in the clinic," Bianca explained. "It went on a few months and that was it. *Finito.* A sweet man but terribly conventional. We couldn't keep going on like this, he said. Either we must marry or end the affair. So I ended the affair."

"Was he serious about marriage?"

"Oh, yes. He was quite infatuated with me. He was outraged when I refused his kind offer."

As any castoff lover had the right to be. But what right did I now have to be annoyed by this information? Before I could come to grips with that question, Bianca said, "I've been wondering. Your Shakespeare had his Prince Hamlet carry out his vendetta by means of a play presented to the murderer. Is that what inspired you to make a film?"

"No. As a matter of fact, although only you and I and Signor Costello know it, there isn't going to be any film."

"But all those people involved in it—"

"They're being very well paid for very little effort."

"I see." Then she came right to the point. "That girl, Grete. Is she your mistress?"

"Somebody else's."

"Good. I've been very jealous of her up to now. I'm too easily jealous really. The old insecurities, I suppose. That week you devoted yourself to Sophia Changouris I used to dream up ways of killing her. Or, better yet, humiliating her. Give her warts that couldn't be removed and a mustache that couldn't be shaved."

"She's not still Milos's girl friend, is she?"

"Not after your mother found out about her. And speaking of your mother—"

"Time to go," I said. "Your plane leaves in less than an hour." I handed her the check for the hundred million lire. "Negotiable at once."

"Molto grazie." She carefully folded the slip of paper. "I'll be waiting for you in Rome as long as I must. I still feel that dealing with those men your way is a kind of madness, but I know it's a kind of madness you won't be released from until everything is settled as you want it to be. So I'll wait."

A kiss? A tender farewell? But no, what she offered was a handshake, so I settled for that. A firm, decisive handshake, all business. Quite a case, the Signorina Bianca Cavalcanti. Dreamy-eyed romantics were one thing to contend with, but a hard-headed romantic?

Harry, the lady's valise in hand, led the way across the marvelously baroque lobby of the Meurice toward the front door where the car was already parked, and we followed without saying a word. Then Bianca suddenly seized my arm, drawing me to a halt. "That man," she said. "The one sitting there against the wall. I saw him at Rome in the airport, then here on the bus into Paris. He seemed to be watching me."

"That's natural."

"No. I had the strangest feeling he was following me. And here he is now."

"Where?" I said. "But don't turn around."

"Behind us there, pretending to read a newspaper. I know it's the same man. He wears a patch over his eye."

"A small man? With gray hair?"

"Yes."

I wheeled around. No one of that description was in sight. Bianca looked bewildered. "He's gone. But he was there. And you know him too?"

"Yes." I motioned Harry over and told him to stand by for further instructions. Then it was back to the elevator and up. In the crowded elevator Bianca opened her mouth to speak, but I shook my head warningly. In the hallway she burst out, "Who is that man? How do you know about him?"

"Well, for one thing," I said, "he tried to kill me last night."

"Ah, no!"

"Ah, yes. But obviously he didn't succeed. Now be patient a few minutes."

"But he tried to kill you! Can't you see what you're doing is terribly dangerous?"

"Pazienza e corragio, signorina."

Costello opened the door, looked at my companion, and remained blocking the doorway. "What's she doing here?"

"She knows all about it, Ray, but take it easy. She can be trusted." I prodded Bianca past him, and he closed the door behind us, not happily. I motioned her to a chair and she seated herself, hands clasped tight in her lap. Costello's face was stony. "I'm listening," he said.

"I suppose I should have told you about it right off," I said, "but somebody tried to knock me off on my way back to the hotel this morning. A little old gent with an eyepatch. First with a hit-and-run, then with a knife. I laid him out before any damage could be done, but a few minutes ago Miss Cavalcanti spotted him in the lobby here. There's no question he's the same man. Is all that clear so far?"

"Sure. Frenchy put out a contract on you."

"But consider this," I said. "Miss Cavalcanti also tells me that our little friend with the eyepatch trailed her all the way here from Rome."

"Used her to bird-dog you?" He turned to her. "You sure?" She nodded, wide-eyed.

"But why?" Costello said to me. "Frenchy knows where you are."

"He does," I said. "That's why I don't think he's the one behind this."

"He has to be," Costello said. "He's the only one in the picture, unless you figure the Dutchman has started putting out contracts instead of doing his own killing."

"I don't figure that."

"Then," Costello said stubbornly, "it's Frenchy. But look. Suppose the guy with the eyepatch was only out to scare you? Suppose the lady here is the real target, know what I mean? If they get hold of her—"

"They could have had her already, Ray."

"They wouldn't have been sure about her until she walked right into your room. All right, all right, I know I'm pushing, but what else do we have to work on?"

I thought this over. "One chance in a thousand," I said. "In ten thousand."

"Even at those odds it's still a chance. You want to risk it?"

Again I thought it over. "No," I said.

Bianca had been worriedly following this. Now, in ripely accented English she said to me, "I do not understand either about this man. But I understand I have made troubles for you. Whatever I can do about it—"

"Troubles for both of us," I said. "Do you know what a hostage is?"

"Hos-tage?"

Costello said impatiently, "Lady, it's just possible that certain people now figure that you and Mr. Shaw have something big going when you travel all that distance just to put in a day with him. So the question is, if they grab you, what the hell is he supposed to do about it? *Kapeesh?"*

"*Capisco, signore,"* Bianca said scornfully. "But I can take care of myself wherever I am. The fact that I am a woman—"

"Oh, sure," said Costello. He turned to me. "How the hell did you get into this?"

"Never mind that, Ray. The question is how to get out of it."

"No sweat," Costello said flatly. "She can stay right here where I can keep an eye on her. For that matter, Harry can be full-time security for her."

"No," I said.

Bianca frowned at me. "Why do you say that, David, if I would not mind to stay here with you?"

"Because you have your work in Rome. That job at the clinic. The money to deliver."

"You know the money can be mailed. And the young man now attending to my work will be glad to remain at it a while."

"There are other considerations," I told her. With Costello taking all this in, I shifted to Italian. "*Mi dica la verità.* You know what the real problem is. What happens if you're always close by, you and your idea that heaven has somehow destined us for each other. A fine comedy that could develop into. And with a very good chance that you'd be badly hurt before it's all over."

She nodded wisely. "I see. You suspect—and with some justice—that if I remain here, I'll be sharing your private life. And your bed. And in the end I'll be left weeping about it like Cio-Cio-San."

"The operatic touch again?"

"That's the opera you're writing," she said. "The way mine goes, you're being made inhuman by this obsession to carry on your vendetta. And my presence is dangerous, because it might make you human again."

"If you think I'm so damned inhuman—"

"I'll settle for you on those terms," she cut in. "Even for the role of Cio-Cio-San if it comes to that, although I don't believe for a moment it ever could."

"What the hell is this all about?" Costello said in exasperation. "If I have to hire an interpreter—"

I said to him, "Harry's waiting downstairs with Miss Cavalcanti's bag. Have him bring it up, and while he's here you can work out the details of his job as bodyguard for her."

"Well, all right," Costello said. Then he had a thought. "Bring up the bag where? She ought to be in one of our rooms along the hall here, but none of them'll be empty until our deadheads take off tomorrow."

There was no sense in game-playing. "My room?" I said to Bianca, and she said placidly, *"Perchè non?"*

Why not, indeed?

Harry entered into his new duties by seeing the lady and her belongings to my quarters. As soon as they were gone Costello said to me, "Now let's have it. How did she find out you were van Zee?"

I told him how.

"Smart woman," he acknowledged. "And she really propositioned you like that? With her looks and class?"

"She did."

"Uh-huh. Well, why not, considering she knows you've got ten million in the bank? Anyhow, if Frenchy had any idea of getting at you through her, that's taken care of. What isn't taken care of is that one-eyed Humpty-Dumpty with the knife. Something has to be done about him."

"I'm dropping in on Marie-Paule this morning. If there's anything at all to your theory about Humpty-Dumpty, she could be the one to handle the problem for us."

"What's that mean?"

"She'll be shown a special van Zee letter as soon as I get it down on paper. It might do the trick."

"It better. But first do me a favor and call His Highness. He's been on the phone trying to get to you."

I didn't have to be told why. As soon as I identified myself over the phone Jean-Pierre said, "What the devil have you done to me, my friend? You offer me a pearl—a magnificent black pearl—and then suddenly snatch it away. Is that an act of friendship?"

I laughed. "Sorry, Jean-Pierre, but it was her choice to make. And like so many flighty young things today, she chose fame and fortune. You can't really blame her for that, can you?"

"Of course, I can, the empty-headed little Venus."

"Then," I said, "let me offer you a replacement for your pearl. Has your mother told you about a dinner being planned in her honor?"

"No."

"Well, the hostess is a dear friend. A charming Siamese noblewoman cruelly abandoned by her husband. If you attend the dinner in my place, you'll be her partner for the evening. After that, it's all up to you."

"Siamese, hey? How exotic. And you have no claim on her?"

"None at all," I said.

When I put down the phone Costello said, "Which combs both of them out of your hair together. Did you have that cooked up in advance?"

"Improvisation," I said. "The old master himself is a great believer in it. Kees Baar."

"Looks like he's a real expert at it too," said Costello.

There were still a few sheets of the Luxembourg notepaper in stock. I took them, and en route to the writing desk saw Bianca hanging away clothing in the bedroom closet.

"*La posso aiutare?*" I asked courteously.

"*Ma no, grazie.* There's not much to help with."

"So I see. As it happens, I have accounts in some excellent shops around town, and all you need do—"

"No. You're not to make such offers to me, David. No clothing. No little extras. No money that magically appears in my purse."

"Pride?"

"Yes. You don't know me at all, do you?"

"About as well as you know me," I said.

"You're wrong about that. In those letters to your mother when you were at school—"

"Jesus, not only the postcards to Grandpa, but the letters to Mama, too?"

Bianca said equably, "She was glad to share them with someone, and Milos certainly wasn't interested. But now and then you wrote about your interest in old films and football and chess. So I took an interest in them. I joined a classical film society and made a point of seeing all the pictures you seemed to like. No sacrifice really. I was delighted by them."

"And in your spare time you played football and chess?"

"Only chess. And very well. But I did lure Umberto into taking me along whenever he attended a football match. I became quite the aficionada. In fact, I run the football pools at the clinic."

"The complete home study course," I said, "in the school for wives."

"At least you seem amused by the idea, not angered. I call that progress. But what's the writing paper for? Battle plans?"

"Sorry," I said, "but any such questions are not in order."

"It's too late for that, David. Whatever you withhold from me now I'll only imagine, and imagination can make things much more frightening than they might really be."

"No. I don't want you complicit in what I'm doing."

"You know I'm already complicit. And Umberto happens to be the saintly one in the family. Resist not evil. Peace at any price. He really lives by those precepts. Not I. And your situation now—"

"*Che cosa è successo?* First you call my vendetta a madness. Now all of a sudden—"

"Not all of a sudden. I've had time to think it over."

"Not that much time," I said.

"Yes, I have. I put myself in your place and asked myself what I would do if I were the victim of those people. Are they to live out their lives happily while I lick my bleeding wounds? And do you know what the answer was?"

"I can't imagine," I said truthfully.

"The answer was that I would do nothing. Even worse, I would tell myself it was because it was morally right to do nothing, and all the while it would only be cowardice that moved me. But you're not a coward. It came to me that I couldn't feel about you as I do if you were. So now I want to know at least as much about your plans as Signor Costello does."

"Very well, have it your way. Kees Baar has so far managed to stay out of range. But the woman who was certainly his accomplice in the hijacking—"

"Marie-Paule Neyna. A Belgian. You were her partner in *Les Amis du Bon Évangéliste.*"

I said with honest admiration, "That's a remarkably shrewd deduction. You really studied those letters, didn't you?"

"And I have an excellent mind. Does that surprise you?"

"I'm beyond all surprises. Anyhow, she's in Paris now, and I believe that if I play my cards right, she may steer me to Baar. I'm going to introduce David Shaw to her."

"Your cards, you say. What cards?"

"She and I had a very friendly time of it in Marseille. More than friendly on her part. I want to produce a van Zee letter for her that'll ignite those embers in her, providing, of course, that any embers remain. If I can convince her that Jan van Zee did not carelessly walk out of her life, but was ordered out by our boss, Kees Baar—"

"I understand. Then you might turn her against Baar."

"I might. The difficulty is in getting the message across to her. I'm not sure how she'll take a love letter popping up ten years after the event."

"Then I can tell you as a woman that she'll believe what she wants to believe. David, let me write that letter."

"You?"

"Yes. At least let me try my hand at it. You can do the translation of it from Italian into van Zee's English."

Nothing ventured, nothing gained. While she was scribbling away I had visitors. Williams and Wylie of Shaw Film Productions. They looked at Bianca with interest, she dipped her head at them, I omitted introductions. Oscar said, "We're throwing a farewell-to-Paris dinner tonight at Maxim's, Dave. It won't be official if you're not there."

Arguing this would only keep them here. "I'll make it official," I said. I hustled them out on that, a hand on each shoulder, and waited impatiently until Bianca completed her labors. She watched intently as I read through the pages of tiny, finely etched script.

"Well," she said, "What's your reaction?"

"Embarrassment."

"That's not surprising. But take this into account. Marie-Paule knows that Jan van Zee was really Jean Lespere. And that the French are capable of expressing love in words. They're not speechless lumps on this subject like the Dutch. Or the Americans."

"Very astute of you, doctor. All right, I'll work up a translation and take my chances on it. Meanwhile, Paris, the city of light, the city of love, awaits you. And so does Harry, who will be happy to drive you around in his fine limousine and show you the town."

"I see," said Bianca. "You find me a distraction." She seemed taken with the idea.

"Well," I said, "that's one way of putting it."

The wrong way.

Not really a distraction. Much more a presence. A light. A warmth.

It was happening too fast.

There had been Anneke. My Anneke. Suddenly, in this light and warmth, the image of her was becoming more and more insubstantial. Unbelievably, another was taking its place.

All wrong to even let the thought enter my mind, but there it was, framed as a question. Two words. Question mark.

My Bianca?

The battered old Hôtel Mazarin on the rue de Vaugirard was solidly French middle class, the kind of place where thrifty, well-to-do farmers and merchants from the provinces stayed for a big week in town. It smelled of respectability and a noxious floor polish. I could see its appeal for Marie-Paule, a great girl during our evangelical stint for respectability and floor polish.

Costello looked around. "Somebody here is one of the agency men. He covers the front way out. There's another who hangs around the side door. They've already been warned that if she tries a getaway they're to stay with her, no matter what."

"A getaway?" I said doubtfully, and Costello said, "You never know what somebody'll do when they're cornered. And little Marie sure as hell knows she's cornered."

She did. When I announced my name through the door she opened it at once, shrugged a greeting, and motioned us in with a sardonic flip of the hand. Physically, she hadn't changed much in ten years, although the hair, once waist-length when released from its schoolmarm bun, was now cropped into a boyish coiffure. She was as lean and sharp-featured and sallow as ever. In style, however, she had traveled the full distance from dowdy to ultra-chic. And, marking the Danish influence, she was smoking a long thin cigar.

"Do you speak English?" I asked, knowing she did.

"Yes."

"And you know who I am? Why I'm here?"

"Yes, of course." She pointed her chin at Costello. "But I don't know who your friend is."

"As you say, a friend."

"A nice way of putting it." Now the chin was aimed at my attaché case. "That isn't wired for recording by some chance?"

I opened the case on her dresser, and she inspected its structure closely. Then, indifferently, she checked the contents of a folder. "The famous van Zee letters," she remarked. "Copies, naturally, considering how valuable the originals are." She dipped into the other folder. "And reports by an unnamed agency on Marie-Paule Neyna and some others of interest. No surprises here. Well?"

"Well," I said, "since there are no surprises, we can get right down to business. The business, of course, concerns Jan van Zee."

"So? But your own records must show that I never knew any Jan van Zee."

"How about a Jean Lespere?"

"That one I knew ten years ago for the matter of a few days. I haven't seen him since."

I said, "Are you trying to tell me you aren't aware they're the same man?"

"Of course, I'm aware of that. I am merely trying to answer you with precision. I understand that your type appreciates precision in these interrogations."

"My type?"

"Yes. You may drop the mask, Mr. Shaw. The stories you've been telling such credulous fools as Simon Leewarden and Yves Rouart-Rochelle are not for me. The charade is over. This must be a painful enlightenment for you, but it's a necessary one if we're to come to terms."

Actually, the enlightenment was not so much painful as stupefying. There were good reasons why Bianca had seen through me. I couldn't, on the spur of the moment, come up with a single reason to explain how Marie-Paule had. And I couldn't just stand here and wonder about it. "Miss Neyna, forgive me if I seem slow-witted, but I have no idea what you're talking about."

"Please." She compressed a world of scorn into that one word. "Almost as soon as you made your appearance on the scene I suspected your identity. After all, it was simply a case of following your activities closely until there could be no doubt about them. An idealistic film producer searching for his lost author? And mustering an army of agents to this end? What a clumsy joke. No wonder your country has a name for being a bungler in these matters."

A ray of light appeared in the darkness. "My country? Then you really do know the nature of my work?"

"As an agent of your CIA in America? Yes, of course."

"Jesus," said Costello in wonderment, and I shot him a look to choke off the next word before it could come out.

Marie-Paule glanced at him. "That one," she said to me scathingly, "even looks as if he had been cast for the role."

"Never mind him," I said. "I'm the one in charge. Now tell me, does Kees Baar know my real identity too?"

"He won't admit to it. When he first decided to let our service sometimes be used as a conduit for your CIA money I warned him that if anything went wrong along the way, you were not people to take it lightly. He laughed it off then. He's got remarkable talents, Kees, but he can be too sure of himself. Then, when van Zee's name and your cover story appeared in the newspapers, I asked Kees if CIA money made up any part of the hijacked million dollars and he said no. He dreamed up a story for me about its being removed from the treasury of some large city in America. Otherwise he'd have to admit my concern was justified from the start, and Kees will never admit to a mistake. Even when you put into motion your elaborate apparatus to search out van Zee, Kees refused to acknowledge it."

"Stubborn, isn't he?" I said. "And what about Leewarden and Yves? Neither of them gave any indication they knew I was a CIA agent."

"Because they were never informed that your agency did now and then use our services. After all, it was Kees alone who brought in that account. Why should they get a share of our commission from it?"

"And van Zee?"

"Knew nothing." One wall of the room contained a bay window, and in the area it provided was a small table, the remains of a breakfast on it, and a couple of chairs. Marie-Paule seated herself on one of the chairs and tapped the ash of her cheroot into a half-empty coffee cup. "Too bad," she remarked, "that van Zee wasn't advised from the start about our dealings with you people. He wouldn't have been so easily tricked into regarding you as a confidant and writing you those letters."

"Perhaps not." I straddled the chair across from her, putting on the expression, or so I hoped, of a CIA agent not to be trifled with. "So you're telling me that it was van Zee who pulled off the hijacking. No one else."

"As if you didn't know that, Mr. Shaw. Otherwise, why would your agency go to such lengths to run him to earth? But what you've been told about his fate is true. My associates were on the way back to Zurich with him to reclaim that money when he tried to escape from them and killed himself in the attempt. A bitter pill to swallow, but there it is. He is dead, and there is no way of discovering where he hid the money."

"Deplorable," I said, straight-faced.

Marie-Paule gave me a sharp look. "You doubt me?"

"Yes. You see, Yves, who once told me that same story, phoned me from Marseille this morning to say he had some fresh thoughts on the subject. He now believes he was tricked by Baar. That it was Baar who hijacked the money and then arranged van Zee's death to cover up his crime and make sure there was no real search for the missing million."

"Ah, l'impileur!" Marie-Paule said in outrage. *"Le batteur!"* and then in expurgated translation, "The filthy liar!"

"Maybe," I said. "All I know is that Yves told me that if I'd meet with him in Marseille he'd describe exactly how Baar pulled off his double-cross. He'd even take me to the scene itself and demonstrate it."

"All lies!" Marie-Paule exploded. "Van Zee himself confessed to the robbery."

"After being beaten half to death, according to Yves. But I'm not making final judgments yet, Miss Neyna, not until I hear what Kees has to say. He may very well explain the whole thing in a few words."

"Then speak to Kees."

"Unfortunately, he's too cautious for his own good. It seems he prefers to keep away from me, rather than meeting with me and settling all questions on the spot. I must turn in a report to my superiors which makes some sense. You can see that unless an interview with Kees is part of it, it won't satisfy them at all."

"And what if I do see that? There's nothing I can do about it."

"But there is," I said. "You can tell me where to find him. Or is it possible"—I timed a pause for maximum effect—"that you yourself share Yves's suspicions and won't admit it?"

"No. All I will tell you is that van Zee was guilty of the hijacking. He was capable of any treachery, that one. I've had the privilege of reading all those self-serving letters he wrote you. You're a fool if you judge him by such nonsense."

"So it may turn out, Miss Neyna, but I have one small advantage over you in this." The translation of Bianca's effort was waiting in my pocket, reduced to three pages of van Zee's jagged penmanship. I took out the pages. "A letter which no one but myself has ever had the privilege of reading. Since it was so intensely personal, and since it offered my agency nothing of value, I simply left it out of the files."

She took the pages. "More of van Zee's wild imaginings?"

"That," I said, "I must leave to your judgment."

She cocked the cheroot at an upward angle between her teeth and read. She couldn't have been more than midway through the first page when her expression suddenly changed. What little color there was in those sallow cheeks drained from them. She abruptly stood up and extinguished the cheroot in her coffee cup. "Pardon," she said, and, letter in hand, crossed the room to the windowless little lavatory there. The sound of its bolt being slammed into place was like a pistol shot.

It was a long wait. As it lengthened, Costello started to look worried. He drifted over to me and said in an undertone, "You don't think she did something to herself in there, do you?"

"No."

"Then you better get ready to bust down that door, because if she just stays locked up in there that's what's left."

"She'll come out."

She finally did, her face expressionless, but her eyes now swollen and reddened. She crossed the room, obviously under rigid control, and reseated herself at the table.

"I'm sorry," I said. "Sometimes in the line of duty one is given a look at things he really shouldn't see. Like that letter."

"Understandable," said Marie-Paule in a tight voice.

"A letter like that—" I said. "Well, I have the feeling that if van Zee knew your address when he was moved to write it, he would have sent it directly to you. You didn't realize until now that he was forced to end his attachment to you, did you? That Kees Baar didn't want any such intensely emotional partnerships within the organization."

"No, I did not know that until now."

"Then I'm glad at least to have that small injustice to van Zee cleared up."

"Yes." She held out the letter. "Your property."

"All yours, Miss Neyna. You have every right to it. And what my superiors don't know about this won't hurt them."

"Thank you. You're very kind."

"However," I said, "what will concern them is my failure to get together with Kees and hear his explanation of events. You know you hold the key to that meeting."

She shook her head. "No more, please. Not now."

"I don't have time to waste. Yves wants me to meet with him by this weekend so that he can explain his charges against Kees in detail. But if I can see Kees beforehand—"

"No." She looked at me unwaveringly, jaw set. "I'll call you before the weekend. I give you my word on it."

I pretended to think it over. "All right. I suppose you know I'm at the Meurice."

"Yes. I'll call you there. Now please—"

On the way to the elevator, Costello stopped to get it off his chest. "The CIA, would you believe it?"

"Aside from that, Ray, what did you make of her? And that story about phoning me?"

"Well"—he gave this close consideration—"she swears easy and she lies easy. Still and all, you worked her right up to where she's ready to cut the Dutchman's throat right now. So she could make that call. Did you watch her while she was reading that letter? You really did one hell of a job on it."

"Give Miss Cavalcanti all the credit. It was her job."

"You're kidding," Costello said. "You got her to write the letter?"

"No. She volunteered."

"Women," Costello said with awe.

In the cab, homeward bound to the Meurice, he remarked, "Couple of cars back, there's a guy with an eyepatch driving a Citroën. Your hit man?"

I turned to see. "Yes."

"Uh-huh. And you never did line up Marie to do something about him."

I said, "She sidetracked me with that weird CIA angle. But I've been thinking about it. Much as she'd like to get Baar in her sights now, wouldn't she want him to finish off Yves first? After all, I gave her the idea that Yves is ready to offer evidence about the hijacking. Since she was in on it, that makes him a threat to her too."

Costello nodded agreement. "It does. How long would it take the Dutchman to get to Marseille from around here?"

"Couple of hours by plane. Eight to ten hours by car."

"Then I'll stay on the line with the agency right through. Hell, there's that good-by party Oscar's giving tonight, isn't there? I guess this leaves me out of it." He didn't sound sorry at the prospect.

"Meanwhile, as long as One-eye is around, don't you come walking home alone from any more parties."

I didn't expect to find Bianca in the suite when I got back, and she wasn't. No need to worry, I told myself without conviction, because Harry wasn't present either. It was well after dark when I heard her give him a hearty *"Ciao, amico"* outside the door, and in she walked, weighted down by a string tote overloaded with books and a bulging brown paper bag.

I looked pointedly at my watch. *"Da dove vengono, signorina?"*

"Where? Oh, the library where I caught up on some research. The bookstalls along the river. A fruiterer who had some splendid bargains. But what happened with you? Did you show Marie-Paule the letter?"

"Yes. Now I'm going to lay down an important rule. You're always to be back here before dark, understand?" I took the string bag from her and planked it down on the table with a thud. The thud made me feel better. "What is this stuff?"

"A few books I could never find in Rome. Some fruit. Or what's left of it, now that you've worked out your temper on it."

I said with great control, "Signorina, take my word for it that room service will be glad to deliver fruit to you any time you call for it."

"It was. At lunch. But I wasn't glad to pay that monstrous bill. And kindly stop addressing me as signorina. Try *bellezza*. God knows I've starved myself enough years to have earned it."

"Very well," I said. *"Bellezza.* Light of my life. Add to the rules that I pay the bills here."

"When we dine together, yes. Only then. Now what about Marie-Paule? Was she affected by the letter? Did she tell you where Baar is keeping himself?"

"Yes, she was affected by the letter. No, she didn't tell me where to find Baar, but she may in a day or two."

"And then what?"

"We'll see. Meanwhile, you can dine off your fruit while I dress for a dinner party to which you're not invited."

Inevitably, attendance at the dinner party was minimal, with Costello and Harry on duty, and with Grete having decided to share a private farewell with Jean-Pierre. That left me marooned for what seemed eternity in the company of Oscar Wylie and Miller Williams who, as a team, were even more stupefyingly dull than they were individually.

At my insistence, the party broke up early and traveled back to the hotel on foot from rue Royale along the rue de Rivoli. I was acutely Citroën-conscious now, curious to know if One-eye was still on duty. If not, would someone else be filling in for him? There was some satisfaction in noting after a few blocks that the hired knife was evidently not in the area, a satisfaction that abruptly evaporated when I gave thought to where else he might be right now. And that I hadn't warned Bianca to double-lock the door after I left.

I quickened my pace more and more, looking around for a phone booth in this wilderness along the Tuileries, my companions falling into a trot to keep up with me, Oscar now and then loudly protesting against the exercise. At last, there was a phone.

"*Pronto,*" said Bianca, her throat obviously unslit. "*'Allo. Qui est-ce qui est là?*"

I told her who, then took a deep breath of relief, and she instantly picked up the clue. "David, why do you sound like that? Is something wrong?"

"No. I just called to tell you that I'm on my way back. And even though Harry's keeping an eye on the hallway, there are extra locks on all your doors. So please—"

"I understand. That little man with the knife. Well, you may as well know that he's been on my mind since you left. I could see him waiting in a dark corner for you. Please don't be too brave about him."

"Of course not."

"Good. I'll be waiting for you, *caro mio.*"

Bellezza.

Caro mio.

God almighty.

And out of all the confusion in me, one thing became terrifyingly clear. I was as vulnerable now as Leewarden and Yves had been in their women. If it had been the voice of the enemy at the other end of that line instead of Bianca's, there would have been no negotiations, only instant and abject surrender.

Costello was at his desk, a map laid out before him, a stubby forefinger tracing lines along it. He swung around to face me. "Little over an hour ago, Frenchy packed some stuff into his car and headed out of Marseille. My guess is the Dutchman phoned him they had to have a meeting right away, and Frenchy fell for it. I'm trying to figure where it'll be."

"How about Paris?" I said.

"But not for sure. I've got two cars on Frenchy now—four men —so they can take turns calling where they are without losing him. Look at this road map. Here's where he is now, heading north. Where would you say he's aiming for?"

I followed his finger on the map. "Too early to tell. He's past Tarascon, so it's not Spain. Actually, Dijon, way up here, would be the giveaway. West from there means Paris, east means the Low Countries. Paris still makes the most sense. It means Baar sits tight and lets Yves do all the traveling."

"Uh-huh. So we just keep watching and waiting. How'd the party go? See One-eye around anywhere?"

"No. We walked home from the restaurant so that I could keep an eye out for him."

"Which," said Costello, "is not the brightest move you ever made. Anyhow, I got the number of that car when it was tailing us and I passed it along to the agency. They already came up with one tidbit. The ownership's held by an outfit that rents out cars for company use."

"Not much of a tidbit."

"So far. But tomorrow the agency'll try to find out just who they rented it to."

"If they do, let me know fast."

"Sure." He nodded at the door opening on my part of the suite. "By phone?" he asked expressionlessly.

"By phone," I said.

Not perfume, but a powerful smell of sliced oranges met me when I walked into the bedroom. Bianca was seated in bed under the covers, half-glasses perched on her nose, her hair piled high and a pencil thrust into it. She was wearing what might be called a good practical pajama jacket and was evidently going through the van Zee letters, the folder of which she had in hand while a large part of its contents were scattered around the bed. Also scattered around the bed were some paperbacks, a bowl heaped high with orange peel, and a face towel dyed with citrus stains.

She lowered her head to regard me over her glasses. "And what do you find so funny?"

"Truthfully?"

"Always truthfully."

"Well," I said, "this isn't exactly what I saw waiting for me. Humor is the fine art of surprise. Let's say I'm surprised."

"Possibly because you anticipated soft music and the Maja Desnuda beckoning?"

"Something along those lines," I admitted.

"Yes. I thought of that when I was getting ready for bed. Then my insecurities got in my way."

"Your insecurities. Of course."

"No, I mean it. I don't really have evidence yet that you're eager to make love to me, and I don't want you to do it just because I'm sending out signals that it's expected. What if you aren't in the mood? Then you'd only feel resentful about it. I think it's much better to let these things take their own course, don't you?"

"Yes."

"Is that all you have to say?"

"Well," I said, tempting fate, "I suppose I should thank you for such consideration and the happiness it promises."

"So?" Her guard was up. "Explain that, please."

"You say you're insecure. Now you've made me insecure. Obviously, we've achieved the kind of relationship everyone is striving for today."

Fate, in the form of an orange peel, whacked me between the shoulder blades just before I made it through the door of the dressing room. She had a good sharp eye and a good strong pitching arm, my analyst.

I disrobed, showered, and, in defiance of the lady's hesitant approach to the Life Force, doused the damp flesh with Cardin's version of myrrh and frankincense. Then I stuck my head through the dressing-room door. "Forgiven?"

She poked a finger into her cheek and twisted it in a gesture right out of the back alleys of Trastevere. "A hard case, all right," she said, "but yes, you're forgiven. Now come out here. There's something I must ask you."

I strolled out and the analyst unabashedly took stock of me. "How did you get tanned all over like that? Do you belong to a nudist club?"

"I did. A very unusual one." In my absence she had at least shifted the debris on the bed to her side of it. I got under the blankets on my side and propped myself in the same sitting position as hers. *"Buona sera, professore,"* I said.

"Buona sera, signore. But there is one question—"

"Basta," I said firmly. "Enough." I placed the bowl of peelings on the floor and tumbled the books beside it. "Time to return those letters to that folder and put it on the convenient table beside you."

While she was at this chore I reached out a foot and pressed it against her leg. She gave a little start but the leg remained where it was. I slowly drew the foot past her knee until it rested against a warm, velvet roundness of thigh. She yielded to the pressure as she divested herself of the eyeglasses and the pencil.

I said, "There's an old joke they tell in America which applies to this situation."

"Yes?" said my analyst warily.

"Well, it seems there was an inspector of lunatic asylums—"

"Oh, please. You must know we don't use such terminology any more."

"Uno manicomio, professore. Uno manicomio. A lunatic asylum. After all, this is a very old joke. Anyhow, this inspector walked into one of its rooms where there was a most respectable-looking old gentleman wearing nothing but a handsome hat. A fine Borsalino. And the inspector said to him, 'Why aren't you wearing any clothing?' and the old gentleman said, 'Because no one ever comes to visit me.' So the inspector said quite logically, 'Then, my good sir, why are you wearing that hat?' and the old gentleman said, 'Because someone might come.' "

Bianca hooted. "That is funny. But you said it applies to this situation. How does it?"

"You're not wearing any pants," I said.

She looked puzzled for a moment, then as the light dawned she shook her head in self-reproach. "I should have seen what you were building up to from the start. And it is even funnier this way because it's so true. David, how marvelous. Suddenly I don't feel at all insecure. Do you mind if I turn out the light now?"

"And leave us in darkness? In a bed this size we'll never find each other without a light."

Long, long after, when we were both satiated into a hard-breathing stupor, she did turn it out, kneeling on my chest to reach the switch, then collapsing on me in an exaggerated torpor.

"Innamorato mio," she whispered in my ear. *"Tesoro mio.* So tender. So skillful. So powerful. And with a joke for every occasion."

I was wakened to pitch blackness by the ringing of the phone. I had to detach myself from my soundly sleeping partner to answer.

"It's Frenchy." Costello spit it out hard. "They lost him."

"I'll be right in."

My watch showed a little after five. Possibly—just possibly—before giving the slip to the agency men trailing him, Yves had traveled far enough to signal his destination.

Next door, the shattered remains of a bottle on a drenched and reeking floor indicated how Costello must have taken the bad news. "An hour ago," he said in answer to me. "I didn't tell you right off because they were still hunting for him. They just now called to say no dice."

"Where did it happen?"

"Dijon. The railroad station. He pulled up, left the motor running, went inside. One car was right behind him down the block. The other came up in a little while, so there they both were, waiting.

Nothing to worry about, because no trains were due through, and anyhow the car motor was running. By the time they caught on he was gone it was too late."

"He could still be around there, Ray."

"Sure. If a meeting with the Dutchman was set up there, he could be lying in an alley right now with a knife in him."

"Then," I said, "Yves is scratched off the list. Which happens to be the name of the game."

"Only we both know the Dutchman is the name of the game. One point for Leewarden, five points for Frenchy, twenty for the Dutchman, that's how we're really scoring it, aren't we? And I'm telling you that whole business at the station has the Dutchman's touch. We were that close to him, God damn it. If we—"

There was a knock on the door. I opened it to Bianca who stood there in robe and slippers. *"Mi dispiace,* David. I knew you had to be here. May I come in?"

"What's she saying?" Costello asked me.

"That she'd like to join the party. Any objections?"

"Not as long as you two knock it off with the Italian and stick to English." He took notice that he was presenting himself to the lady in a pair of drooping underwear shorts and a wristwatch. "And if you let me get on a pair of pants."

"If you think it necessary," said the lady. She leaned against the wall, arms folded on her chest, while Costello got into his trousers. Then he nodded at her with what could only be interpreted as admiration. "I wanted to tell you. That was one hell of a letter you wrote for little Marie. I was there, so I know."

"Thank you," said Bianca. "But now I must tell you a thought I had about those people."

"Not now," I said. "First we have a little crisis to attend to."

"A crisis? A trouble?"

"So it seems." I gave her the gist of it. "In any event"—I aimed this at Costello—"we're left with three areas to keep under surveillance day and night. The Mazarin, Vahna's place, and Chouchoute's. Then, if either Yves or Baar shows up—"

"But," Bianca cut in, "that is what I must tell to you. David, what if Yves killed Kees Baar soon after the robbery in Luxembourg? What if he is already dead?"

"Kees Baar?"

"Think, David. You met all the others these past weeks. You spoke to them. You saw with your own eyes that they exist. But for Baar you have no such evidence."

"Look," I said, "I appreciate your scientific approach—"

"No, you do not, because you want Kees Baar to exist. You want that with desperation. But please. Try to see it as I do, from a little distance."

I reined in my temper, "All right, and what do I see? The murder of an American named Gardiner Fremont that took place when everyone but Baar was accounted for. The murder of Simon Leewarden when everyone but Baar was accounted for. Eliminate Baar as their killer, and who does that leave in his place?"

"A paid assassin. Is it so difficult for Marie-Paule to find one? At this moment there is such a one with his knife out for you."

Costello said, "We know that. But Marie? What gave you the idea she was the one behind him?"

Bianca shrugged. "Last night I read the letters again and considered all the events that followed after them. It came to me that Kees Baar never appeared in any event. But Marie-Paule? Who, of a sudden, has a fortune to spend on the buying of brothels? And if it is the stolen money, why is it now in her hands?"

Costello looked at me. "The Dutchman dead?"

"I'll believe it when I see it," I said.

"Not even then!" Bianca said fiercely. "You made his destruction the whole meaning of your life, and you will not be cheated of it, will you?"

It was cold and gray here on Square Nine. Now, alarmingly, there was a siren call to the light and warmth this woman offered.

No.

Because sharply outlined in the cold grayness were the images of Anneke accusing and Kees Baar gloating, and all the light and warmth in the world couldn't dispose of those images. Only I could.

I said in Italian, "I'm sorry, signorina. You specialize in clever argument and cut-rate psychotherapy. I can do without either."

Too late, I knew I shouldn't have said it.

"Hey," Costello said, uncomprehending but reproachful. He took in the stricken expression on the lady's face, the sudden high color in her cheeks. "If this is too private for me—"

"I think it is," I said. "I'll see you later."

Back in the bedroom the lady immediately curled herself up on the bed, knees to chin.

"Molto interessante," I commented. "The fetal position. Regressive behavior under stress. Now what would you prescribe for that, doctor?"

"Just leave me alone."

I sat down beside her. When I placed a hand on her arm she flung it off. "No," I said. "Don't do that."

"I choose to do it."

"Obviously. But let's come to an understanding about this one thing. No matter the feelings of the moment, when either of us reaches out a hand to the other it must never be rejected."

No response.

I waited.

Slowly Bianca twisted around to face me. "Is that how it was with you and Anneke?"

"After she taught it to me. I'll admit I wasn't the fastest learner in the world."

"I see. You know, the little time I had with her she impressed me as a very gentle and forgiving soul. Was she?"

"Always."

"Well, I'm not." Bianca draped an arm around my neck and drew me down on her, straightening out those long legs so that I was half lying on her. "I'll forgive you, but I must also inform you that you have a vile temper. And a vile mouth. And that your arrogance is almost frightening."

"And to think that's my good side."

"No, your good side is that when you insult me publicly, at least you do it in a language that an outsider can't understand."

"Costello? Far from an outsider. Already your devoted admirer. He should have done wonders for those insecurities."

"He did," said Bianca soberly. "He understood what I was trying to tell you about Kees Baar. He could see the logic of it. You're past all logic. The way the Church needs Satan to war against, you need Kees Baar."

"Bellezza, you forget too easily what he's done to me."

"No. I hate him bitterly for what he's done to you. But I hate him

---

251

even more for what he's doing to you now. Controlling your life. Directing you down the road you're taking. Why can't you just tell yourself he's dead and beyond reach?"

"Because," I said, "he isn't. And, since I'm not quite as simpleminded as Signor Costello, I'm not buying your kind of logic. I think there's more to it than meets the eye."

"How?" She was too ingenuous about it.

I said, "You were violently opposed to what you called my vendetta. Suddenly you changed sides, you actually became my partner in it when you wrote that letter. Now, just as suddenly, you've changed sides again." I released her arms from around my neck and sat up to see how she was taking this. "What made you do it? There must be some reason."

"There's a good chance Baar is dead."

"Not that good a chance. What made you do it? The truth."

She closed her eyes. "I woke up and you were gone. I started thinking—"

"Yes?"

"If Baar isn't dead—"

"We're making progress," I said.

"I'm not saying he isn't, I'm just conceding the possibility. But if he isn't, in the end it will come down to you and him alone, face to face."

"It will."

She opened her eyes very wide. "Don't you see? He must know that too. He must know that if he doesn't kill you, you'll certainly kill him!"

"But you understood that all along."

"I didn't! I've been telling myself that if he could stay at a distance from you, sooner or later you'd give up your obsession. But now that I know so much about both of you I don't believe that any more." She sat up, planted a hand on each side of my face, and gave me the full power of those eyes. "Listen to me. You have enough evidence against Baar to put him in jail for life. You must go to the police with it."

"Only if I'm ready to openly admit that I'm Jan van Zee who traveled under a false passport and committed some crimes of his own. In that case, Baar might possibly wind up in jail, but I certainly would. And under any conditions this is not police business."

"Meaning you're determined to end up either a murderer or a corpse!"

I drew her hands from my face and took a tight grip on them. I said, "It's obvious that this arrangement isn't working at all. We can't stay together under these conditions. I'll get you a place somewhere safe. Harry can stay on as your bodyguard, and I'll hire some agency men to back him up."

She sat there, very white of face, bringing herself under control. Then she said calmly, "It's true, of course. I have been making difficulties. That was wrong of me."

I waited.

"No," she said, "there's nothing to be suspicious about. Baar may already have been disposed of by his friends. I'll comfort myself with that thought. Meanwhile, as long as you restrain your temper and your tongue, I'll be the ideal lover. Forbearing, passionate on occasion—that comes easily as you must have observed last night—humorous when the light touch is called for, and yes, I think I'll try to give up smoking again."

"Very funny."

"Not altogether. Do you know how I feel about you?"

"I'm not even sure you do."

"Then consider, signore, that whoever you choose to be, I am hopelessly, painfully, happily in love with you. Now if you have the courage, tell me your feelings for me."

"Confused."

"You're not as brave as you look. Try again."

"My God," I said, "how long have we known each other? Two days?"

"Eighteen years and three months. And too many of them wasted. I'm not wasting any more by saying good-by to you now and setting up house in a fortress surrounded by armed guards."

"If anything happens to you—" I said.

"Ah, so there it is at last. I'll settle for that. And look, it's getting light. Open the shutters and we can lie down and watch the sunrise together."

I opened the shutters on a downpour. We fell asleep watching it together and slept until noon.

At the lunch table she maintained the same placid mood even while explaining that mama and papa had never accepted her independence and that poor Umberto had to act as her go-between.

"That reminds me," she said. "I must phone him and tell him your gift will soon be on the way. You can't imagine what it'll mean to him. He's a splendid doctor but a terrible administrator, and this business of scrounging for pennies to maintain the clinic is simply beyond him. He'll find it hard to believe his troubles are over. He'll heap blessings on you."

"It was supposed to be a bribe," I reminded her.

"So it was," she said equably. "You see how God moves in mysterious ways?"

She reported after the call, "He was grateful almost to tears. And he insists on paying you an honor I'm not sure you'll appreciate all that much. But there's no changing his mind about it."

"About what?"

"The clinic is to be renamed after you. It's never really had a name of distinction anyhow. It is now to be La Clinica David Hanna Shaw. What do you think of that?"

"Not much," I said. "But who knows? It may come in handy some day having my own devoted obstetrical service standing by."

"Perhaps even sooner than you think," said Bianca, smiling.

That smile—?

"I don't believe it," I said. "Signorina, there is a marvelous device in the form of a pill—"

"Yes, of course. And no, I'm not using it."

"Bianca."

"You can stop looking so reproachful, David. There are devices men can use. If you so object to fathering our child, why didn't you take measures against it? Why assume I would? I have no such objections."

I was trying to come up with a sane and suitable response when Costello walked in. He was disheveled, a little unsteady on his feet, and triumphant.

"Yves turned up," I said.

"No. The agency just reported that One-eye's car is rented to a company works out of Rome. A tobacco and produce factor. Does that ring any bells?"

"No."

"The company name is Periniades and Souloukis."

"Milos," I said.

"That's right," said Costello. "His rental car, his hit man, his contract. It looks like your grandpa's ten million really got to him, didn't it? He knows your dumb-as-hell mama is next in line for it if you kick off, and he'll be right there to spend it for her."

"Milos," Bianca said. "But of course. When I told your mother I would come to Paris to see you he must have known it at once. He could count on me to lead that murderous little man right to you. Horrible! But, David, what happens to your mother now when she learns about this?"

Costello nodded grimly. "That's a fact, Davey. I can take care of him easy, but breaking the news to her—"

"How do you take care of him?" I said. "That comes first."

"I've got that file about his payoffs and kickbacks to top people in the government there. I just tell him over the phone that either he gets One-eye off your back fast or that stuff goes right to the newspapers. So that leaves mama. How do you get her to walk out on him without letting her know why she has to?"

"I don't see why she has to," I said.

"You mean," said Bianca, "you would let her remain with him even after you know what he is capable of?"

"She's in no danger from him. And what she doesn't know won't hurt her. Breaking up the marriage would. At her age and weight, she's not likely to find a replacement for him very easily."

"David—!"

"Basta, signorina. Remember your vows."

She looked stormy. She looked guilty. She remembered her vows.

I spent the rest of the day in Costello's room, starting every time the phone rang, and it rang regularly as the agency men kept reporting in turn. Even traveling from Dijon to Paris by donkey, Yves should have reached here by nightfall if this was his destination, but according to the men on the job, no one of his description had come near any of the territories they had staked out.

Late in the evening Bianca and I dined out at her insistence— anything, she said, to bring me out of my mood—and then, with Harry trailing close behind us in the car, we walked back to the hotel under the streetlights. We found Costello asleep, the phone planted on the pillow beside him. "Poor man," whispered Bianca. "Caught in someone else's nightmare."

Costello opened his eyes and focused them on me with an effort. "Any sign of One-eye?"

I shook my head.

"Figures. I finally got through to Mister Peritonitis in Rome and scared the hell out of him. Told him I knew what was going on and to get his little pal off your back right now, or else. He made a noise about not understanding what I was talking about, but he understood all right. Especially after I reminded him about those files. So that takes care of that."

"Anything from the agency?"

"Nothing. You still think Frenchy'll turn up in town here?"

"If he doesn't," I said, "we're down to that phone call Marie-Paule promised to make. And if she doesn't make it, we're nowhere."

"You said it," Costello remarked. "I didn't."

There was no finding sleep for me that night for a long time, and I was aware, from the occasional tuggings of blanket and poundings of pillow on the far side of the bed, that Bianca was also having trouble in this direction. At last, just as I was slipping into unconsciousness, her voice penetrated it. "David, if it works out as you hope it will—if Yves leads you to Kees Baar—would you really kill him?"

"Yes."

"But I don't want you to! I don't want you to kill anybody!"

"I haven't yet."

"I don't even like the way you say that. Look, if nothing happens by tomorrow, would you do me a favor? Would you come to Rome with me?"

"Bellezza, if you're planning to reunite me with my mother—"

"No. It's the clinic. Its business affairs are always in a tangle. Everyone means well there, but no one seems able to take charge. You have the right to do that now. They'd be glad if you did it."

"I have other plans," I said. "When they're attended to I'll consider your offer. Now good night and pleasant dreams."

"Pleasant dreams?" she said. "That's as bad a joke as I've ever heard."

I opened my eyes to see Harry tiptoeing around the room closing windows. Another downpour. I said to him, "Miss Hansen and the others make their plane in time?"

"Yes, sir. Three hours ago. Breakfast in bed, sir?"

"No, I'll have it in Mr. Costello's room. Let Miss Cavalcanti sleep. And, Harry, if she goes out, stay very close to her whether she uses the car or not."

She didn't leave the hotel but later showed up in Costello's room to spell me at my waiting and, finally, to order me out of that fog of cigar smoke for a breath of fresh air and a chance to stretch my legs. I was stretching my legs, quickstep, back and forth across the sitting room when I heard voices raised next door. I hastened in. Bianca was clutching Costello's arm. Costello, trying not to do any damage, was making an effort to detach himself. He said to me, "I told her to get you in here, but she said no, not to bother you. Bother you, hell!"

"About what?" I said.

"The phone call you've been waiting for. Frenchy's back in town."

Bianca released his arm. She said pleadingly to me, "It does not mean Baar will come here too, does it?"

I disregarded this. I said to Costello, "Where is Yves?"

"Look," he said, "let me tell it the way it happened. Schefflin, the agency guy, is staked out across the street from Choochoo's. This morning he sees Marie walk in there. A little later, along comes a priest and what looks to be a doctor, little black bag and all, and they go inside."

"Yves and Baar together?"

"Just listen. They go inside. An hour later, out comes the priest, and right after him all the girls carrying suitcases and such. And the two guys who tend the place. But no doctor and no Marie. This time Schefflin gets a good look at the priest, and he's legitimate all right, runs the church around the corner. As for the girls, they all head off one way and another.

"But one of them is our contact there, Avril, so Schefflin takes off after her. When he gets her alone she tells him the old lady is almost done for, that's why the priest and the doctor. And no, she never saw that doctor before. He asks her to describe him, and she says kind of chubby, neat little mustache, slick black hair. Frenchy, all right. As for everybody being cleared out of the place, it seems Marie told them that with the old lady on her death bed the shop would be closed for a couple of days."

I said, "Leaving Yves holed up there waiting for Baar to show."

"Right. And don't forget Marie's in there too. If the Dutchman wants to wipe out both of them together—"

The phone rang. I got to it a step ahead of Costello.

"Mr. Shaw?"

"Yes, Miss Neyna."

Costello whispered, "Right on schedule." When he picked up the extension phone Marie-Paule said sharply, "What is that?"

"My partner wants to hear this too, Miss Neyna. I assure you the call is not being recorded. For obvious reasons, my agency does not want any of this on the record."

"Understandable. Mr. Shaw, I have been in communication with Kees Baar." The voice was emotionless. "I have given him your message."

"You convinced him of my official status?"

"As an agent of the CIA? Yes. So he is now willing—but entirely on his own terms—to meet with you and explain the events surrounding van Zee's death."

"And his terms?"

"A train to Luxembourg leaves the Gare du Nord at five minutes past two. You will be on it, traveling first class. Kees will join you in your compartment some time before you arrive at Luxembourg. In Luxembourg he will provide a car, and the two of you will view the scene of the accident together. Is that satisfactory?"

"If the trip can be postponed a day or two, yes."

"No. Kees will board that train whether you are on it or not. If you are not, he will regard it as a breach of faith, and that will be the end of it as far as he is concerned. He put it very simply, Mr. Shaw. Today or never."

"All right, Miss Neyna, I'll be on the train. He won't have any trouble recognizing me?"

"None. Good journey, Mr. Shaw."

That was it.

"Hell," said Costello. "Him buying that CIA story? Inviting you to get close to him? That's not the Dutchman's style, Davey."

"No, but trying to get me out of town is. They don't know we've spotted Yves walking into Chouchoute's, but they do know we've been watching the place. Steer me away from it for a day, and that'll give Baar enough time to settle with Yves and then take off."

"So," said Costello heavily, "it's today."

"Please, David," Bianca said, "I heard nothing of what she told you. What was it?"

"A trick to get me away while Kees Baar attends to Yves. A little train ride to nowhere."

"Oh." Then her jaw set. "But how do you know it was a trick? I think it is better to believe her. If we all went together on that train—"

"A nice try," I told her, "but I'm not going on any trains. I am now going to visit some old friends at a former place of employment. Alone."

"No! David, understand one thing. If you do this, I leave for Rome at once. I will not wait here for the police to come tell me the terrible thing that happened to you. Or the terrible thing you did."

I said, "You'll do as you're told. While I'm gone you will remain here with Signor Costello and Harry and with the doors locked." I turned to Costello. "You heard that, Ray. She's to stay here, whatever it takes. She's not to get near any phone either. Let Harry know that too."

"Look," Costello said, "in one way she's right. How do you even figure to get in there?"

"You're forgetting that Jean Lespere knows that territory inside and out. Don't you worry about it. He'll get in."

"Madman!" Bianca said. She was almost through the door when I caught up to her. I clamped a hand on her shoulder and wheeled her around to face me. "No," I said, "there's to be no calls to the police. Or anyone else."

"How clever you are at reading minds," she said with contempt. Then in Italian, "You're hurting me, do you know that? But what does that matter? You'd kill anyone who stood in your way now, wouldn't you?"

"Behave yourself," I said. I flung her down on the bed and not trusting her at all I kept an eye on her as I said to Costello, "In London, you told me you'd get another gun to make up for the one you had to junk. Let's have it."

He went over to the locked drawer of his desk, scrabbled in back of it, and came up with a holstered pistol. He drew it from the holster. "You sure you know how to handle this thing?"

"Yes." I reached for it, but he shoved it into his pocket and said, "Better if I'm the one carting it around meanwhile. At least I'm licensed for it in the States."

It took me a moment to understand what this meant. Then I said harshly, "I'm not walking in there, Ray. I'm climbing in. And if you don't mind my saying so, you're too fat and out of shape for exercise like that."

He looked totally bulldog. "I mind your saying so. It doesn't change anything. And if you want to find out how out of shape I am, you can take the first punch right now. Only remember I'm not the kind of soft touch you just manhandled onto the bed there. You could be in for a surprise."

"Ray, your part of the job is finished."

He shook his head grimly. "Wherever your grandpa is right now, Davey—and most likely he's up to his neck in red-hot coals—he wouldn't go along with that, so neither can I. You figure on being locked up in there with Frenchy when the Dutchman walks in, don't you? Well, even counting Marie out that still makes it two against one. Two against two is a lot smarter odds."

I was wasting time with this.

"All right," I said, "get Harry in here and give him his orders about the lady. Tell him to sit on her if he has to. And the way it is outside, you'll need a raincoat."

Bianca stood watching in silence, fists clenched at her sides, as I changed into jeans and sneakers and found what I hoped was a waterproof jacket among the stock in my closet.

"Goodbye, David," she said when I was at the door.

"Arrivederci, cara mia."

"No," she said. "It's good-by, *cara mia.* Very much good-by."

L e Chat Louche, half a block down rue Houdon from Chouchoute's, was one of those dismal cafés where I had served as kitchen hand ten years before. As dismal as ever now when I led Costello into it, it offered one advantage. The small-time hustlers and big talkers at its greasy tables were too street-wise to display interest in any pair of tough-looking strangers who strode purposefully past them.

Costello followed close behind as I headed through the smoky kitchen in back—the chef there didn't even turn from his stove to glance at us—and then we were in the cul-de-sac behind the café, only partly sheltered from the downpour by the overhang of the fire escape.

There was a stench of rotting garbage here from the cans lined up against the wall—my nose must have grown sensitive over the years —and I had to hold my breath as I dragged one under the drop-ladder of the fire escape and climbed on it. Now I could grasp the bottom rung of the ladder and hoist myself up. I climbed to the first landing, unhooked the ladder and lowered it to the ground for Costello's easy use.

When he joined me on the landing we pulled the ladder up and latched it in place again, then climbed three more flights of slippery fire escape to the roof of the building. Here Costello got a full view of the steeply pitched, coppery-green mansard roofs and the thicket of chimney pots that marked the course ahead, a course that wouldn't be made any less tricky by the rain water sheeting down those slopes. "Crazy bastard," he said under his breath, and I had a feeling it was as much a judgment on himself as me.

I said, "No sweat, if you plant your hands against the slope and inch your way along. Just don't put your weight on one of those rain gutters because they can go right out from under."

In this fashion, inch by inch, we made our way across the roof to the next one, where the pitch was even steeper. Costello's dress shoes weren't made for this combination of mountain climbing and water-skiing. I saw him slip, then, as his foot went into the gutter and knocked it loose, he let out a yell and started sliding after it. I managed to get a grip on his coat collar before he was completely gone, and between the two of us he was hauled back to safety. He lay there cursing softly between gasping breaths, then said angrily, "What the hell are you waiting for? We can drown here like this."

This time I let him set the pace, so that it took an endless time to cover the remaining distance. But cover it we did, and then were on Chouchoute's roof where halfway up the slope was the skylight window of her bedroom. Here, flat on my belly, I provided support for Costello's soggy shoes, this way shoving him up to where he could take a position directly under the window, hanging on for dear life to its outside sill.

Somehow I managed to get enough handhold and foothold to work my way up beside him. Peering through the skylight, I could dimly make out a form on the bed and no one else in the room. I heaved up on the window frame, it gave way and opened enough to let me crawl through. Inside, I hung suspended, measuring the long drop below, felt my fingers slipping and willy-nilly made the drop. Costello was already through the window and hanging there. I reached up to break his fall, he came down in my arms and, a solid weight, almost bore me to the floor with him. But we were in now, and, I could only hope, had not roused those occupants capable of being roused.

Chouchoute was certainly not one of them. There was little left of her but a pair of glittering eyes sightlessly fixed on the ceiling, and if it weren't for the slight rise and fall of the meager chest under the coverlet, it would be easy to mistake her for dead. The room was stifling hot, the radiator hissing and clattering away, which, from my experience, was an unnatural condition for the house once winter had passed.

Costello had gun in hand when we opened the door to survey the hallway, and when I motioned him to give it to me he surrendered it only grudgingly. As it turned out, the hallway was empty, the rooms along it were empty. The same for every room on the floors below, checked out one by one. We moved down to the ground floor as silently as we could—not too silently the way each step creaked in protest—and on the ground floor at the foot of the stairway we waited for some sound to guide us in the right direction.

There was no sound.

I led the way to the kitchen, found the back door bolted from the inside, and from there traced a route through the ground floor that took us back to the staircase.

"Beautiful," said Costello. "When we climbed in the top they walked out the bottom."

"We're not at the bottom yet," I told him.

The door to the cellar wasn't locked. And the dim light over its stone stairway was lit. From the head of the stairs I looked down at the familiar collection of empty cartons, waste paper, and crates of discarded wine and beer bottles that Madame, her packrat instinct always working overtime, could never bring herself to throw away. I descended the stairs, gun at the ready, Costello breathing down my neck. There had been a noise from some remote part of the cellar, a bang and a clank, muffled but clearly audible.

The furnace and coal bin were at the far end of the cellar, and the door in the partition that separated them from the storeroom was partly open and showed a light behind it. I made my way toward it and stopped at the door to look through at whatever was going on. Costello crowded me to get a look for himself. "God damn," he whispered in awe.

Marie-Paule, naked except for a pair of unlaced work shoes, was furiously stoking the furnace fire which, from the glare of it, was already close to white hot. Her hair was dank, her lean body poured sweat in rivulets that shone under the drop-light, but there was good reason for the nakedness and the labors.

A large plastic sheet had been stretched out on the stone floor. On the sheet, also naked, bound hand and foot, lay the object she had been working on. The skin was slate-gray, the lips blue, and the pattern of long, deep gashes on chest and belly oozed trickles of blood to join the puddles of it on the plastic sheet. There were all the signs here that this cadaver had been brought to its end very slowly and painfully.

I took that one look and everything in me churned up into my throat, choking me until I could force it down again. Then I managed to wrench my eyes away from the sight.

"Frenchy," whispered Costello.

Wrong.

The hair had been dyed black, the thin line of newly grown mustache had been dyed black, but there all resemblance to Yves Rouart-Rochelle ended.

"Kees Baar," I said.

An exquisitely slow and painful end at the hands of a fanatically neat workman. Paring knives, carving knives, and cleavers, those instruments for torture and dissection, were all arranged in a neat row outside the plastic. When the job of dismemberment was complete and the remains thoroughly cremated there would be no misplaced blade left behind.

I walked into the room, Costello at my shoulder, as Marie-Paule slammed the furnace door shut with the blade of the shovel. She turned and saw us there, the pistol aimed at her. For a few ticks of the clock, she looked like Lot's wife halfway to becoming a pillar of salt. A few seconds, and then I could actually feel her charge herself with the nerve and cunning to meet this crisis.

"A gun," she said contemptuously. "How brave."

I motioned with it at the shovel. "Drop that thing."

She glanced at the shovel in her hands as if unaware she was holding it, and only after she had dropped it with a clatter did I thrust the gun inside my belt.

"Now," I said, keeping my eyes averted from her handiwork,

"cover him up. Find something to put over him. Quick."

She found something in a stack near the coal bin, an old canvas drop cloth, stiff with splashes of dried paint. She hauled it over the body and stood back from it facing us. "There's no use your killing me," she said calmly. "You'd gain nothing. You'd only lose everything."

"Everything?" I said.

"Your agency's share of the hijacked money. After all, it is the money your CIA must be interested in, not the useless killing of people. And the money will be returned to you. I swear to it."

"Never mind that now. Where's Yves?"

She pointed at the paint-encrusted cloth. "That—"

"No," I said, "that is not Yves. That is what's left of Kees Baar. Now the truth. What happened to Yves?"

"Very well, the truth. He's lying dead in his apartment in Marseille where Kees settled with him. You know the rest. Kees took his car but abandoned it at Dijon when your men came too close. He traveled the rest of the way here by bus. I had told him to meet me here."

"So that you could kill him?"

"Yes. He deserved killing. He deserved worse than killing. And that is what he got."

"Because of van Zee's letter? The one telling of his feelings for you, and the way Kees forced him to give you up?"

"Yes. And whether you intend to shoot me or not"—she motioned at her nakedness—"do you mind if I put on some clothing? I find this very embarrassing."

This was embarrassing to her. The sliced-up body under that cloth wasn't.

The clothing was neatly folded on a box against the partition. She dressed with deliberation, slipped on her shoes, shrugged her arms into a jacket. She came back to the body and pointed a now handsomely shod toe at it. "Consider, Mr. Shaw, I've only done to him what you would have been forced to do in the end, because as long as he lived you would never have seen one dollar of your money. This way it will all be returned to you, and the whole thing can be forgotten. No one need ever know what has taken place here."

"Watch it!" shouted Costello.

I had been listening to her, not watching her, and that was my mistake. I hadn't even seen the motion of the hand that slipped the gun from her jacket. All I knew was that I was suddenly looking right into it, and, though it appeared to be a small-bore automatic, it was like looking into the mouth of a tunnel.

"No!" Marie-Paule suddenly said, and Costello who had shifted his position had sense enough to freeze where he was. She frowned at me. "I am surprised, Mr. Shaw, that you did not take into account that I must have used some device to persuade Kees to take the walk down here with me. You are not really very good at your work, are you? Now it appears that all problems will be resolved in my favor."

I said, "Easily done, Miss Neyna. A matter of saying good-by to you and forgetting all about this."

"Too late, my friend. What both of you will do is place your hands on your heads."

We did. This was a killer who, from the look of it, enjoyed killing. And there was the furnace ready, as capable of incinerating three as one. And here she was, moving up close, the gun never wavering from its mark between my eyes. "Now turn around, please," she said.

So it was to be in the back of the head. Safer for her that way, because the second bullet would explode in Costello's skull before he could do anything about it. Costello slowly turned aboutface. I didn't.

"Marie-Paule," I said, "look at me. Even with the surgery that was done on my face, is it possible you still don't know you're looking at Jean Lespere?"

Her lips quirked. "A curious gambit, Mr. Shaw. And a foolish one."

I said, "I once saved your life. In Marseille, two thugs hired by a man named Renaudat were ready to knife you until I came along. Would I know that if I weren't Jean Lespere?"

"Why not? You people must know every last detail of the company's business. But I knew Jean as none of you ever could."

"You did, Marie-Paule." I shifted to the hard-boiled Boulevard de Clichy French of Jean Lespere. "You came to my room that night in a shabby old robe. You opened the robe wide to show me there was nothing underneath it. And you said to me, 'Do you find this of interest to you?' knowing how desperately I did. *C'est moi, ma chère! C'est votre Jean!*"

"Ah, mon Dieu!" she gasped, her eyes searching my face, the gun wavering. I lunged for it, by a miracle caught hold of her wrist and turned it upward, and felt the shock of the explosion from wrist to elbow. Marie-Paule stood there, that expression of incredulity still stamped on her face, then went down full-length, the gun gripped in her hand even in that final convulsion.

Costello said weakly, "Jesus," and kneeled down to look closely. "Finished," he said. "Under the chin and right through the top of her head."

"Finished?" I said, trying to understand it.

"That's right. She had us all wrapped up, and you told her you were the old boy friend, and she blew the whole works." He shook his head, marveling. "She really had a big thing going for her Johnny, didn't she? Never got over it."

No, she never did. A fatal condition, too.

We left by the kitchen door, which opened on the congeries of unlighted alleys leading away from rue Houdon. On Costello's advice, we used the metro rather than a cab for the ride back to the hotel.

When Harry opened the door of the sitting room to me I was once again faced by the spectacle of a body bound, and, in this case, gagged, but unlike the macabre object in that torture chamber on rue Houdon, this one was very much alive. Bianca was planted in an armchair, her wrists fixed to its arms by a couple of neckties, with a handkerchief and another tie sealing her mouth. On the floor nearby stood her valise, evidently packed in such haste that the edge of a feminine garment stuck out of it.

Harry seemed close to panic. "Mr. Costello told me not to let her go out, sir, or get near a phone, and she tried both of them. This was the only thing I could do about it."

"A gag?" I said. "She didn't really yell for help, did she?"

"I don't know if it was for help, sir, because it was in Italian. But she started yelling so loud anybody outside could hear it and that would have meant bad trouble. I'm sorry sir, but—"

"No, it's all right, Harry. You did fine."

I nudged him through the door and locked it. Then I went over to confront Bianca. *"Allora, Signorina Prima Donna,"* I said.

She glared at me and made a noise in her throat which, if not muffled, might have been a roar.

"Not yet," I said. "First, like it or not, you're going to hear me out."

She shook her head violently.

"Oh, yes, you will," I said. "And what you'll hear is the truth. I could easily lie about what I've just been through, and Costello would back me up in it, but I'd rather risk the truth." I described the scene in that basement, not sparing my captive audience any of the details. "So," I concluded, "Marie-Paule is now dead, along with all the others. For that matter, so are Jan van Zee and Jean Lespere. All dead and gone forever. That leaves David Shaw and Bianca Cavalcanti, and what becomes of them, I think, is very much up to you."

Again she shook her head violently.

"At least," I said, "are you in a mood to behave reasonably if I reclaim my neckties?"

She nodded, and when I undid her fastenings and the gag she sat there stonily. Finally she said, "I warned you that if you went this far with your madness, it was all over between us. I'm grateful you're not dead. Deeply grateful. But whatever the reason, you ended up killing that woman. That makes you a killer, don't you understand? I couldn't live with you, knowing that. I don't see how you'll be able to live with it."

"I do understand. That's why I just now used Signor Costello's phone—with his unhappy permission—to call the police and tell them about it. They'll be paying me a visit in a little while. I'll fight the case as hard as I can, *cara mia,* but of course when my past comes out it'll mean at least a few years in prison for me. If I know you'll be waiting—"

"Prison?" she said with horror. "You'll go to prison? Ah, no! Never! I'd never live through it!"

I was still kneeling before her, the neckties in my hand, and she hurled herself at me so unrestrainedly that she sent me flat on my back, and there she was, sprawled over me, my face clutched between her hands while she rained kisses on it, sobbing, "I'll die, do you hear? *Mio amore.* What a fool to send for the police! *Caro mio.* For you to be in prison even one day—!"

I managed to get my arms around her, and she yielded whimpering to the embrace as I comforted her.

Ah yes, I was going to have a stormy time of it with her when she sooner or later realized that I hadn't called the police.

And after that, considering the temperament of my woman, I could forecast other stormy times for God knows what other reasons.

But certainly never a dull moment, and certainly never an empty one.

About the Author

STANLEY ELLIN has been called "a master storyteller." His novels have been translated into twenty languages and have won him an international reputation. He has been honored with seven Edgar Allan Poe awards; and his works have been made into movies by such directors as Joseph Losey, Clive Donner and Claude Chabrol, and into numerous television plays, most notably by Alfred Hitchcock. Mr. Ellin is married, and his year is divided between his homes in New York and Miami Beach.